FOREVER
Lies

Print Edition ISBN: 978-1-7330721-3-7

Cover Designed by Hang Le
Photography by Chris Davis at Specular
Cover Model Adam Cowie
Edited by Personal Touch Editing

❁ Created with Vellum

FOREVER LIES

JILL RAMSOWER

CHAPTER 1

Alessia

The sight of the silver elevator doors closing before I could reach them caused my chest to clamp tight with desperation.

"Hold the doors, *please!*" I called out over the clatter of my stilettos on the marble floor.

Hiding from my boss would be so much harder if I didn't get my ass tucked away in my office before he arrived. If he'd simply been the overly chatty sort or socially awkward, I wouldn't bother with my elaborate evasion schemes, but it was so much worse than that. I would do whatever I could to avoid spending a single unnecessary minute with that man.

If I missed this elevator, would I be forced to ride the next one with my boss? He'd be arriving at the building any minute. Ten floors, alone, in an enclosed space with the creep.

My heart seized painfully.

A second before the doors could seal shut, they froze with a jerk, then retracted, allowing me to scramble aboard.

"Thank you so much. You really don't understand—" My words trailed away when my eyes landed on the man who had saved me from potential misery.

He was masculine beauty personified—dark hair, perfectly styled back and closely cropped on the sides. He had a dusting of dark hair on his angular jaw, and his deep-set eyes were so dark that they were almost black. Without saying a word, easy confidence wafted from his expensively suited form like steam from a rain-soaked summer street.

I had never seen him before. I'd come to recognize many of the building's occupants, but there was no chance I would have forgotten the sight of him.

He was the most breathtaking man I'd ever seen.

Towering over me, despite my four-inch heels, he owned every square inch of the small elevator car. While he was only a few years older than me, he had the powerful presence of a much older man.

"What don't I understand?" The amused purr of his voice was a warm caress that stole the air from my lungs.

Fortunately, the elevator doors closing behind me jarred me from my trance, reminding me I'd been unabashedly devouring him with my eyes. I exhaled a shaky breath as I turned and pushed the button for the tenth floor.

"Just that I needed to get upstairs. Don't want to be late for work." I forced an awkward chuckle, looking anywhere but at the gorgeous man directly across from me until I realized I could feel the penetrating touch of his eyes. I didn't have to look up to know he was staring at me, daring me to meet his gaze. Unable to ignore his unspoken command, I lifted my eyes and peered at him through my lashes.

When my gaze reached his face, one corner of his mouth quirked up just a fraction. Had I not been so keenly aware of the man, I would have missed the fleeting movement. Leaning back against the wall, hands clasped casually in front of him, he was perfectly at ease, amused by my flustered reaction.

I, on the other hand, was coming apart under his scrutiny.

Why was I so affected by a man I'd never even met? He was nobody to me. What did I care what he thought of me? There were loads of attractive men in the city.

This man is different.

His commanding stare stripped my defenses and left me raw and vulnerable.

Just when I thought I would blurt something to fill the uncomfortable silence, the elevator shuddered, then ground to a stop, lights flickering. My hand darted out to catch myself against the wall, and I gasped in surprise. The man, on the other hand, needed no such balance assistance. Aside from a glance around the elevator car, he was seemingly unfazed.

Why should the laws of physics affect someone so clearly not of this world?

"Looks like we're stuck," I murmured after it became clear the doors were not opening, nor were we resuming motion. "I suppose we should call for help." I glanced down at the phone labeled for emergency use on my side of the elevator, and when I looked back up, the man's piercing gaze was still fixed on me.

He pulled away from the wall and closed the space between us, making my breath catch in my throat. Leaning across me, just inches from touching me, he opened the call box and retrieved the phone. I released a shaky exhale and took a small step back to give him room and to collect myself.

"Yes, my companion and I are stuck in one of the elevators in the Triton building … No emergencies, just stuck … Thank you." He hung up the receiver and turned to where I now stood in the back corner, having inched away from him as he spoke. "They've sent someone to check on the situation, but there's no telling how long it will be." His deep voice resonated throughout the small space, each syllable oozing control. The sound was the perfect complement to his unflappable demeanor.

My heart pounded so fast, I became lightheaded. I'd been around assertive men all my life, but this man's presence filled up the small space so completely, there was no oxygen left to breathe. My eyes flitted to his, and I offered him a glimpse of a smile. "It's not the first time I've been stuck in an elevator. Live in the city long enough, and you come to expect these things." Relief coursed through my veins when I managed to utter something semi-intelligible.

"You work in the building?" Leaning his shoulder against the side wall, he continued to focus all his attention on me, not returning to his side of the elevator.

"Yes, I work at Triton. You?"

"No, I'm here to meet someone."

He stared at me for a long moment. It felt as though he was measuring my worth, as if he could see deep inside of me and was perusing my most personal thoughts.

The tension in the small space was more than palpable—it was a physical force pressing against my skin.

"Luca," he rumbled as he extended his hand, finally breaking the silence.

He was introducing himself. What did that mean? Was he merely being polite in an awkward situation, or was he taking the opportunity to hit on me?

"Alessia."

His hand was rough but warm, and he held my much smaller hand for longer than was necessary.

Hitting on me. Okay, Alessia. You can do this. Play it cool.

As he released my fingers, his thumb stroked along the back of my hand, sending tingles across my skin, cascading up my arm and down into the pit of my belly.

"That's Italian, right?"

"Yes," I breathed. "You as well?"

"I am." His head angled to the side. "Are you seeing anyone Alessia?"

My eyes danced from one shiny metal wall to the other. Was this really happening? Was this god-like man asking me out while we were trapped in an elevator together? Had I hit my head and dreamed this entire situation while comatose in a hospital bed? It seemed too fantastical to be real, but I had no other explanation.

Answer the man, Les. Before he thinks you're crazy.

"Um, no. No, I'm not."

The first hint of a smile formed on his perfect lips, but before he could respond, the elevator lurched back into motion.

Luca reached forward and pressed the stop button, and the elevator ground to a jarring halt again.

My brows creased in confusion.

"Give me your phone," he ordered softly, palm outstretched.

Common sense should have screamed at me not to turn over my sole source of communication while this man had me trapped with him, but I'd apparently woken up low on all forms of self-preservation. Something about his commanding tone spoke to deep-seated need within me to comply.

Eyes wide, like a lamb to the slaughter, I placed my phone in his hand.

He arched a brow. "Unlock it, Alessia."

My name on his tongue was the sweetest nectar I could have imagined—delicious, tempting, and dangerously addictive. The slightest twinge of fear pricked at the back of my neck. Somewhere deep down, I sensed this man had the potential to undo me—take me in, rearrange my insides, and spit me back out after I was unrecognizable.

I chided myself for overreacting. This was a five-minute conversation with a man in an elevator, not an arranged marriage. I needed to get a grip on myself. As soon as he pressed the button again, we would be on our way, and I would likely never see him again.

He tapped at my phone before a buzzing sounded in his breast pocket. He pulled out his own device and began to type, my phone still firmly cradled in his other hand. "I'd like to hear more about you and your family, but it looks like our ride is almost over, so we'll have to continue the conversation another time."

He closed the space between us, and instead of handing back my phone, he reached over and slid the device back inside my purse, bringing us within inches of one another. Heat radiated off him, tugging at me to close the gap and press my body against his. My eyes leapt up to his, my mouth softly parted as I struggled to keep my wits.

"It was a pleasure meeting you," he rasped before stepping back and pressing the button behind him without severing our connection. "I'll be in touch." The moment the doors opened, he was gone.

Holy fuck, what just happened?

It was like a scene from a movie—that crap didn't happen in real life. Yes, I was an attractive woman, but that usually meant I got cat-calls from construction workers and hit on by slimy douchebags. Rarely was the attention wanted, and the feelings were almost never reciprocated on my end.

I only had a matter of seconds to gather my thoughts and collect myself before the elevator doors opened onto my floor. With uneven steps, I entered the Triton lobby, a bemused grin plastered on my face.

What a surreal start to my day!

Thoughts of Luca were almost distracting enough to make me forget about my lecherous boss.

Almost.

Each step I took closer toward our adjoining offices brought back a renewed sense of doom. Not to mention a healthy dose of anger.

Roger Coleman was the smarmiest, most disgusting man I'd

ever met, but he was also damn good at hiding his true nature. He'd held his position at Triton Construction for well over a decade and was an established member of the good 'ol boys club. A brotherhood of men led by the owner of the company—a man who also happened to be my father.

Dad had built Triton into the largest construction company in New York with a lifetime of dedication and a ruthless mind for business. Triton was his pride and joy, and I desperately wanted to join him at the helm of his company. More than anything, I wanted to make my father proud, and I wouldn't accomplish that by running to him every time I had a problem. I needed to handle Roger on my own. He was just a misogynic sleaze, after all. If I could grow a spine and be firm with him, he wouldn't be an issue.

Admittedly, I'd done an abysmal job so far.

I wasn't the best at handling conflict, and he always seemed to catch me off guard. No matter how many scenarios I rehearsed in my head, his veiled innuendo and unsettling looks left me speechless. I'd heard of fight or flight, but my default setting was most definitely to freeze, and overcoming that instinct had proven more challenging than I'd hoped.

Roger's advances had started out small—telling me how lovely I looked or commenting on my hair or eyes. In romance novels, having an older executive pursue the young professional sounded sexy and exciting, but when my fifty-five-year-old boss with a fake-and-bake tan and leathery skin started hitting on me, it was repulsive and unsettling. I'd done my best to discretely brush aside his advances and discourage his behavior in the hopes he would take the hint and move on, but after a year of working in the office, he had yet to cease his efforts.

Only once had his pursuit escalated to a physical level. Six months ago, at the company Christmas party he cornered me in a hallway and pressed me against a wall, his dick thrust against my stomach. He'd been drinking heavily, and I made the mistake of walking to a restroom alone. I'd been so repulsed and terrified, I didn't even hear the unquestionably revolting comment he made. I gave a stuttered excuse and tore from his grasp, leaving the party without another word.

The incident had been seared into my brain. I tried to tell myself it was an isolated incident that wouldn't have happened had alcohol not been present, but I couldn't shake the lingering anxiety that he'd try again. I took every effort to distance myself from the man, both professionally and physically. I made certain I pulled in coworkers to help on projects, so there was always an extra set of eyes working with us.

Our offices, along with several others in the suite, were constructed with glass walls, which helped give me a certain degree of security—no hiding behind closed doors outside of the conference or break room. Another fortifying fact—Roger's advances weren't a daily affair, not even weekly. The problem wasn't their frequency; it was the uncertainty of not knowing when they might occur that was the most stressful.

This week I was in for a treat. Today was the only day I'd have to deal with Roger before he left on a week-long business trip to L.A.

I could survive one day with the devil.

Most of the morning passed uneventfully. I was left to my own devices, preparing for a full week of project meetings and impending deadlines. It wasn't until almost eleven when the intercom on my phone blared with Roger's voice.

"Alessia, can you come in here, please?"

A seemingly harmless request, but it stirred an overwhelming sense of dread in the pit of my stomach.

I didn't answer—there was no need. He could see me as I stood from my chair and made my way to his office next door. While I didn't so much as glance his direction, I had no doubt his beady eyes would follow my every step. Our offices lined the outer wall of windows—the glass walls allowing the rest of the employees to enjoy the soaring views from our building. It was a double-edged sword—no privacy was a good thing, but it also meant there was no escaping Roger's stare.

"Did you need something?" I stopped several feet from his small conference table where he'd laid out his presentation materials.

"You sure you can't come with me? You know the material as well as I do and would be an enormous help when I make the pitch. It's not too late to get you a ticket." He arched a brow, hands propped on his hips where he stood on the opposite side of the table.

"My sisters would kill me if I'm not there to help get ready for Mom's party this weekend. It's her fiftieth and—"

"I know, I know," he cut me off as I began to blather about my mother's pretend birthday. She'd turned fifty years ago, but the party had been the best excuse I'd come up with on the spot when Roger had initially asked me to accompany him on the trip. There was no way in hell I was traveling with the man. Fortunately, he hadn't bothered verifying my story, so I continued to uphold the ruse.

"You told me already. Well, get over here and let's run through everything one more time before I head to the airport." He waved me over with a frown, clearly disgruntled I hadn't caved to his pressure to accompany him.

The project was a relatively minor remodel proposal for a building in Brooklyn owned by a corporation headquartered on the opposite coast. I'd worked on the project along with a couple other people from our team. It was too small-scale for Roger to do the grunt work, but he was presenting our proposal because the contact was a friend of his. We had already given him all the pertinent information on multiple occasions, so I wasn't sure what I was supposed to say.

The chairs had been pulled around to clump on my side of the table with the various documents and exhibits spread out for viewing from the other side. His setup left little option except to come around to his side of the table, but I kept as much distance between us as was reasonably possible.

"It looks like everything is here," I offered as I perused the materials.

"What about the schedule of work?" he asked as he leaned forward to retrieve the document. "I noticed we listed a completion timeframe of six months, but I thought we had discussed moving that out to nine." His right hand snaked out to curl around my waist and pull me next to him while his other hand held out the document as if showing me its contents was the purpose behind his flagrant violation of my personal space.

Stunned by his action, I took the papers and stared at them dumbly. I didn't see the words on the page—I was entirely focused inside my head where my thoughts raced at a frenzied pace in an attempt to grasp my situation. My boss's hand lingered at my lower back, the insidious warmth seeping into my skin, before slowly dropping down to caress over the curve of my ass cheek.

I ceased breathing, and my ears began to ring.

His repulsive touch in such a private area made my skin crawl, but I couldn't seem to move a muscle.

I was frozen—horror battling with mortification.

The glass walls gave me a perfect view of the bustling office where a dozen employees scurried about their business. Never in a thousand years had I imagined he would make a move on me in plain sight of our coworkers, but he'd done a masterful job keeping his actions unseen. To all the world, we looked as though we were simply examining a document—his wandering hand only visible to the New York skyline out our tenth-floor windows.

"Um … we decided … to subcontract the welding work," I sputtered out. "Our guys will be busy on the Merchant project. Outsourcing will enable us to keep the six-month timeline the client requested." As I said the words, I frantically debated what to do. If I allowed him to continue touching me, it would no doubt encourage the asshole to take more liberties. If I confronted him or in any way made a scene, the entire office would know in seconds. Before I had a chance to decide, the intercom in his office crackled to life.

"Mr. Coleman, your flight leaves in two hours."

The instant his assistant, Beverly, began to speak, I pulled out of his grasp and fled the office. Bypassing my own office, I hurried to the restrooms and locked myself in a stall. Leaning against the door, head back and eyes closed, I tried to regulate my erratic heartrate.

Did that really just happen?

Could I have imagined the whole thing? Surely, my boss hadn't assaulted me in front of the entire office. As much as I wished it had been a nightmare, it wasn't. Each agonizing second had played out in living color, and I had stood immobile like a squirrel starring down an approaching car. What was wrong with me? Why hadn't I pulled away instantly? Why hadn't I swallowed my pride and told my father the truth months ago or just turned Roger's balding ass into HR? I'd had my reasons at the time, but they seemed less and less valid with each new day. My conflict and self-doubt brought on a barrage of guilt and blame that bowed my shoulders with their oppressive weight.

I needed to get out of the building.

I exited the stall and went through the motions of washing my hands before walking to my office with my eyes lowered to the geometric patterns of the grey commercial carpeting. Grabbing my phone, I texted my cousin to move up our lunch date, then snagged my purse and scurried out of my office. Normally, I would inform a coworker if I was leaving early, but I couldn't do it. I felt exposed—like anyone who looked at me would know what I had allowed to happen. I couldn't force myself to take that chance—to let them see the shame in my eyes. Instead, I kept my head down and hurried out the closest exit.

I couldn't allow my boss's behavior to continue.

The realization was daunting.

Now, I just had to figure out what I was going to do about it. Would I confront Roger myself? Would I file a complaint with HR or go straight to my father? If I told my dad, would he believe me or think I was overreacting? Roger was his friend, after all. And if Roger wasn't immediately fired, would he know I'd reported him? How would a man with such little moral character respond when he found out I'd put his job in jeopardy?

The possibilities paralyzed me.

You have the rest of the week to figure it out, Les. Try not to panic.

I wasn't normally the type to procrastinate, but in this case, I needed time to process. I needed to talk through everything and make sure I took the proper steps, because once I started that ball rolling, there would be no stopping it.

Fortunately for me, I already had lunch scheduled with my cousin, Giada. She would be the perfect sounding board. Until then, I would ignore all thoughts of Roger to protect my sanity. I shoved the incident into a dark corner of my mind—somewhere next to the misery of my first period and getting lost as a child in the subway—and prayed my dramatic morning had no more surprises in store for me.

CHAPTER 2

Alessia

Giada was a firework laced with gasoline—her presence electrified a room and enchanted everyone she came into contact with. Where I was cautious and a touch introverted, she was bold and always the life of the party. She'd been my best friend for as long as I could remember. Our mothers were sisters-in-law, and we were born one month apart. Where she was the oldest of three girls, I was the middle, but we might as well have been twins we were so close. Yin to my yang, the opposite nature of our personalities kept us perfect in balance.

It was as if we were born to be close friends—soul sisters.

We ate lunch together at least once a week, often at the same deli where I was currently headed. It was close to my office and had the best Kaiser rolls around. I reached the place first after moving up our lunch so unexpectedly. Grabbing one of the four tiny tables inside, I played a game on my phone while I waited.

I'd never been big on social media. My parents didn't let us girls get on Myspace or Facebook when we were younger, and now that I was on my own, it had never felt all that necessary. Outside of Giada, I didn't have a ton of friends, which was fine with me. I had two sisters and three female cousins—that was plenty of girl drama in my life.

"Hey cuz, what's going on? Hope you didn't have to wait long. I got here as quickly as I could." Giada plopped down in the seat across from me, impeccably dressed, as always, long auburn hair falling in thick waves down her back.

"Hey G! Not long at all. Sorry to spring the time change on you."

"Not a problem. I hope everything's okay."

"Yes and no. Let's grab our sandwiches, and I'll tell you about it over lunch."

"Please tell me it's not your dickhead of a boss again."

I rolled my eyes and grabbed her hand. "Food first, then talk."

We ordered and took our food back to the table as the deli slowly began to fill with people on their lunch hour. I quietly relayed the events of the morning, attempting to keep the conversation just between us in a restaurant the size of a shoebox. I started easy with my sultry elevator encounter, and once I had her distracted with lust-filled ideas of romantic rendezvous, I quietly recounted what had happened with Roger.

As I suspected, Giada was fuming by the time I finished. I had hoped the elevator story would take the edge off her anger, but no luck. G was a mama bear ready to throw down on my behalf. "Al, I know you don't like conflict, but you can't let that man keep doing this shit."

"I know. I realize it's not going to stop if I don't do something about it. You know how hard I've worked to make a name for myself at Triton and for Dad to see me as an equal. I wanted to handle the situation discretely, but it's not working."

"You don't have to raise a stink, just tell your dad. He'll fire that guy's ass in a heartbeat—no one has to know why." In theory, her suggestion seemed like the easy answer; however, life was rarely so simple.

"That's the very last thing I wanted to do. Crying to him for help would ensure he still sees me as a child incapable of handling my own problems."

"Then go to HR and file a complaint. That's not asking for help—that would be you handling the matter with the proper authority. Hell, file a police report for assault while you're at it. Better yet, we'll find a guy to take out his kneecaps. It'd be a lot harder for him to put the moves on you when he's in a wheel-chair. The slimy toad deserves it."

I choked on my diet soda. "No, G. We aren't committing any felonies."

She shrugged. "Suit yourself."

"I will, thanks." I gave her a wink. "But I get what you're saying with HR. That would show a degree of assertiveness, even if it's not me grabbing the bull by the horns. I just want the employees at Triton to respect me. That's why Dad didn't just give me a job at the top to begin with—I'm supposed to earn my position—and I want to give him that. Show him that Triton would be in good hands under my leadership."

"I can't say that I totally understand. You don't even *need* to work. Your family has plenty of money."

"What else would I do with my life? Go shopping and host parties? I'm not my mother, that's not enough for me."

"Too bad," she mused. "I'll have to find someone else to accompany me on my shopping runs and spa treatments."

"Whatever. That's not you either, and you know it." I narrowed my eyes and tossed one of my chips at her.

She laughed, her vibrant green eyes shining. "I know no such thing. What I *do* know is if you don't do something about that boss of yours, I'm going to come up there and raise holy hell. Got it?"

"I get it," I smiled at my best friend. "And I promise I'll file a complaint with HR. In the meantime, he's gone for the rest of the week!"

"Fabulous! We should take a long lunch break and hit Saks later this week."

"You're incorrigible."

"So, is that a yes?"

I threw my head back and laughed. "Yes, I think that could be arranged."

"Boom! Now, get your ass back to work and file that damn complaint," she ordered with every ounce of moxie in her five-foot frame.

"Yes, sir, Colonel, sir." I saluted her as I stood, then hugged my amazing friend. Not every girl was lucky enough to have a Giada in their life. I thanked my lucky stars on a daily basis that I'd somehow managed to score the best cousin ever.

I walked back into work feeling optimistic and empowered. I would file the dreaded HR complaint and finally get Roger out of my life, not to mention prove to myself that I could handle the matter. I wasn't sure how my dad would react, but I could only control so much. I'd be proud of myself. That would have to be enough.

MY DAD'S office was the only one along the wall of windows that was fully enclosed for privacy. It was on the opposite end of the floor as my office, so I didn't run into him all that often. In fact, my job in marketing didn't require a whole lot of interaction with the CEO's position, but every now and then, I'd have a budgeting issue or some other business matter that needed to be signed off on by my dad.

On this particular occasion, I had budgeting paperwork that needed his signature. When I approached the open door, I heard my dad's steady voice as he spoke to someone from within his office. I listened at the door for a moment to decide if I should wait or come back later.

"I called to speak with the concrete rep this morning, discovered the guy killed himself," came my father's voice.

"The Venturi kid? The one you met with last week?" I recognized that voice as well—it was my dad's long-time best friend, my Uncle Sal. I wasn't sure if Sal was technically related to me—he wasn't an uncle but had carried the honorary title since I was little. He'd been a part of our family for as long as I could remember. He'd even been a pallbearer at my brother's funeral.

"Yeah. Hung himself just a day after I talked to him. Not sure how that will affect my price negotiations. If that cousin of his takes over, it'll be a nightmare." My dad had never been particularly empathetic, so his comment didn't surprise me.

"Frederico?"

"Yeah, that man's a lunatic," my dad grumbled.

I decided their talk wasn't overly-sensitive, so I poked my head around the corner. "Excuse me, am I interrupting?" I cautiously cut in.

"Alessia—my favorite marketing pro!" called Uncle Sal. "You aren't interrupting at all, come in."

"Hey, Uncle Sal! What are you doing up here?"

"I was nearby and thought I'd steal your dad for lunch. How have you been?" He rose from the chair he'd been occupying and gave me a hug, kissing my cheek like he always did.

"I'm great, just had some paperwork for Dad."

"Enzo, this girl of yours is going to run you out of a job soon!" he joked with a warm smile.

"We shall see—she has a way to go yet," he said coolly. My dad had remained seated behind his desk, not including himself in our exchange.

Sal waved him away like my father's comment was rubbish. "This one's a hard worker. I have no doubt she'll be sitting in this office soon enough."

"Alright, let's head to lunch before you have me forced into retirement." My dad slowly rose and walked to where his jacket hung on the wall. "Alessia, you can leave the paperwork on my desk. I'll have a look at it when I get back."

I offered the two men a tight-lipped smile as they said goodbye. I had no delusions I would be invited to lunch. Whether it was because I was still a child in their eyes or merely because I was a woman, I wasn't sure, but whatever the reason, I was not a welcome addition to their party.

A part of me desperately wanted my father to take me under his wing and include me in things like the occasional lunch with associates. My father had never guaranteed me any position at Triton, and there were times like this when I wasn't sure he truly considered me an option to replace him. Unless he outright told me there was no chance, I wasn't giving up hope I could rise in the ranks and would continue to do everything I could to make that happen.

BY THE TIME I made it home that night, I was exhausted. I never got around to filing the complaint but swore I'd do it by the end of the week. The emotional toll of dealing with the incident itself had been enough for one day. I'd save the drama of dealing with HR for another day.

After changing into something comfy, I warmed up one of the dinners delivered by the meal service I used and poured myself a glass of wine. Deciding to take advantage of the beautiful May evening, I opened a couple windows and sat at the kitchen table.

My apartment was my sanctuary. What Giada had said about money had been true—my family had always been wealthy. I was exceptionally fortunate to be able to afford a beautiful two-bedroom place in downtown Manhattan straight out of college. The living area and bedroom boasted floor-to-ceiling windows, and even the backsplash in the kitchen was a series of horizontal windows looking out onto the city. I had accentuated the light, airy feel of the space with cream-colored fabrics and a glass-top dining table. Paintings and throw-pillows offered bursts of color and added a homey feel to the contemporary design.

Unlike most twenty-three-year-olds in the city, I wasn't forced to live with a roommate—the apartment was all mine, and I loved it. I didn't have to worry about someone eating my food or bringing home uninvited guests. It was my space to unwind and allow the stress from the day to fall from my shoulders like an unwanted scarf.

The atmosphere was perfect, assuming there were no interruptions or disturbances, such as my mother calling. I should have expected her call—she'd been in constant contact about my youngest sister, Sofia's, upcoming graduation party. I'd had dinner with my parents just the day before, but we hadn't discussed the party. My father had already declared himself fed up with the discussions and forbade the topic at our weekly Sunday dinners.

It would never have been an issue if Mom had settled for a small affair, but that wasn't her style. She was throwing a graduation gala and planned to invite a few hundred of her closest friends. I was certain Sofia would have preferred no party at all, but she had humored our mother and allowed the production. We were closing in on the final weeks, so my mom's calls had been coming more and more frequently.

"Hey, Mom. How's it going?" I said brightly into my phone.

"You are not going to believe this," came her coarse voice. She had been a smoker for many years when she was younger, and though she had quit, she still bore the scratchy voice of a smoker.

"What happened? The caterer running low on pâté?" I teased.

"If only! Vica decided she's bringing a man. Can you believe that? I'd already made all the table assignments, and now she's gone and screwed it all up."

Maria Ludovica Francesca Elena Genovese, Vica for short, was my father's younger sister. She was an Italian wild-child who gave her two big brothers, and their wives, constant grief. She'd been married three times already but had refrained from having children—a small blessing, according to my mother. Apparently, Vica had met someone new and wanted to bring him to the party.

"The graduation is still three weeks out; there's plenty of time to rearrange things," I reminded her, hoping she would realize how absurd she sounded.

"I don't suppose you've decided to bring anyone," my mother prodded questioningly. "It would keep things even, that's all."

Of course, I should have known.

"Yeah, Mom. Your question has nothing to do with you wanting me to get married and make babies."

"Of course not!" She paused, and I knew what was coming. "Not that it would be such a bad thing."

"Yeah, yeah. I'll get right on it," I muttered.

"You do that, and make sure he's Catholic—that makes everything easier."

"Alright, Ma. I'm in the middle of eating dinner, so I'll let you go." She hated the use of the term 'ma,' but I threw it in there just to rib her. Every other New Yorker used the term, but not our family. My mother had always said it sounded like a dying sheep and demanded we girls called her Mom or Mother.

"I heard that."

"I'm sure you did. Love you, Mom."

"Love you, baby girl."

I hung up and sighed aloud. Every bit of tension I'd eased out of my shoulders had snuck back in and begun to pulse in my temples. My parents loved me unconditionally—I knew that. That knowledge should have been enough, but somehow, it wasn't. I wanted them to respect me and be proud of me. Maybe they would say that was the case, but I always felt a dollar short—like who I was and what I did was never quite enough.

When my mom would sneak in a reminder while I was in college that I could always find a man and quit school, it made me feel like she didn't believe in me. I was sure she simply wanted me to know I had options and didn't want me to feel pressured to be a working woman, but that's not how it felt. The same went for my dad. When I first brought them to my apartment after I'd bought it, he suggested I could buy the unit next door and combine the two to give myself more room. Instead of simply congratulating me, there was always a suggestion on how things could have been done differently.

It was my own fault I continued to seek out their praise, but I didn't know how to break the cycle. I had always been the parent pleaser; I didn't know how to be anyone different. That was the part of my personality that made dealing with my boss even more difficult. Confrontation was not my strong suit, but I was going to have to start learning.

CHAPTER 3

Luca

I had never wanted to fuck someone in an elevator more than I had wanted to fuck Alessia. I wasn't convinced she wouldn't have let me. The way her lips parted, and her breathing became shallow when I was close to her had been ample evidence of how deeply I affected her. I hated to admit it, but her effect on me wasn't far off.

The red dress she'd been wearing was professional yet molded to every curve of her beautiful body like the glossy coating on a candy apple. I had wanted to peel back that layer and see the sweet flesh underneath—she promised to be delicious. There were no obvious panty lines. The image of her wearing nothing underneath had my dick swelling as if I was a thirteen-year-old kid again.

Alessia's thick, dark hair, had been pulled up loosely on top of her head. The style drew my eyes to the delicate column of her neck, not helping the situation in my pants. Her eyes were dark brown and unusually expressive—I could see each and every thought and emotion as it crossed behind those wide, intelligent eyes.

The woman was sophisticated, gorgeous, and dripping with a surprising amount of innocence. That guileless innocence warred with her desire—she had clearly been torn—both drawn to and scared of me. She hadn't let the fear win out. Most people, even when they had no clue who I was, withered in my presence. A part of Alessia had wanted to withdraw, to cower in a corner of the elevator and keep her eyes downcast, but she hadn't. She stood tall, and even more intriguing, she had held my eyes. It was surprising how few women or men were capable of that feat.

The woman was even more enticing than I had expected.

Sure, she was gorgeous, which was why I'd zeroed in on her to begin with, but there was something else about her that called to me. She seemed to possess the unusual combination of backbone with a natural inclination to submit. I found most often women with fortitude had trouble surrendering control, and submissive women were often too weak to hold my interest. There was a sweet spot right in the middle where a woman was strong and confident but also able and willing to bend her will to a man. It made me naturally curious just how far a woman like her could be bent. She would probably argue with my assessment, seeing herself as a strong, independent woman. However, her instant response to my commands was more telling than any argument she could make—her innate tendency was compliance.

If I wanted to get close to a woman like her, I would need to play my cards just right. Too much force and she'd run. Not enough, and she'd lose interest. I would have to set the stage carefully to draw her in.

It was a good thing I loved a challenge.

Interrupting my thoughts, my phone began to buzz in my pocket. I hated the damn thing, but it was a necessity—I did most of my business over the phone.

"Yeah."

"Our guy's report came back—the handwriting's a fake," said Rafi, one of the few people I trusted in the world. He'd had it rough growing up, and I'd done what I could to help him, which meant he'd been my shadow ever since.

"It's all connected—it's got to be them," I murmured. "We just have to pinpoint who he's working for."

"I'm not sure how much time you have before all hell breaks loose."

"I'm on it." I hung up the call and attempted to stretch out the tension that coiled in my neck. This job could make or break me. There were people at the very top expecting me to come through —disappointing them was not an option.

The last time I had to worry about disappointing anyone was when my mom had still been around. There was Ari, but she'd probably have thrown a party if I disappeared off the face of the Earth. Proving myself to her had never been an issue. Ma was different. There was nothing worse than seeing her eyes shimmer with sadness when I'd gone off half-cocked or failed in some way to live up to my potential—the potential she saw in me.

I'd been a dumbass kid who thought my mom would be around forever. In two seconds flat, that childish delusion had been shattered. One minute, I was a normal kid, itching to graduate high school, the next, my world became unrecognizable. There was no longer anyone to keep me in line.

The only thing that mattered was revenge.

Ma had been one of the good ones, and I had tested her patience at every opportunity. I spent far too many hours out on the streets with friends, especially during hours of the night when no good can come from wandering about. She raised Ari and me on her own, giving us every advantage she could scrape together. It hadn't been much, but it was a hell of a lot more than some kids got. She was a hard worker, patient, kind, but also firm. She had expectations of us. That alone was a gift many kids never received, and one I hadn't appreciated until she was gone.

Often, I'd look to the sky and wonder if she was watching. If she knew the things I'd done. For a while, it weighed on me—the guilt. Over the years, I'd come to terms with who I was and my role in the world. I'd shed my worries about her disappointment like an ill-fitting skin, sluffed off on the rocks, never to be seen again.

Times change, however. Just as my world shifted when my mom died, I could sense a new shift in my trajectory. For the first time in many years, other people were counting on me—watching and waiting to see how I'd perform. I may have fallen short where my ma was concerned, but this time, I wasn't going to fail.

I was ten years older and a hell of a lot wiser. Wise enough to know that tangling myself with Alessia probably wasn't the brightest move. I needed an in, and while I could have chosen someone a little frumpier and less appealing, I'd convinced myself the moment I'd seen Alessia that she was the one.

She would make the job far more enjoyable—where was the harm in that?

Two birds, one stone. I was all about efficiency.

It had been weeks since I'd gotten laid. I wasn't the indiscriminate teenager anymore who fucked anything in a skirt. Whether they knew better or not, women regularly offered themselves up to me on a silver platter. I'd learned over the years that the old adage, quality over quantity, had merit. Any guy with a dick could stick it in a hole—there was no satisfaction in that. The pursuit of something far more refined was infinitely more appealing.

Alessia was the definition of refined.

She would be the perfect quarry, and the hunter in me was clawing to start the chase.

CHAPTER 4

Alessia

I had tried not to obsess over the elevator incident, watching
television and playing games on my phone that evening,
trying to clear my mind. But when I'd laid down in the
darkness of my bedroom, all I could think of was the soft curve
of his lips and how they'd feel pressed against mine. By morning,
I was little more than a puddle of female hormones.

I hadn't expected to hear from Luca immediately, but I was
still disappointed the next morning when my phone showed no
missed calls or messages. He didn't strike me as the type to
engage in silly games, but he also didn't seem like a man who
would be desperate for a woman's attention. He said he would be
in touch, and I believed he would, in his own time.

Until then, should I run into him at work, I wanted to make
certain he knew what was at stake. I spent a solid hour on my
hair alone that morning, ensuring every detail of my appearance
was perfect. I may have been a hot mess emotionally, but I was
one damn good-looking hot mess.

When I crossed the marble floors of the lobby on my way into work, my eyes were drawn straight to Luca. I wondered if I'd ever get used to the sight of the man. Each time I saw him, he rendered me breathless. He wasn't just attractive; he was animal magnetism personified. He was every crush and craving, each desire and fantasy, all rolled into one. Something about him called to me on a visceral level, and I was powerless to deny it.

He stood with two other men near the center of the room, listening to one of them talk. Another day and another expensive suit, this time accented with a simple black tie. Compared to the two men he was with, Luca was a formidable presence. Where others were simple evergreens crowded in a forest of trees, he was an ancient redwood, statuesque and imposing. It wasn't merely height that made the man stand out, it was the powerful aura that surrounded him. People stepped out of their way to give him a wide berth while their eyes were drawn his direction, unable to look away from the man who exuded power from his every pore.

My hands tingled in anticipation at the sight of him, but I refused to give him the satisfaction of knowing how he affected me. Instead of walking over to say hello or letting him catch me staring, I turned my head just before he began to look my direction and took the escalator without a backward glance. Inside, I may have been a teenager fangirling over her celeb crush, but on the outside, I forced an impervious air all the way to the office.

Work was infinitely more enjoyable without Roger there. We had a quick staff meeting in the morning, and I was able to catch up with a couple coworkers I hadn't spoken to in a while, which made the morning pass quickly and kept thoughts of Luca from occupying my mind. When I finally returned to my desk, I had a text waiting for me.

I saw you watching me.

My body thrummed with excitement at receiving his text. I thought about admitting the truth, but I decided there was no way he could have seen me staring at him. **I don't know what you're talking about.**

His reply was almost instant. **Don't lie to me, ever.**

The words sent a shiver prickling down my spine. Had he truly known I'd been watching? How? And how did he manage to be domineering even over a text? I felt like I was back in school, being reprimanded by a teacher, and it automatically elevated my defenses. **I'm not making any promises.**

I didn't ask for promises, just honesty.

Well, damn.

When he put it that way, I felt like an ass for resisting. Asking for honesty wasn't so unreasonable—it was a far cry from demanding the truth. Funny the difference a few words could make. **Alright, I'll do my best.**

There was no response for several minutes. His other replies had been immediate, and I wondered where he was and what might have his attention. I debated putting the phone down and getting back to work, feeling foolish for staring at a screen, waiting for a reply, but the conversation dots appeared before I could force the phone from my hand.

Let me take you to dinner.

I noted the absence of a question mark—yet another command. Did the man ever ask politely for anything, or was every word out of his mouth an order?

I had an intrinsic reaction to his domineering behavior in person, but over text, I felt more in control. **No, I don't even know you.**

Take that, Captain Pushy Pants. Let the man work for his dinner. He may have been above playing games, but apparently, I was not. Plus, Luca was clearly a man who would lose interest in a woman who fell at his feet. No doubt, he had plenty of those in his life.

Isn't that how we get to know one another?

Yes and no. I usually only go out with people I have a connection to. You could be an axe murderer, for all I know.

How has that been working for you?

Well, fuck.

He was right. I hadn't had a decent date in months. The last man I'd been out with was an accountant my mom set me up with—the son of some friend of hers. He'd sent his food back three times, complaining about too much garlic, used an inhaler halfway through the meal, and refused to leave a tip because of the imaginary garlic. I couldn't get out of there fast enough.

Touché. I'll think about it.

Don't think too long.

A giggle slipped past my lips at his reply. My immediate reaction was to text back *or what*, but I didn't cave to the temptation. A man like Luca was accustomed to getting his way, and something inside me reveled at denying him the satisfaction of a response. I tossed my phone back in my purse and buried myself in work.

I was successfully able to distract myself all day, but twenty-four hours later, Luca was all I could think about. I didn't see him the next morning on my way into work, and I was getting twitchy about not giving in to his request for a date. Could my little show at playing hard-to-get backfire on me? He certainly hadn't reached out to push for an answer—could he have decided I wasn't worth the effort?

My thoughts were consumed with questions about Luca, so much so that I was a distracted mess. I had turned on the ancient industrial coffee maker without any water in it, sent out an email to the wrong person, and had put a handful of letters into outgoing mail without any postage—all before ten a.m.

I scolded myself, insisting when I returned from lunch, I would get my head on straight before I made a major mistake and got myself in trouble. I likely wouldn't get fired—that was one of the perks of being the boss's daughter—but explaining a screw up to my dad would be a far worse punishment. Memories of past reprimands would likely forever haunt me—I didn't need to add to their numbers.

One of the most vivid of those memories danced around in my subconscious every time my father grew agitated. At the ripe old age of seven, I had left the water on in the bathtub while I ran to collect some toys for my bath. Distracted by a Barbie my older sister had mutilated, I forgot about the water. Manufacturers make those little drains on the inside of tubs to catch overflow, but I'm not sure why—they don't work worth a flip. The water flooded the bathroom and into my bedroom before I discovered what had happened. Even better, my room was on the second floor. The water leaked into the floor and dripped down into our living room.

My mother made me face my father after he came home from work and tell him exactly what had happened. The veins in his temples had pulsed with anger. He'd berated me for acting like a baby and suggested I returned to wearing diapers. He never raised a hand to me or punished me unfairly, but his disappointment and anger had been enough. I'd only been seven, but I remembered that day like it was yesterday. I hated seeing the disappointment in my father's eyes when I let him down, and if I didn't pay more attention, that was exactly the direction I was headed.

The problem was, Luca was nearly as captivating as my father was intimidating. Everything about the man screamed '*stay away, danger*'—but did that stop me from daydreaming at every opportunity? Hell, no. I was drawn to the cool control Luca exercised over himself, and likely everything in his life. Girls should be drawn to men who are sweet and respectful, not controlling and domineering. He made me nervous, but in a good way—as if being the sole focus of his attention could make the world disappear.

Nothing else would matter, only him.

It was a terrifying and intoxicating prospect.

I stepped into a crosswalk as I made my way back from lunch, absorbed in my thoughts, and was suddenly yanked back into a hard body as a small delivery truck whizzed by right where I'd been about to walk. Adrenaline surged through my veins, and I turned wide-eyed to look back at my savior.

Luca glared down at me, eyes blazing with fury.

"What … how?" I was too disoriented to formulate a clear thought.

"What the fuck, Alessia? You almost walked straight into traffic," he growled down at me, hands still gripping my arms.

"I was distracted," I replied, still breathless from the incident. I glanced down at his hands, and they slowly released me, but neither of us stepped apart.

He looked up at the buildings above us as he took in a deep breath, some of the tension softening from his features. "You have to be more careful," he chided when he brought his gaze back down to me. "I haven't gotten my date yet."

I coughed out a laugh and took a small step back, relieved he had lightened the mood. "I'd hate to disappoint you by getting killed." I sobered and dropped my chin, feeling suddenly shy. "Thank you for saving me."

Luca stepped forward nonchalantly, not letting me put space between us, and slowly lowered his mouth to my ear. My breath hitched as he drew closer, his cheek mere inches from mine. Who was this man, and why did he affect me so profoundly? Just his nearness rendered me incapable of breath or thought.

"Thank me by coming to dinner tonight." The low timbre of his voice resonated against my sensitive skin and brought on a wave of goosebumps down the length of my arms.

How could I say no?

The man had saved my life by pulling me out of the street before I was flattened. I could tell myself the only polite thing to do was to accept his invitation, but the reality was, I wanted more than anything to have dinner with him, regardless of customary civilities. I wanted to know this fortress of a man who exuded practiced control. I wanted to know what made him tick and why he was the way he was. I wanted to be the sole recipient of his focused attention.

"Alright," I breathed out as he pulled away and met my eyes. "But I'm driving myself, just tell me when and where."

His lips curved with a hint of amusement. "Del Posto on 6th— I'll reserve a table for us at seven."

I nodded and glanced toward my building. "You headed back?"

"Just leaving."

"Okay, I guess I'll see you this evening." I smiled, suddenly feeling awkward, and started to turn when he called my name.

"Try to pay attention—I may not be there next time to save you." With those words, he turned and disappeared into the river of pedestrians flowing along the city sidewalk.

My skin tingled with unease at the realization of just how lucky I'd been. Most of the people around me were too absorbed in minding their own business to stop a woman from being hit by a car. Not that they were bad people, they were simply trained to keep their eyes down and thoughts to themselves. That was city life.

I'd been three blocks from the Triton building—what were the odds at that precise moment, someone I knew would be nearby, and that someone would be Luca? In a city of millions, the odds were astronomical. I wasn't sure if I should take it as a sign of kismet or a harrowing red flag. Regardless, the outcome was the same—I had a date with Luca, only hours away.

BACK AT THE OFFICE, I spent a good amount of time stressing about my impending date. I did far less work than I should have, which wouldn't have been a problem had I not received an email from my boss informing me he would be back from his trip early.

The presentation went well, and I was able to catch an earlier flight. I want to run through the Gold Street project tomorrow morning, so have a progress report ready for me.

Fuck. Fuckfuckfuck.

Roger would be at the office tomorrow, which was bad news on its own, but to make matters worse, I had no idea what the status was on the Gold Street project. At four-thirty in the afternoon, there was hardly time to gather information, put together a report, and still make it to my date with Luca. I could go in early, but Roger often went into the office early, and there was no way I wanted to chance being alone with him in the building.

I refused to sit down with my boss the following morning and tell him I was clueless about a project I'd been supervising. That only left me with one option. I would have to cancel my date and stay late to prepare for my meeting.

Reluctantly, I took out my phone and texted Luca. **Change of plans—I'm going to have to cancel tonight. I'll text you later.**

I knew he'd argue, and I didn't have time to explain, so I turned off my ringer and dove into work. I spoke with several coworkers about where we were in the bidding process and had begun to review the drafts of our proposal documents when I sensed a presence in the doorway of my office.

My eyes rose and took in all six feet and change of an angry Luca leaning against the doorframe. His casual stance was not to be confused for indifference—a storm raged in his obsidian eyes. I sat motionless, eyes wide, hands frozen over my keyboard.

"How did you find me?" I asked, stunned.

"The elevator—you said you worked at Triton, remember?"

Of course. How could I have forgotten? My eyes danced around the room as I stood, at a loss for words. He'd come because of my text—did he plan to argue with me? There were no private conversations in my office, and Luca didn't do subtle.

Panic had me surging forward to grab Luca's hand and drag him down the hall toward one of our private conference rooms on the interior of the building. Pulling him inside, I closed the door behind us and rested my back against it.

"What are you doing here?" I hissed quietly.

He stalked to where I stood until we were toe-to-toe, his hand reaching out to clasp the back of my neck. "Don't you know it's rude to send a text like that, then disappear?"

"Don't you know it's rude to show up at someone's workplace uninvited?" I shot back.

"I'm not letting you back out tonight."

"My boss is coming back early from a trip, and I have to prepare for a meeting we're going to have in the morning."

His blazing eyes narrowed. "Go in early."

"I … I can't."

He scrutinized me to cipher out what I was leaving unsaid, but I kept my lips tightly sealed.

"We'll push dinner back an hour." He gave me an expectant look, demanding I concede to his terms.

This man I hardly knew had sought me out in my office and was insisting I have dinner with him—everything about the situation implied I should walk away—not just walk, run. And yet, in my twisted mind, it was the sexiest thing a man had ever done. The little warnings voiced in my head were lost in the tornadic winds of lust he conjured inside me. A part of me was starving for whatever it was he offered—escape, protection, explosive desire. I'd been with men before, but no one like him. Nothing even came close. He was a tsunami, and my small island had no hope of surviving his battering effects.

Head still cupped in his large hands, I nodded my acquiescence. His eyes sparked in response, pleasure radiating from those dark depths. My chest swelled with warmth at the knowledge that my surrender had brought him such satisfaction. I had always been eager to please, but that side of me became all-consuming when I was around Luca.

His thumb traced a path along my jaw, came around to my chin, then lifted to pull gently on my bottom lip. My eyes were transfixed on his face while his gaze stayed glued to my parted lips. I could almost see the thoughts as they passed behind his expressive eyes, and I wondered what he'd decide—to kiss me, or not to kiss me. I was shamefully tempted by the former.

"I'll come by the office and pick you up," he said as his hands fell away.

Not to kiss. Too bad.

"No, I'll meet you there." Some small portion of my self-preservation instincts managed to overcome my desire to please.

"Stubborn, aren't you?"

"Not normally—you seem to bring out the best in me."

He stepped back with a wicked grin. "Eight sharp, be there."

CHAPTER 5

Alessia

After throwing together some notes sufficient to get me through my morning meeting, I texted my driver to let him know I wouldn't need a ride after work. Having a driver in the city wasn't necessary, but it was one of the luxuries I allowed myself to indulge in. Plus, it had been one area in which my father had been unyielding—he didn't want any of us girls living alone in the city without a driver to get us around at night.

I had no issue with using a driver, but on that beautiful spring evening, I decided to walk to the restaurant. It was only a couple blocks from my office, and I needed the fresh air to clear my head before facing Luca. He was overwhelming in every sense of the word. There was a very real chance I would lose myself in him if I wasn't careful—drown beneath the sheer force of his will and the alluring pull of his magnetic personality.

My cheeks heated in the brisk evening air, and there was something else that caused my skin to tingle—something that set me on edge. Had I not been so focused on paying attention to my surroundings, I never would have noticed. It was the feeling of someone was watching me. Perhaps long-ingrained from our prehistoric days, I sensed an awareness of possible danger, a sixth sense that couldn't be explained.

I took a casual glance behind me, scanning the area for signs someone was watching me but saw nothing unusual—no suspicious man in a trench coat, skulking behind me or sketchy thugs eyeballing me from a distance. The city street looked like it did on any other evening, so I tried to calm my overactive imagination. Assuring myself it was likely just my anxiety over having dinner with Luca that had me worked up, I tucked my chin and continued toward the restaurant.

The place he'd chosen was an elegant Italian bistro nestled in downtown Manhattan. Despite the soaring ceilings, the room felt cozy, thanks to the rich wood accents and dimmed lighting. It was the type of place you might find a politician or movie star dining—a place that discretely catered to important people. If I hadn't been used to such establishments my entire life, I might have been unnerved by the place. As it was, I had been to Del Posto before and was well acquainted with the experience.

I arrived before Luca, but he entered only minutes after. I hadn't had the wherewithal to admire how he looked in his black suit at either of our earlier exchanges—both having been too intense to allow for a casual perusal of his suited form. The sight of him crossing the foyer toward me liquified my insides. The fabric of his suit pulled taut where his biceps flexed against the sleeves, and the broad expanse of his shoulders over his narrow waist made my mouth go dry. As if he knew the effect he had on me, a wolfish grin spread across his face.

"I may not have said it earlier today, but you look stunning." He took my hand and pressed his lips to the back, just below my knuckles, lingering briefly. The sensation edged my heartrate up from a gentle thrum to a fluttering frenzy.

"Thank you. You look rather handsome yourself."

Not releasing my hand, he led me to the hostess station where the young woman on duty snapped into motion.

"This way, please." She led us to the back of the restaurant toward a table in the far corner.

"I'm impressed you could get a reservation moved on such late notice," I whispered to Luca.

"The owner is a friend of mine," he murmured near my ear as he helped me into my seat.

Blushing at his nearness, I glanced down at the white china place setting. "I guess it pays to have friends in high places."

As soon as he was seated, our server brought waters and took our drink orders. The moment I gave my wine selection, Luca instructed the server to bring a bottle.

"That's not necessary," I cut in.

The young man looked between us, and Luca gave him a stern, raised brow. Without looking back to me, our server scurried off to obtain the bottle.

"Do you always get your way?" I asked with amusement.

"Quite often, yes."

"And yet you still manage to have friends?"

"Having friends is an important part of my business."

"And what business is that?"

"Banking."

I tilted my head, looking him over appraisingly. "You don't strike me as the banker type."

"No?" he mused. "What type do I seem like?"

The question was a tricky one. I'd already thought about it after our encounter in the elevator but had come up empty-handed. His features were so striking, it was hard to think of him as doing anything outside of modeling. Then again, his dark intensity lent itself to positions of power and a job that would require a great deal of drive. "Maybe a pro athlete or an actor?"

He took a sip of his freshly poured wine, eyes still bright with amusement. "Nothing so exciting as that, I'm afraid."

"What bank do you work for?"

"You probably wouldn't know it—we're a relatively small-scale operation."

"Do you like what you do?"

He peered at me for long seconds, seemingly weighing his answer. "It's my life; it's who I am."

There was silence between us for a moment as his words lingered in the air. It was a bold statement. I could relate because my company was family-owned, but not many other people in my experience felt the same sense of ownership regarding their job.

"What about you—what do you do for Triton?" he asked, bringing the discussion back to me.

"I work in the marketing department currently."

"And do you enjoy it?"

I rolled my eyes playfully. "When my boss isn't around." Bringing my glass to my lips, I took a healthy sip of wine. I could feel Luca's assessing gaze attempt to read between the lines, but I wasn't going to give him more information.

"What is it about your boss you dislike?"

I should have known he wouldn't leave that one alone. What did I tell him without saying too much? I hadn't told my sisters or anyone but Giada about my boss—I certainly wasn't going to tell Luca, who I'd only just met.

"He's … bossy, that's all." I smiled, hoping to lure him away from the subject.

Taking the bait, his eyes sparked with mischief. "I could have sworn you liked that in a man."

"It's more tolerable in some men than others."

"And do you have any other bossy but tolerable men in your life?"

Was he asking if I was seeing anyone? Surely, he knew the fact that I'd come to dinner meant I wasn't involved with anyone else. "No."

He lifted his chin, acknowledging my answer as the server came to take our orders. "Captain's menu, please."

"Yes, sir. And your antipasti selection?"

We both gave our orders and had our glasses topped off before the man scurried off to the kitchen.

"It's refreshing to see a woman who knows what she wants," Luca remarked. I had hardly perused the menu, knowing what I would order well before I arrived.

"There's hardly a bad choice on the menu. I grew up eating most of these dishes or simplified versions." I smiled to myself, remembering my mother's mother who used to cook for us at every opportunity. Food is a cornerstone in any Italian home.

"Tell me more about your family."

"There's not much to tell. There are lots of them—as is the Italian Catholic way—but otherwise, we're a pretty standard lot."

"Are you close to them?"

"That depends on what you mean by close. We have Sunday dinner each week, per my mother's orders, but I wouldn't say we're close in the true sense. We're all pretty private, I guess. What about you—are you close with your family?"

"My dad wasn't around, and my mom died years ago. I have a younger sister, but she's a pain in my ass—always finding herself in some kind of trouble," he grumbled.

It made me smile to think of tough-guy Luca attempting to parent a younger sister. If she was half as gifted in the looks department, I could see how she might be quite the handful. "It's good that she has you. A protective older brother could be an asset in this life." The realization of what I'd said made my breath catch.

I'd had an older brother once, and the memory of his loss, though many years ago, still weighed heavily on my heart. Not wanting to darken the mood with such thoughts, I cast them away with a silent apology to the boy who lived on only in memory.

Our food arrived at that moment, giving me a chance to collect myself. Each course was more delicious than the last. I chided myself for relying so often on my meal delivery service. Their catered meals were as good as pre-prepared food could be, but it couldn't compare to a freshly cooked meal.

By the time dessert arrived, I could hardly take a single bite. There were only a couple fingers of wine left in the bottle, which Luca poured into my glass.

"I can't possibly drink anymore—I'm stuffed, and I need to be able to get myself home," I said with a wry smile. The food had helped to mute the effects of the wine, but I had a nice buzz going. Not so much to be stumbling drunk, but enough that I felt light and airy.

Luca's eyes heated, and the muscles in his jaw twitched. "I'm sure I could get you home."

"I bet you could, and I'd probably lose my clothes in the process."

"Undoubtedly," he admitted confidently.

We held each other's gaze for a pregnant moment. The hunger in his eyes was an erotic promise, challenge intrinsic in his stare. As if he could project thoughts into my mind, visions of Luca bare-chested and thrusting inside me, making me scream his name in pleasure, infiltrated my head. With a shaky breath, I dropped my gaze, breaking our contact.

"I should probably get going—I have an important meeting in the morning." My voice was breathy, and my words sounded uncertain, even to my ear. When I took a hesitant glance back up to Luca, he wore a wicked smile.

"Let's get you home."

After he paid the check, and we made our way outside, I turned to tell him goodnight.

"Let me walk you to your car," he offered.

"I don't have a car. I walked." I didn't want to tell him I had a driver. He was decently well-off in the money department, but I didn't want to look ostentatious.

"You're not walking home," he said irritably. "We'll take a cab; come with me." He tugged at my hand, but I held my ground.

"I don't need a ride—I live nearby."

Luca stepped close, his gaze burning through me, leaving his mark on my soul in a way that I'd feel long after we parted for the night. The air around us became charged with anticipation, heavy like the moist air of a sultry Florida evening.

In that frozen moment of time, there was only me and Luca.

Weaving his fingers into my hair, he slowly lowered his lips to mine. He was gentle but firm, his lips molding to mine as perfectly as I'd imagined they would. I could feel his restraint as if he were holding a delicate butterfly and trying not to crush its wings. Tasting. Testing. But before long, his control snapped as his touch dug into my flesh, and his kiss became demanding. He seized my mouth like he couldn't get enough—like I held the cure to whatever darkness seethed inside him.

I should have been alarmed, but instead, a moan slipped past my lips, spurring him on. I lost track of the city around me. People walked past us, and horns honked in the distance as cars wove in and out of traffic, but none of it penetrated my senses. I was ensnared in his kiss, his touch lighting my body on fire as I gave him everything he demanded.

Eventually, he pulled back, eyes hooded and black as night. "Come, I'll walk you home."

His warm fingers took hold of mine, a current running between us, electric and inviting. He led us down the sidewalk without a word from me until I realized we were walking in the correct direction without me telling him where to go.

"How did you know which direction?" I asked curiously.

He glanced at me wryly. "Lucky guess—I had a fifty-fifty shot."

I arched a brow. "Do you often play by chance?"

"I very rarely leave anything to chance. I'm far too controlling to rely on luck to get me what I want."

"You don't say," I mumbled just loud enough for him to hear.

He cut his eyes to me, and there was a hint of humor in their dark depths. "I see you, on the other hand, like to live dangerously."

His teasing made my heart sore, and I offered him a beaming smile to which he shook his head with a laugh. I led us to my building where trepidation and awkwardness set in, at least on my part. Nothing about Luca could ever be awkward or uncertain. He pulled me aside, just outside the entry steps.

"When do you go to work in the morning?"

"Why?" What did it matter to him when I went to work?

"I'll drive you. I'm heading to the Triton building, so I might as well give you a ride—there's too much crime in this city for you to be walking."

"Actually, I have a driver," I admitted reluctantly. "I don't tend to tell people because they often treat me differently when they realize I have money."

"I'm not like other people; surely, you've figured that out. No lies and no omissions, not with me. Understand?" His hand gently secured a stray strand of hair behind my ear, and I could see in the softening of his features, he was genuinely pleased I wouldn't be walking. He lowered his lips and gently kissed my temple, hands threaded through my hair. "I'm not coming upstairs with you tonight … but soon. I suggest you get used to the idea." He spoke against my skin, the soft caress of his lips sending waves of chills down my spine. Pulling back, he gazed longingly at my lips. "I'll see you tomorrow," he promised, then drifted away down the sidewalk, leaving me cold and alone.

We'd had no plans to see one another again, but his parting words indicated there would be more—much more. I had never pictured myself with a man like Luca. I figured I'd find a stockbroker or some executive and have a standard suburban life similar to my own upbringing. Luca made it hard to see anything but him—like looking into the sun, blinding me to everything else.

There was only Luca.

My mind became entrenched in thoughts of when I'd see him next. It didn't matter that I had an important meeting in the morning, that laundry needed to be done, or that I had Sunday lunch plans with my family—I wanted to spend that time with Luca. Would he call or text before then? Would I let him fuck me the next time we went out? Could I tell him no even if I wanted to? The question was pointless—I'd wanted to see him naked since the moment I spotted him walking through the Triton lobby. I might have given in to him after dinner had he pressed the issue.

I started to worry I was becoming obsessed, which wasn't like me. Even as a young girl, I never lined my bedroom walls with posters of my favorite celebrity or doodled hearts around a boyfriend's name. I was rational and intentional about my choices in life, but nothing about my desire for Luca was rational. My interest in him defied logic and consumed my every thought. He was a poisonous fruit, and I was a woman starved. He was likely bad for me, but my mouth watered with hunger for him. I would convince myself one taste wouldn't hurt, and that would be the end of me.

I would no longer be Alessia—I would be his.

CHAPTER 6

Luca

When I first asked Alessia out over text, she'd made me wait longer than I'd expected for an answer. Most of the women I'd been around fell over themselves to spend time with me. Had I not stopped her from walking into traffic, I wasn't sure she would have agreed to a date at all. The reminder of seeing her nearly killed had me clenching my fists until my knuckles ached.

What had she been thinking, being so careless on a city street? The drivers in New York were lunatics; it was a miracle more pedestrians weren't killed each year. It made me livid to think about what might have happened if I hadn't been following her.

When I'd leaned in to tell her how she could thank me, my lungs filled with the sweet scent of her. My gut clenched, and I was overtaken with the need to know if she tasted just as delicious—like raspberries in the summer breeze. I thought I'd all but guaranteed I'd get the chance to taste her that night until her text came through, canceling our plans. If she'd thought she could shake me off so easily, she had sorely misjudged me.

I hadn't crawled my way out of the gutter without a little determination and an unwillingness to take no for an answer. It had been time for her to get a glimpse of who she was dealing with—a hint of the cutthroat man who lurked beneath the outer façade of restraint and civility. I was endlessly curious how she'd respond to him.

When I walked into her office and saw her almond-shaped eyes round with surprise and her painted red lips part on a silent gasp, all I could think about was how I wanted to see that red lipstick smeared all over my dick. I wasn't sure what she thought I was going to do in her glass-walled office, but she'd obviously been worried. She was out of her chair, tugging me down the hall before I'd gotten a single word out. I would never have jeopardized her job, but she hadn't known that. Her fear played into my hand perfectly—once she had tucked us away into a secluded room, I was free to do whatever I pleased, and it wouldn't have taken any coercing.

She had practically begged me to kiss her.

The way her lips had parted… The way her chocolate brown eyes had liquified … I'd had to blow my load afterward to get my raging hard-on under control. She was the epitome of everything I found sexy in a woman. It had only taken a couple of strokes, she had me so on edge. My lack of control had been an embarrassment—I hadn't come that quickly since my voice had first changed in the eighth grade.

Had I given in to my urge to kiss her in the conference room, caved to that raw need, there was no telling how far it would have gone. Fortunately, I managed to maintain control of myself, knowing it was more important to leave her wanting than to quench my own desire. She had already proven as skittish as a frightened rabbit. I didn't want to give her any additional reason to pull away.

Alessia was a study in contradictions. The more I learned, the less I understood, and the more fascinated I became. She was prickly yet soft, spoiled but grounded, independent while remaining pliant. The most intriguing part of her was her guileless innocence—as if she were clueless to the world around her.

Could it all be an act? Or was the sexy siren truly as naïve as she seemed? If so, the right thing to do would be to keep things aboveboard—get my information and get out. She would be better off not tangled up in my world. Unfortunately for her, I was never very good at doing the right thing for anyone but myself. It was her own fault she was so fucking tempting, at least that's what I told myself.

However, chances were slim to none the gorgeous career girl was as pure as she seemed. I had discovered a crucial bit of information when I'd gone in search of Alessia at her office. What I found indicated she likely didn't have an innocent bone in her body.

What I found changed everything.

If she was truly more wolf than lamb, it was even more reason for me to keep our interactions purely platonic. I didn't need that kind of complication in my life. And yet, what I wanted to do and what I should do were two totally different things. Whether she was innocent or not, it would be best to keep a tight rein on my raging libido, but it was clear that wasn't happening. The taste of her lips on mine wasn't going to satisfy the beast within me. He wanted every piece of her—not just a kiss and a few tidbits of information. He wanted to crawl beneath her skin and see inside her soul.

The insistent craving was distracting.

Regardless of what was right, what I should do, or what I wanted, I was there for a purpose, and that purpose was not my dick. I was looking for someone, and now I knew Alessia could likely give me the answers I needed. That was far more important than anything else.

I needed to get my information and walk away—that would be best for both of us.

But that seductive voice in the back of my mind whispered sweet words of temptation—wasn't I allowed to have a little fun on the job? It was only sex, nothing more. I desperately wanted to sink myself inside her, and if it helped me get the information I needed, more's the better. Right? Once I'd felt the creamy skin of her inner thighs wrapped around my waist, the pulsing need to have her would subside.

Hypocrisy is a tricky thing. It parades itself around like rationale and reason, deceiving you into believing your thoughts are sound and just when they are anything but. I had demanded honesty from Alessia but was attempting to pull the wool over my own eyes. I could tell myself all day long one taste of her would be enough, but I knew deep down inside, I had no intention of letting her go.

Consequences be damned—she was mine.

CHAPTER 7
Alessia

My meeting with Roger went better than I had anticipated. At the last minute, I pulled in one of our contract managers to join us in the discussion, seating him between us, despite the disgruntled glares from Roger. The report I'd scrambled to prepare had been enough to satisfy my boss, and our third wheel had ensured the meeting didn't last any longer than necessary.

My thoughts drifted throughout the morning to my dinner with Luca. It had been one of the best dates I recalled ever having. Our conversation had flowed naturally, setting me at ease in what otherwise would have been an unnerving situation. He was respectful of the staff, polite but firm. I found that I loved watching him in action—the way he spoke to people and how he carried himself.

I'd been on a date with a man once who could hardly summon the courage to ask for a refill—there had never been any hope for him. If he couldn't ask a waiter for water, how could he possibly earn my respect? Being physically appealing was only a portion of the attraction equation. Financial responsibility, shared interests, respect, and numerous other elements were all just as important. For me, one of the most important qualities in a man was confidence—meek and simpering was a total turnoff.

The control Luca exercised in every situation was a testament to his unerring confidence. He was sure of himself and comfortable with who he was. He didn't suffer from the burden of societal pressures like most people. Luca was unapologetically himself, and that was just as alluring as any Hollywood smile or perfectly chiseled abs.

I also appreciated that he told me about his family. Men were often guarded about their families, and him sharing about his mother's death and his struggles with his sister helped me see a more human side to the otherwise stoic man. I had desperately wanted to ask questions but felt it might be too forward on the first date.

Thinking about him losing his mom brought me to thoughts of my own family. Aside from Giada, the person I was closest to was probably Sofia. Neither of us had ever connected well with Maria, who was the oldest of us girls. Aside from a few words with her at our family dinners, I couldn't remember the last time I'd spoken to Maria. Sofia, on the other hand, had been my playmate as a child and was somewhat of a confidant through our teen years. Since then, we had maintained a decent relationship with periodic phone calls and the occasional lunch date but nothing so constant as my friendship with Giada.

I realized I hadn't spoken to Sofia in what felt like ages. She had been preparing for finals during our last family dinner and managed the impossible feat of bowing out of the obligation. I could count on one hand the number of times I'd been allowed to miss a Sunday dinner. Since I hadn't seen her in two weeks, I grabbed my phone, noting no new missed messages or calls, and dialed my sister's number.

"Hey, Lessi. What's up?" came Sofia's angelic voice. When she was little, she couldn't say my name, instead using the moniker 'Lessi.' The nickname stuck for many years, although no one else in the family still used the endearment.

Sofia was the golden child—literally and figuratively. Her hair was a dirty blond highlighted with natural golden streaks, and she had the fairest complexion of all of us. From the time she was little, she'd been a talented artist and was fiercely independent. She never seemed to feel the need to strive for acceptance by our parents or anyone else. She was just about perfect in every way—even her voice sounded like it came from heaven above.

At different stages in our lives, I'd been jealous of my little sister, but no longer found myself ensnared in that pitfall. With age had come the maturity to understand that nobody's life was perfect, even if it appeared that way. I kept my issues to myself, and she no doubt did the same. Who was I to say her problems were any less than mine?

"Hey, Sof! Nothing's up, just wanted to see how you were doing."

"Ugh, I've still got one more final to go," she groaned.

"You excited to be done?"

"Yes and no—when I'm done with school, I have to move back home for a few weeks until my new apartment is ready."

"Can't say I envy you."

"Yeah, and if that isn't bad enough, I have to suffer through my graduation party. I keep telling Mom I don't need a party."

"Good luck with that," I laughed in response, knowing Mom would never cancel at this rate. "How are the job prospects going?"

She paused with indecision. "Actually, I got a job in a small gallery on the lower east side."

"Sof, that's great news! Have you told Mom and Dad?"

"No, although, I suppose I'll have to at some point," she grumbled.

"Why don't you want to tell them?"

"I just don't see a reason for them to know every aspect of my life."

"You and Maria are so freaking secretive."

"Hold up—don't go comparing me to Maria. We are nothing alike—it's not even apples and oranges. She and I are like apples and bicycles."

It seems I'd struck a chord. Sofia was almost always even-keel, but I'd clearly ruffled her feathers. "Okay, my bad. Maria definitely takes secrecy to a whole other level—I didn't mean to offend."

I heard a sigh drift over the line. "Sorry, I'm just stressed and exhausted."

"No problem—we're all just doing the best we can. I suppose I can relate a little. I haven't told Mom and Dad, but I met someone," I offered quietly, not wanting anyone in the office to overhear.

"Oh, yeah? Tell me about him!"

"There's nothing to tell, yet—I just started dating him."

"But?" she prompted with the word I'd left unspoken, too scared to admit the intensity of my feelings.

"But there's something about him; he's not like the other guys I've dated." I was trying to share with my sister, but there was only so far I was willing to open up. There was something mysterious and intriguing about Luca that I wasn't ready to share with anyone else.

"You going to bring him to dinner on Sunday?" she asked coyly.

"Hell no! Are you crazy?"

"Come on, Lessi, that would take the spotlight off me," she pouted playfully.

"Wouldn't dream of it, little sis. That spotlight is all yours."

"Fine, be that way," she pouted.

"I will, thanks. You get back to studying. I'll see you on Sunday," I said the last part in a sing-song voice.

"You better. I don't want to face the inquisition alone," she muttered.

"Never. I shall be your faithful protector."

Sofia giggled. "Love you, Lessi."

"Love you, too," I returned warmly before hanging up, a smile plastered on my face as I dove back into work.

An hour later, I made my way downstairs to get lunch and run a couple of errands. My eyes were immediately drawn to Luca where he stood talking on his phone. The moment his eyes landed on mine, he ended his call and began stalking my way, not taking his eyes from me.

I'd say he moved with a predator's grace, but that wouldn't be accurate. He didn't just move like a predator—he was a predator. The question was, just how ruthless were his instincts? Did he merely enjoy the hunt, or was he one who liked to toy with his prey?

Luca stepped close, only speaking when we were near enough not to be overheard. "If I didn't already have work obligations, I'd insist you join me for lunch." His words spoken softly in his deep, rasping voice felt like an intimate caress in the crowded room.

"That's okay," I offered, feeling my cheeks heat. "I have some errands to run anyway."

"I want you to spend the afternoon with me tomorrow."

"Okay." My reply was instant. I gave no thought to any other obligations I might have had for my Saturday. That's what the man did to me—he intoxicated me with his presence until I thought of nothing else but him.

His lips curled in a knowing grin. "Let me sort some things, and I'll be in touch." He leaned down and placed one of his tender kisses on my temple, and I melted onto the floor of the lobby as I watched his retreating form exit the building.

Scraping myself off the marble tiles, I followed in his wake toward the busy New York street when I heard my name hollered behind me. I looked back for the source and was surprised to see a man I'd been friends with at school. Jackson Byrne had been a fellow business student at NYU, and we'd had some shared friends who hung out occasionally. Despite a mutual attraction between us, we'd never dated. The timing had never been quite right—either I was in a relationship when he was interested or the other way around.

It occurred to me Luca would never have allowed something so silly as a boyfriend to come between him and a woman he wanted. In that regard, the two men were worlds apart. However, Jackson bore his own brand of devilish, Irish charm and rugged good looks. Deep dimples were the perfect accent to his affable nature, and his curling dark hair and mocha eyes were warm and inviting. We hadn't stayed in touch since graduating more than a year ago, and I was pleased to run into him.

"Jackson! What a pleasant surprise. How have you been?" I asked, giving him a hug when he caught up with me.

"I'm really well. And you?"

"I'm doing great. It's been ages since I've seen you. Are you working in the building now?"

"No, I work for Investors Bank in the commercial department and was meeting with a client. I take it you're still working at Triton with your father?"

"Yes, climbing my way up the ranks."

"I still can't believe your dad didn't put you straight into upper management."

"That's not the way he works, and it's not that bad. I've learned so much in just a year."

He smiled at me, but wariness crept into his eyes before they dropped to his hands.

"Is everything okay?" I asked warily.

Returning his gaze to me, his features hardened with resolve.

"I know it's not any of my business, but I saw you earlier with that man in the lobby. How well do you know him?"

His question caught me off guard, and I stumbled for words. "I … we went to dinner last night—that's about it."

"He's not a good man, Alessia. You should stay away from him." Jackson's voice was sharper, his eyes harder, than I could ever recall seeing the handsome playboy.

"What do you mean?" My stomach churned with unease.

His lips pursed, and he exhaled a frustrated sigh. "I can't really explain, but I've heard things about him. Bad things. I'd hate for you to get hurt."

Heard things? What did that mean? "You can't give me any more than that?"

Lips pressed tightly together, he shook his head.

"Alright, thank you for the warning."

His eyes softened. "I really have missed seeing you. We should grab dinner and catch up sometime. Is your number still the same?"

"Yeah, that sounds nice." I forced a smile, pushing aside my worry.

Jackson gave me one more hug before disappearing down the busy sidewalk while I was momentarily rooted to the spot. What had he meant with his cryptic warning? Was he simply trying to tell me Luca was a player, or had there been a more nefarious meaning behind his words? Then again, maybe Jackson finally wanted to date me and was trying to push away the competition.

Without a more concrete explanation, it was hard to put much weight into his words. I wasn't about to ignore him, but I didn't think a vague warning was sufficient to act on. I would tuck away the cautionary words to revisit later if needed.

CHAPTER 8
Alessia

Luca texted that evening, telling me he would pick me up at three the next afternoon. He also instructed me to dress casually and bring a sweater but refused to tell me where we were going. I laid awake that night for ages, wondering where we would go, and what Luca would look like in casual clothes. I hadn't seen what was under the suit, but his sculpted physique suggested he would look mouthwatering in anything he wore.

Despite a short night of sleep, I woke easily, excitement thrumming in my veins the moment my eyes opened. Wanting to release some of that pent-up energy, I went to the gym inside my apartment building and ran until my muscles were thoroughly fatigued. I tried to keep a regular exercise regimen, but lately, I'd been too busy to do anything more than get a run in whenever the chance presented itself.

After the run, I wobbled down the block in my sweat-soaked gear to the corner coffee shop and loaded up on caffeine. No, it didn't make sense to wear myself out just to stock up on caffeine, but we can't all make sense all the time. Sometimes, we just have to do what feels right, and that first sip of creamer-rich coffee tasted all kinds of right.

On my way back to my building, the sensation of being watched crept into my awareness, just as it had a few days earlier. Rather than trying to be discrete, I stopped mid-step and spun around, searching the street behind me. It was early on a Saturday morning, and while the area was far from empty, it was less crowded than it would be later that day. Not a single person looked suspicious or out of place. No one startled at my abrupt about-face or even noticed me, for that matter. I decided to march my crazy ass back home and attempt to chase away my newfound case of paranoia with a shower and some breakfast. The coffee might not help matters, but there was no way I was giving that up.

It was just after ten in the morning when I arrived back home, still hours and hours away from my date, with nothing to do but get myself ready. I jumped in the shower, ridding my body of all unnecessary hair, scrubbing myself within an inch of my life. Once I was fully buffed, shaved, shampooed, and conditioned, I started the chore of deciding what to wear.

Dress casually.

Any woman would know that was a joke—there were infinite degrees of *casual* in a woman's wardrobe. A slight heel on a sandal or the thickness of the straps on a blouse could drastically affect the feel of an outfit. Casual dress to ride the New York Circle Line ferry would be far different than the casual dress for a Broadway matinee.

I tried on dozens of outfits before deciding on mint skinny jeans with a sleeveless floral top and ivory cardigan. Using the curling wand, I gave my long hair gentle waves, then applied a full face of barely-there makeup. To my utter dismay, it was only one o'clock when I applied the last strokes of mascara. I had drawn out my routine as long as humanly possible and still had two hours until Luca would arrive.

The clock ticked by agonizingly slowly. By the time two forty-five rolled around, I had watched an hour of Naked and Afraid, organized my kitchen junk drawer, and cleaned the lint out of my dryer. When the text came through from Luca saying he was waiting downstairs, relief that the wait was over helped balance out my nerves—until I walked outside and saw Luca leaning against the sleek lines of his black Audie R8.

I'd been right. Luca in a suit was a sight to behold, but Luca in jeans blew a circuit in my brain. My thoughts dissipated in a puff of smoke before a surge of nerves threatened to overwhelm me. Luca, on the other hand, was unruffled as always in a casual button-down shirt rolled up to his elbows, his jean-clad legs crossed at the ankles. He was every girl's spank-bank goldmine. Images of him standing there like a ruthless god could get me through a year-long dry spell.

"Hey," I greeted breathlessly, overwhelmed by his beauty.

"Hey yourself, gorgeous." He pushed away from the car with a smirk, placing a soft kiss on my cheek, then opened the passenger door for me.

I glanced around the interior of the car, appreciating its luxury touches while Luca walked to the driver's side. He was surprisingly graceful, folding his large frame into the compact sports car.

"Now will you tell me where we're going?" I asked playfully as he started the car and looked for oncoming traffic.

He grinned without taking his eyes from the road. "We're going to the beach."

"Coney Island?" I asked excitedly. "That's way more romantic than I pegged you for."

"Are you saying I can't be romantic?"

"I don't see you as a flowers and poetry kind of guy, no."

"Good," he huffed, unable to hide his smirk. "Because I'm not."

"I haven't been to Coney Island in ages, but I loved it when I was growing up."

"Me too," he mused. "Did you grow up in the city?"

"Staten Island, so close enough. You?"

"Hoboken."

"New Jersey, but still practically in the city," I pointed out more to myself than for his benefit. "Did you like growing up there?"

He glanced over, a hint of darkness clouding his eyes. "I didn't have the childhood you did. We didn't have much with my father gone, so I spent a lot of time on the streets."

Hoping he didn't think I was prying, I continued to ask questions, trying to sate my unending curiosity. "How did you end up where you are now?" The odds weren't great for a kid who started out on the streets to become a successful banker.

He came to a stop at a light and gave me a long, hard look that sent a shiver down my spine. "After my mother died, I was adopted into a new family. They instilled a work ethic and taught me how to survive."

Caving to the pressure of his piercing gaze, I dropped my eyes to where his hand rested on the gearshift. His knuckles bore the telltale remnants of scars. *How had I not noticed before?* My chest ached as I wondered what Luca had gone through during those years on the streets. My hand reached of its own accord to ghost my fingertips along the mutilated remnants of his past. The car lurched forward when the light turned green, snapping me out of the morose spell I'd fallen under. I quickly pulled my hand back into my lap and turned my gaze out the window.

"You know," I said thoughtfully. "I realized this morning that I don't even know your last name."

The lines of his jaw softened with the change in subject. "Romano."

Luca Romano.

It suited him. The name commanded respect without being flashy or overbearing.

"Aren't you going to ask mine?" I prodded.

"Alessia Genovese—I came to your office, remember?"

"You're always one step ahead, aren't you?" I sighed, dropping my head back on the headrest. "I feel like you know everything about me already, and I hardly know you at all."

"I like to be on my game, yes, but there's still plenty I don't know about you."

"Like what?"

"Like whether you scream when you come," Luca offered in a lust-filled rumble.

That was unexpected. His comment had rendered me speechless, but my body had reacted instantly—nipples pebbling, my heart thrumming in my chest.

"And if I don't?" I asked softly.

"Honey, what I've got planned for you, you won't have a choice." His eyes cut to mine, his lips pulling back in a wicked grin.

Turns out, he did make me scream … by forcing me on the Cyclone rollercoaster.

Once we got to the boardwalk, we rode a dozen different rides, which all looked far more dangerous than I remembered. The Ferris wheel was the only one he didn't have to drag me onto. It probably wasn't any safer since it looked far older than the others, but the slow rotation gave the illusion of safety, and I'd really wanted to see the area from up above.

The sun had begun to close in on the horizon, not quite setting but low enough to cast long shadows across the landscape. "The city is beautiful from up here," I absently noted as we took our turn paused at the top of the wheel.

Luca draped his arm behind me and pulled me in close against his hard body. "I love this city—can't imagine living anywhere else."

"I think when you're from New York, it becomes a part of you. The diversity and opportunities, anything you could ever want is right here—why would anyone want to leave?" When I stopped speaking, I realized I could feel the weight of his stare.

Luca's fathomless gaze searched my face, for what, I was unsure. He brought his hand from my shoulder up to the back of my head, weaving his fingers into my hair, and pulled me in for a tender, sensual kiss. As the car slowly rocked, we tasted each other in an achingly sweet kiss. Lust began to stir deep in my belly but was doused when the ride jerked back into motion, startling us away from one another and sending me into a fit of giggles.

Luca shook his head playfully. "Reminds me of getting caught making out in my bedroom as a kid."

"You fooled around in your house when your mom was home?" I couldn't even comprehend doing that.

"I did a lot more than that," he said with a fiendish grin. "I was hell on wheels. My poor ma never had a chance."

"What did she do when she caught you?" I was pretty sure my dad would have locked me in a basement until I was fifty.

"She'd chase off the girl, then slap me upside the head while she cursed me out in Italian. She would spit fire once she got going; it was impressive, really."

"Do you know Italian?" I asked in surprise.

"Nah. My dad didn't speak it, so ma didn't use it much—she was more Italian than him. Your family speak it?"

"No, my mom's mom did; she lived with us for a while when I was young. I wish I could—it's a beautiful language. I've thought about buying software or taking a class but haven't ever taken the time."

"Think I'd rather just go spend a month or so in Italy," he mused, gazing off toward the beach.

"That sounds great in theory, but I couldn't just leave for a month."

"Why not? You taking care of an elderly relative or have kids in school or something?"

"No."

"Life is short, Alessia. You should live it to the fullest. You are the only one who dictates the parameters of your world. If you say you can't do something, then you can't, but if you believe you can, you'll find a way. You want to go to Italy, spend a summer, find a way to make it happen."

I had no response. He made it sound so easy, it almost felt possible. The bold way he seized life made me feel alive when I was with him. I never realized I'd been living life in a hazy dream state until he swept into my world. Now, he'd roused me from my sleep, and I saw the world in bold new colors. When my time with him was over, I wasn't sure how I'd survive if he took that vibrancy with him.

We were quiet for a few beats as the car rounded closer to the ground, both lost in our thoughts. Eventually, the ride ended, and Luca helped me from the car, leading me away from the throng of people clustered near the ride entrance.

"What do you want to do next?" To my endless embarrassment, my stomach took that moment to rumble its insistent need for sustenance.

"Sounds like it's time for dinner," Luca teased. "Come on, let's get you some food." He took my hand in his and led me out of the amusement park area toward the boardwalk where he bought us each a hot dog and a bag of cotton candy for us to share.

The sun had begun to drop below the horizon as we sat at a table under a blue umbrella. We'd been lucky to get a table—the boardwalk was packed with people, even more so than it had been hours before when we'd arrived. We ate quickly, fending off the bold seagulls who lay in wait for the smallest window to swoop in and snatch our food.

"Blue or pink?" Luca asked when we'd finished our dogs.

"The cotton candy?" I asked in confusion. "There's no difference."

"Don't be absurd—blue is way better than the pink," he said as he tore off a chunk and dropped it into his mouth.

I reached over and tore off a section of pink. "I suppose if blue is your favorite, I shall have to suffer through eating the pink."

Luca winked at me as he tore off another chunk, then reached his non-sticky hand out for mine. "Come on, let's go walk by the water."

We removed our shoes and made our way through the thick sand toward the shore. Most of the beachgoers had packed up and gone home for the evening, leaving the beach open for walkers and sightseers. The sand was still warm and felt amazing beneath my feet as we strolled toward the water. It wasn't exactly the Caribbean, but it was a nice change of pace, and the setting sun was a melted rainbow of colors over the placid waters.

"Which ride was your favorite?" Luca asked, extending a clump of pink candy toward my lips.

"The Brooklyn Flyer," I replied around the dissolving sugar.

"The swings?" His nose scrunched up in distaste. "Come on, you loved the Cyclone, admit it."

"Sorry to disappoint, but I've never been much of a thrill-seeker. I was more of a piano and art kind of girl growing up than soccer or lacrosse."

"I wasn't one for organized sports either actually, but I could play a mean game of handball. We could go to the Y for free and play for hours. I'd come home with jammed fingers and bloody knuckles, but I loved it."

"That sounds awful."

He shrugged. "It kept us out of trouble and didn't cost anything—no equipment or fees, and no coaching necessary. There was always basketball too, but my friends and I always gravitated toward handball."

"Do you ever play as an adult?"

"Haven't in years. Most of the guys I played with moved to different parts of the city. If you weren't into sports, does that mean you didn't play anything?"

"I did cross country and still run about three times a week. It's a lot less risky than most other sports."

"You're rather risk averse, are you?" he peered at me with a mischievous glint in his eyes.

"Certain types of risk, yes," I admitted with a defiant tone.

Luca pulled me in close, my body pressed snuggly against his, and lowered his face until our noses just barely touched. "We'll have to see what we can do about that. The riskiest ventures can yield the greatest prizes." His eyes dropped to my lips as they parted in breathless anticipation; but instead of kissing me, his lips pulled back in a boyish grin. "Speaking of prizes, I think the carnival awaits." He stunned me when he pulled away and tugged me back in the direction of the brightly lit boardwalk.

What a tease.

I couldn't be upset, though. Luca's eyes lit with excitement at the prospect of carnival games. The enthusiasm was contagious, my heartrate picking up its pace at the prospect of playing for a prize.

The beautiful Saturday evening had drawn out droves of people, which meant every food stand and game booth had a line. After a careful scan of the options, I committed to the ring-toss game and failed miserably. Luca was a different story. He went straight for the shooting game, perfectly picking off each target like a practiced marksman and earning me a large stuffed bear.

"How in the world did you learn to shoot so well?" I gawked at him over the head of my new furry companion.

"Lots of practice at the range," he explained matter-of-factly.

"We have gun ranges in the city?" I wracked my brain and couldn't recall ever noticing signs for any gun ranges.

"Of course. Most of them are underground."

My steps faltered, and the woman walking behind me nearly

collided with my back. "You go to illegal gun ranges?" I hissed as he pulled me aside out of the way of the flow of traffic.

"When I said underground, I meant that literally," he said with an amused grin. "They aren't illegal—they're built in basements to make use of the concrete walls."

Oh. "Illegal sounded much more exciting."

"Sorry to disappoint—I'll try to be more lawless with my future hobbies."

I peered up at him curiously. "What other hobbies do you have?"

His eyes became hooded, and a lazy smile spread across his face. "There are a number of things I excel at—shooting is only one of them." The heat in his eyes was so prolific, I could feel the warming effects across every inch of my skin. Luca closed the distance between us and slammed his mouth down on mine, devouring my surprised gasp with his hungry kiss.

We were starving for one another, tongues tangling with urgency, hands groping frantically. I wasn't normally prudish—public displays of affection never bothered me—but I had always had enough common decency not to be overly showy. In Luca's arms, with the cool ocean breeze blowing through my hair, there was no such thing as decency. There was only me and Luca, and I couldn't get enough of him.

He made me feel desired and precious.

He made me feel … everything.

Before we got too carried away, his phone began to ring. The interruption was probably for the best, but I still wanted to throw the infernal device in the ocean. Luca pulled away reluctantly, sucking at my bottom lip, his eyes simmering pools of liquid heat. He groaned at the caller ID.

"What is it?" he snapped at the caller, surprising me with his clipped anger. "You can't handle that on your own?" He shuffled his feet agitatedly as the person on the other end answered his question.

I couldn't hear if it was a man or woman, let alone the nature of the call, but an urgent call on a Saturday evening had me curious.

Luca offered a resigned, "I'll be there in thirty," then hung up the phone. His lips pursed as he peered off toward the water and took in a deep breath. "I have to take you home," he said coolly.

I stepped close to him and laid my hands on his chest. "What was that all about?" I asked quietly, knowing my question was likely prying into private matters.

He dropped his gaze and cupped my jaw with both hands. "Just business."

"On a Saturday night?"

"Some of my associates can be more demanding than others. This one's a pain in my ass."

I smiled up at him, and he placed a soft kiss to my forehead.

"Come on, let's get you home." Luca wrapped his arm around my shoulders and led me back to the car.

As he drove, I wondered why a client might need his banker on a Saturday night. Credit card fraud? With twenty-four-hour internet sales, bankers might be on call longer hours than I had originally assumed. Perhaps corporate lending was more time-intensive than I realized. There were viable reasons for the call, but I couldn't shake the feeling that it was odd. However, I'd had such an amazing night, I refused to let the phone call spoil the evening.

Luca had been fun-loving, engaging, and even romantic, despite his claims otherwise. I was hardly out of his car before I was already longing for the next time I'd see him.

CHAPTER 9

M y driver, Leo, was supposed to pick me up at five to take me out to my parent's house for Sunday dinner. Until that time, I spent the day moping around the apartment. It was insane. I'd only just met Luca less than a week before, but I'd seen him each of the last five days, and a day without him felt like an eternity. I hardly knew the man, but it didn't seem to matter.

Luca had swept into my life with the force of a freight train. When the train passed through the station, the only thing left was dirt wafting in the air, making it hard for me to breathe. Everything about the situation was crazy. How could I be so caught up in a man I'd just met? The intensity of my feelings for him worried me, and I wondered if I needed to put distance between us to regain my bearings.

The thought alone made my chest hurt.

These intense emotions weren't like me. I didn't sit around and pine for men. Time spent with Luca was changing me as I expected it would. The process had begun, and the only question now was, how would it end? Would he leave me malformed and broken or fill in my missing pieces so that I was stronger and more complete than before?

If I walked away now, I ensured I would survive my encounter with Luca Romano. It would still be difficult, even after only a week, but I could do it. Much more time with him, and I wasn't sure I could drag myself away. However, ending our relationship before it had begun felt weak. My dad would say only a coward walks away in fear, and that's what I would be doing—running in fear when there was no way to know I was in any real danger to begin with.

Had there been some tangible reason to back up my fears, some legitimate concern that supported the fact that he would be bad for me, I might have had reason to push him away. As it stood, I had no viable complaints with Luca—my only issue was my fear that I was already in too deep with a man who could destroy me.

I was no coward.

Fear would not dictate my decisions. Allowing myself to fall for him would be risky, but it might be the best thing to ever happen to me. There was no way to know unless I allowed our relationship to play out. That didn't mean I couldn't keep my wits about me rather than let my hormones run the show.

First and foremost on that front would be keeping myself from sitting around and pining for the man. Attempting to keep busy, I spent the day doing laundry and other household chores. I refrained from texting Luca, which I considered a success—I wasn't trying to play games, but I didn't want to be that clingy girl who couldn't stand on her own two feet. I had lived many years without Luca and would easily survive a day without him now, or so I tried to tell myself.

When five o'clock rolled around, I was relieved for the distraction. Our weekly family dinners were often a chore, but on a day when I didn't want to think, I welcomed anything that might draw my attention, for however long, from the beguiling man who haunted my thoughts.

My parents lived in my childhood home on Staten Island in a small waterfront community named Annadale. It was near the city, but we always stuck close to our neighborhood, so it was almost like growing up in the suburbs. The house was a two-story Mediterranean home with customary marble columns and glossy marble floors. It had been updated through the years but held much of its original old-world charm. The best part of the house was the expansive back patio looking out over the bay. The patio was outfitted with a wealth of wrought-iron furniture and was often used to host family gatherings.

I had loved growing up in that house. There were darker moments, but most of my childhood memories were good. I was comfortable in my parents' house, and each week when I crossed the threshold, a part of me always drifted back to my youth. It was hard not to regress when surrounded by the people and things of the past. I had to make a concentrated effort to pull forth the successful businesswoman I'd become and not allow my inner angsty teen to resurface.

On this particular instance, when I entered my parents' home, I found my Uncle Sal in the entry, preparing to leave.

"Hey, Uncle Sal," I greeted as I gave him a warm hug.

"Alessia! My God, you look more beautiful every time I see you."

I chuckled an embarrassed laugh. "You aren't sticking around for dinner?"

"No, I was just heading out. We'll have to have you girls over to our place soon so we can spend more than a couple minutes catching up."

"I'd love that. How's Aunt Tina?"

Uncle Sal had married a woman much younger than himself. Martina, Tina for short, was plenty nice, but I was pretty sure Sal married more for function than substance. He was still an attractive man for his age, and I could see how he'd snagged a woman twenty years his junior. I didn't understand why, but I could see how.

"Tina's great. She's buying me out of house and home," he teased playfully. "Alright, I gotta get outta here. You enjoy your dinner, and I'll see you soon."

"Sounds good, see ya."

I closed the door behind him and made my way toward the back of the house, which overlooked the patio and waterfront. Crossing paths with my dad just outside the dining room, I offered him a hug, and he wrapped his strong arms around me.

"Hey, Dad."

"Alessia, I'm glad you made it." As if I had a choice. "I have to make a quick call; I'll be right back." He strode down the hall, and I momentarily watched his retreating form. He may have had high expectations for us, but he wasn't a bad man. I loved my father. I just wished he looked at me the way he looked at Maria.

My older sister was already seated at the expansive dining table—she was never one to help in the kitchen. Mom and Sofia entered the room from the other door, placing dinner on the table. We all took our places—the three of us girls sitting in the same spots we'd had since we graduated from our highchairs. Dad joined us minutes later, and we began the ritual dance that was Sunday dinner.

Mom asked what we had been up to that week, and we each volunteered some scrap of information to satisfy her curiosity. Dad mostly ate in silence, occasionally interjecting a question or brief comment. Once our portion of the show was over, Mom launched into her lengthy updates on her bridge group, charities, family gossip, and latest projects.

"Enzo, I know you said no party discussions, but I just want everyone to know I was able to rearrange the seating charts to include Vica's plus one," Mom informed us as if this had been a great feat of engineering. "I need to know now, though, if any of you are going to end up bringing someone. Sofia, this is your party, sweetie—surely there's someone you want to bring."

All our attention turned to Sofia. Her eyes flitted about like a little mouse trapped in a cage until they landed on me apologetically. I knew instantly what she was about to do, but there was no time to stop her.

"Alessia is dating someone," she blurted out to everyone's astonishment.

As one, the group all turned their eyes on me.

I glared at Sofia, promising payback. "We've only gone out a couple of times—there's nothing to tell. I don't have plans to ask him to the party, so don't worry about that."

I was stunned when my father was the first to respond. "What's his name?"

"Why?" I asked cautiously, making sure not to sound too flippant.

Dad wiped his mouth with his napkin before leaning back in his chair. "I want to know if we know this man. There are too many predators out there to be handing yourself over to someone we don't know."

"Sticking to people we know makes for a pretty small dating pool, Dad." I didn't want to argue with him, so I tried to respond with as much respect as I could and still say my piece.

"This guy could be a pervert or a serial liar, and you'd never know. It's good to find someone with references—people who can vouch for him."

"Just because we know people doesn't mean we know if they're *good* people."

"No, but it helps reduce the risk. There's no reason to reinvent the wheel—we have plenty of friends and family who could recommend good dating options—might as well give those a try first before you branch out to random people on the street."

Stunning us all, Maria chose that moment to interject her

opinion. "I have to agree with Alessia. There's no telling what goes on behind closed doors. Even the people we know could be completely different when no one's around." She so rarely contributed to our conversations, we were all speechless. I wasn't sure if she even realized what she'd done, but I was enormously grateful she'd backed my position.

"It's not like I'm marrying the man," I said, downplaying the relationship. "We just started dating, so there's nothing to worry about."

Dad frowned but picked up his fork and returned to eating. "What does this man do for a living?"

"He's a banker."

His eyes looked me over for a brief moment, then nodded as if in answer to an unspoken question. A few awkward seconds passed in silence, so I used the opening to divert the conversation away from me.

"Speaking of news, Sofia failed to mention she got a job." I looked over at my younger sister, who's eyes rounded in surprise. No doubt she would have kicked me under the table if she could have reached me; instead, she stuck out her tongue, and I responded with a wink. Payback was a bitch.

CHAPTER 10

Alessia

The following Monday morning felt far different than its predecessors. The anticipation of hearing from Luca was a shot of adrenaline to my system. I wasn't sure if it was excitement or fear—maybe a little of both. Regardless of the cause, I was up early, ready for my day.

As if he knew I was thinking about him, my phone chimed while I ate breakfast.

I'm coming by to take you to work this morning. Just like Luca—no question about when I needed to be at work or what plans I had. He simply informed me he was taking me and expected my compliance.

I appreciate the offer, but there's no reason for you to come all the way over when I have a driver to take me. I wasn't crazy about relying on anyone, and I certainly didn't want him to see me as a chore.

You can argue all you like, but I'll be there in twenty.

I must not have felt too strongly about the matter because his words made me smile. The man was ridiculously overbearing, and damn if I didn't love it.

Of course, it had only been a week. Would I still feel the same way after a month, a year, or ten? Would his domineering tendencies mellow, or would they grow into a problem? I didn't necessarily mind a man who threw his weight around. Who was I kidding? It could be unbelievably sexy when done right, but there was a fine line between sexy and a dictatorial asshole. I had no desire to be kept under the thumb of an egotistical man.

Jackson's warning whispered in the back of my mind, along with my father's words about dating someone I didn't know. Luca seemed like a decent guy, but that didn't mean I truly knew him.

The chime on my phone drew me from my thoughts. Luca was downstairs waiting. I gathered my things and made my way down and out to the street. Luca's sports car was blocking traffic, a number of impatient motorists stuck behind him. I ducked my head in embarrassment and hurried to his car as fast as my pencil skirt would allow.

"I suppose you're aware you're blocking traffic," I murmured as I buckled my seatbelt.

"Waiting a few minutes isn't going to kill those people."

"I doubt that would be your opinion if you were the one stuck behind someone."

"You'll learn quickly, Alessia, that I only care about myself … and what's mine." He turned his head and captured my gaze as he said the last words.

Did he consider me his? Tiny butterflies came to life and danced around in my stomach at the possibility of being Luca's girl. Is that what he meant, or was I jumping to conclusions? I certainly wasn't going to ask for clarification. If that wasn't what he meant, I'd look pathetic asking.

"Thanks for the ride," I said instead, choosing to sidestep his remark.

His lips twitched upward at the corners as he checked the rearview. "The other thing you'll learn about me is I'm a selfish man. The way I see it, giving you a ride is purely self-serving—it means I get to lay eyes on those sexy fucking legs. The only way starting my day would be better is if I was naked between them."

My heart stuttered in my chest. His comment had been the most presumptive, lewd thing any man had ever said to me, and I loved every word. I pressed my thighs together, attempting to soothe the ache in my core that his words had provoked.

"When I offer to do something for you," he continued, "rest assured, I'm not being put out. I'm doing it because I want to— you may not be clear on my motivations, but that doesn't mean I'm not getting something from my actions. Got it?"

"Yes," I breathed in the suddenly sauna-like heat of the car.

I thanked my lucky stars when the phone began to ring through the car stereo system. I'd needed a moment to recover. His words had stirred up a whirlwind of emotions inside me, and I had no idea how to organize the chaos and decipher how I felt.

Before Luca answered, he switched the call from the overhead speakers to his phone for privacy. "This isn't a good time," he said brusquely, then paused as the caller spoke. "My gut tells me it's him, but I need more time to be certain … Well, tell them to calm the fuck down—nothing's going to change in the matter of a week … That's what I thought."

The caller hung up, and Luca tossed his phone back into a dashboard compartment. Tension filled the car until I could feel the oppressive weight of it pressing against my chest. I wasn't supposed to hear his conversation, that had been clear. Not only had I heard Luca's end, a snippet from the caller rang clear in my ears.

Venturi is demanding blood for blood.

"Sorry about that—more work shit," he bit out, still radiating anger from his conversation.

"No problem." Fuck, yes, it was a problem. Blood for blood?

What the hell had that meant? In what other dimension did banking involve conversations where 'blood for blood' would be applicable? Was that code for something? There was no way I was going to ask for more information, not while he was angry, and certainly not while I was captive in his car.

Both the subject matter and his emotional response created a deep-seated unease inside me. I had told myself I wouldn't walk away just because I was scared he would hurt me, but the words I'd overheard changed everything. There had been no humor in the man's voice and certainly none in Luca's response. Both men had been dead serious about the subject matter, and in my gut, I knew I should have the same reaction.

Thank God, my mother had instilled in me the crucial ability to maintain appearances. On the outside, I carried on as if nothing had happened, asking about his plans for the day and thanking him for the ride.

On the inside, I was coming apart.

As much as I wanted to ignore the faint smell of smoke and the warnings I'd received, the conversation had been a red flag I couldn't disregard. Where there was smoke, there was fire. I had said I needed something more concrete—how much more concrete were angry phone calls talking about blood?

Something about Luca made me wary, and now, I had a sound reason for that fear. He was captivating and alluring in ways no other man had been, but there was something more sinister lurking beneath that tempting façade—how sinister, I had no idea. It could merely be a bad temper, or he could be a psychopath. The problem was, I'd never know until it was too late.

Luca told me he'd give me a ride home after work. I didn't argue. He pressed a kiss to my lips, and I offered a warm smile in return before hurrying to my office, where I fended off a panic attack. I needed an exit strategy. How did you walk away from a man like Luca who didn't take no for an answer?

My concern wasn't that he was going to attack me physically —quite the opposite. He'd lure me back in. Using the magnetic charisma he possessed, he'd whisk away my concerns until they were a distant memory. Luca was the most tantalizing dessert I'd ever seen. No matter that I'd been on a diet for weeks and didn't want to ruin my good health, the moment I got a whiff of the rich, creamy decadence, every ounce of my resolve would disappear until I couldn't remember a single reason why I should say no. The only chance I had of not giving in was to avoid him completely. I couldn't eat the dessert if I was never near it.

A finite plan would be necessary, but for now, I decided on simply escaping him for the day. I would figure out a more thorough solution once I was home. As the end of the workday rolled around, I texted Luca, explaining I had an unexpected late meeting and would have my driver take me home.

Just text me when you're done, I'll pick you up.

Fuck. I knew that would be his response. **I'm headed into the meeting and already have my driver lined up. I'll text you later**.

I turned off my phone and gathered my things, not wanting to risk a surprise visit from Luca. I texted Leo to pick me up around the corner and used the service elevator to exit out the back of the building. The entire walk to the car, I fought the overwhelming urge to look over my shoulder.

"Is everything alright, ma'am?" asked Leo as I slid into the black Cadillac.

"Yes, I was just behind on my walking today—needed to get those steps in," I replied airily, relieved I'd prepared an explanation for my change in pickup instructions.

Leo eyed me with a hint of suspicion. He was close to me in age and attractive if you liked that meathead sort of look. I didn't know what he did in his spare time to bulk up, but he obviously spent ample hours in the gym. His muscles had muscles.

I raised my brows somewhat haughtily, reminding him he was

paid to drive me, not act as my chaperone. He huffed out a laugh and pulled the car away from the curb.

Not until I safely entered my apartment did I breathe a deep sigh of relief. Tension had crept into my shoulders, which now ached from being clenched tight all day. I set aside my purse and work satchel, then bee-lined for my bathroom, where I filled the oversized tub. The warm water was a balm on my sore muscles and even soothed my racing thoughts.

As the anxiety melted off me into the steaming water, I was left with a resounding sense of sadness. I had wanted things to work out with Luca more than I'd realized. Walking away from him meant facing the loss of the fantasy I'd envisioned in my head.

I had never gone out with a man who made me feel as special or beautiful as Luca did, nor had I dated a man who enchanted my senses the way he could. Whether it was his musky scent, the sight of his chiseled features, his masterful touch, or the reeling emotions brought on by his words, Luca was a masterful magician, using his tricks to bewitch me in every way.

In a short time, I'd grown attached to the way he made me feel, and losing that was going to be agonizing. Just as painful, I would have to put on my big-girl panties and tell him I didn't want to see him any longer. It would be a difficult conversation, but I was capable of doing hard things, or so I told myself. It would take a bit of time to scrounge up the courage, but I could do it.

Tomorrow.

After I'd had a chance to wallow in bed and spend the night eating ice cream.

After the bath, I put on my favorite pair of pajamas—an oversized shirt from an old boyfriend and a worn pair of blue-plaid flannel bottoms from college. The outfit was atrocious, but a blanket of comfort wrapped around me simply wearing it. I'd just sat on the couch with a pint of cookies and cream when a knock on my door resounded through my quiet living room.

My muscles locked down in mid-motion. It couldn't be Luca, I reminded myself. I hadn't received a call from the security desk telling me I had a visitor. It was either Giada, popping over unannounced, or more likely, the older lady two doors down who frequently went in search of her missing newspaper. I jumped into motion but stilled when the pounding knock sounded again.

That was no gentle wrap from old Mrs. Cohen.

I tiptoed toward the door and tried to take a quick look through the peephole. There was no mistaking who stood outside my door. Clad in a navy suit and leaning against the opposite wall, Luca had come for me. I debated not answering. Whether he knew I was home or not, I could hide in my apartment. And how long would that last? Luca wasn't the type to give up. I would have to face him at some point—better to get it over with now.

I could do this.

I could remain strong, explain my position like a mature adult, and he would abide by my wishes.

Right.

"Alessia, I know you're there. Open the door." His forceful voice resonated through the thick wood and kicked my heartrate up to a frenzied pace.

I turned the deadbolt and opened the door, attempting to look unfazed. "Luca … how did you know what apartment I was in?" How did you get past the security desk? How did you know I was home?

He eased forward, forcing me to retreat into the apartment and allow him entry. "The mailboxes in the lobby are numbered with last names—not particularly safe." His words were spoken calmly, almost in a resigned tone. He helped himself inside, peering around my home.

Great. I had a potential psycho giving me security advice after breaking into my building.

It was strange having him in my space, my sanctuary. I rarely invited people over—that was one of the awesome things about living in a big city—there were plenty of places to meet people outside of the home. His dark suit was a stark contrast to everything light and airy in my apartment. In a way, it was nice. The muted tones were that much softer next to his sharp outline.

"You have a lovely apartment," he finally said as he turned back to face me.

"Thanks," I replied awkwardly, unsure whether to ask him to have a seat or order him to leave.

"It suits you."

Huh? "What do you mean?"

"Everything in its place—you like order in your life, and it shows." There was an odd vibe emanating from him, and I didn't know what to make of it.

"Luca, why are you here?" I asked softly, deciding to pass on the games.

He leaned against the island counter and studied me, his eyes scrutinizing me until I was sure he could see straight into my soul. "How was the meeting?" he finally asked in a deadpan voice.

"It was fine. What's this all about?" If he was going to play games, I could play dumb with the best of them.

"I want to know why you lied to me. I told you from the very beginning never to lie to me, did I not?" He didn't seem angry. Rather, he was more like an iceberg, distant and brutally cold.

His removed demeanor should have been a good thing, should have made it that much easier to explain things were over between us. However, that plan didn't take into account how wounded I'd feel at his cold disposition. It was like standing before my father, all over again, explaining why I'd forgotten to turn off the bathtub water. I didn't want to disappoint Luca.

Every one of the practiced explanations I'd rehearsed in the bathtub evaporated. Instead, tears pooled in my eyes as I wrung my hands together. "You scare me, Luca. I don't know you, and you've rammed your way into my life in such a short time. I'm developing feelings for you, even though I can sense you have secrets. For all I know, every word out of your mouth could be a lie. I'm so torn, and it terrifies me."

There. I'd laid myself bare.

I hadn't exactly ended it, but I also hadn't been a coward and run. I had confronted him with my fears, and no matter the outcome, I would feel good about how I'd handled the situation.

Luca closed the distance between us, trailing his knuckles down the side of my face. "I will never hurt you, Alessia. I know you're scared, and you have every right to be, but I don't want you to run from me. If you have a problem, you come to me, and we'll work through it together."

I dropped my gaze to the buttons on his white dress shirt and chewed on my bottom lip. "What about the phone conversations?" I asked in a small voice. "Work calls that require your presence at night—talking about blood for blood—those things aren't normal. How do I reconcile that if you aren't lying to me?"

Luca pulled me close and lifted me against him, wrapping my legs around his middle. He walked me to the kitchen counter and placed me down, keeping his body pressed firmly against mine. "I'm not a normal man, but that doesn't mean I'm going to hurt you," he whispered, eyes peering deeply into mine. "Sometimes, people like us are different. Surely, you've felt it. We aren't like the other sheep out there, pissing away their lives at menial jobs. We're different, the both of us."

I breathed in Luca's warm breath, reveling in our nearness. "All I know is, I can see me losing myself in you, and I don't even know you. I need this to slow down."

"Have I done anything to hurt you? Pushed you to do anything you didn't want or given you any reason to fear me?"

I slowly shook my head as a stab of guilt wracked my resolve.

Luca had been nothing but gentlemanly toward me at each of our encounters—a roguish gentleman, but a gentleman, nonetheless. I'd taken a couple of one-sided phone conversations and let my imagination run away from me. Although, I did note he hadn't explained what I'd overheard.

Luca's gaze dropped to the framed photo beside me. It was a picture of my sisters and me with our parents on our last family vacation in the Bahamas, all sunburned and smiling—it was one of my all-time favorite shots of us. He picked up the frame to look more closely at the photo.

"You're different than I expected—none of this was supposed to happen." He spoke almost under his breath as if the words weren't meant for my ears.

"What's not supposed to happen?" Had he meant for us to be a one-and-done when he first asked me out? It wouldn't have surprised me if he wasn't used to relationships. Men like Luca weren't picket fence type of guys.

"I'm not supposed to want you," he said as his eyes returned to mine.

"Sometimes, it doesn't matter what we want or need. Sometimes, life just is. I can feel in my gut you're not good for me, but that doesn't seem to change anything," I admitted softly.

He set down the frame and turned back to me. "You're not the only one who knows this is wrong."

"Why would it be a bad thing for you to want me?"

His jaw flexed, and his hand caressed down the length of my arm. "Because you complicate things immeasurably."

Ouch. I pursed my lips and glanced out my living room window, suddenly wishing I could walk away from the conversation. The telltale prick of tears stung at the back of my throat. *This* was exactly why I'd tried to walk away from him—Luca was heartache waiting to happen. Anger swelled inside me that in a matter of minutes, I'd let him slink his way back under my skin.

Luca turned my face toward his and swiped at a threatening

tear. "Complicated isn't always bad. In fact, lately, complicated has looked very, very good." Then he kissed me, softly, sweetly, his lips moving achingly slow against mine.

Instinctively, my hands lifted to his jacket to pull him closer. His lips curved in a smile before he deepened the kiss, his assault making my lips feel swollen and tender. I liked the gentle kisses, but I also liked the frenzy—as if his need for me was insatiable, a yawning cavern that couldn't be filled. He stole the air from my lungs and swept me away on a river of desire.

We only came apart when a knock sounded at my door. I pulled in shaky breaths, trying to ground myself back in my body.

"You expecting someone else?" he asked in a rasp, his eyes narrowing just a fraction. Was he jealous? The thought did funny things to my insides.

"It's like Grand Central Station up here," I muttered as I slid off the counter. "It has to be Giada, my cousin—she's the only person who shows up unannounced." Until you.

As I moved toward the door, Luca placed his arm out and stepped in front of me to look through the peephole. Who did he think he'd find?

When he stepped back, I glared at him. "Satisfied?" I asked smugly.

His responding glare promised retribution for my smart mouth. He never had to say a word. It was there in the glint of his eyes and the gentle pursing of his lips. His brand of retribution wouldn't be painful—it would be torturous, and I would love every second. Just the suggestion aroused a heat inside me that made me want to jump him and forget about Giada.

I sighed as the knocking came again.

Everyone was so damn persistent.

Opening the door, I smiled at my cousin who grinned in return until her eyes landed on Luca.

"Oh," she gasped. "Am I interrupting?" Her eyes met mine with a silent apology.

"Actually, I was just leaving," offered Luca. He came over and planted a sensual kiss on my lips, nodded to Giada, then disappeared down the hall.

"Sweet baby Jesus, who the fuck was that? And where do I get some?"

I busted out laughing and closed the door to my apartment. "That is every flavor of trouble—I'm in way over my head."

"Tell me *everything*," said Giada as she plopped down on my couch.

I followed suit, sitting next to her with my legs pulled up to my chest. "We've only been out twice. It's not a big deal."

"Honey, everything about that man is a big deal."

She made me laugh, as usual. "He's crazy intense, and for all I know, he may be legit crazy, period. But I can't seem to walk away."

Giada's eyes narrowed, and her smile faltered. "You don't think he's dangerous, do you?"

"Not to me, no—at least, not physically."

"What does that mean? You think he could be emotionally abusive?"

"No! It's just that he's addictive, and I have this feeling he's going to break my heart. I can't stop thinking about him, and I love the way I feel when I'm with him, but I know he has secrets. Dark secrets."

"Yikes, that is rough. What are you going to do?"

"Hell, if I know. Eat ice cream and watch movies—care to join me?"

A wide grin spread across her face. "I thought you'd never ask."

CHAPTER 11

Luca

I knew the minute she texted—she was running.

My intuition about people was impeccable. There was no meeting. She'd used the excuse to avoid me. As pissed as I was to have her run from me, I was also pleased to confirm she had a decent head on her shoulders. Some women loved to get a taste of danger—enjoyed a walk on the wild side.

A smart woman would be wary of associating with me.

Alessia had not been blind to the dangers and was wise enough to heed the warnings. Not only that, I'd been impressed with her practiced ability to remain composed when she'd overheard my phone call. A part of me even questioned if maybe it hadn't bothered her, but the text had verified her calm demeanor had been an act.

Fucking Rafi.

I'd been using him to handle my affairs while I gathered information, but there was only so much he was capable of. The others knew he spoke on my behalf, but he had no authority. He was too low-level to give orders, not that I was particularly high up. I'd been surprised when they called me in to do the job, but as they explained, my history made me more qualified than most. I'd get the answers they were looking for, and when I did, it would help secure my future in the organization.

I understood Rafi's need to call for help, but that didn't mean it didn't piss me off. I considered censoring my words while Alessia was in the car, but an overwhelming part of me wanted her to know, wanted her to put the pieces together. She needed to understand I wasn't some Johnny Homemaker, but there were rules I had to obey. More than my career was at stake if I gave her more information than I should. I had to put the pieces before her and hope she not only put them together, but she didn't walk away for good.

I needed her. I needed her to open up to me, and that wouldn't happen unless she trusted me. It would be easy if I pretended to be someone else, but I didn't have it in me to play weak. I could only be myself and trust I could win her over on my own.

Our exchange at her apartment had been reassuring. She was scared, but she wasn't beyond my reach. She was just as much a victim to the magnetic pull between us as I was. I craved to be near her when she wasn't around, and when she was, all I could think about was getting inside her. All of her. I wanted to sink my cock inside her and penetrate that sharp mind of hers. I wanted to possess her inside and out. I wanted to know why she exercised such strict control over all aspects of her life and how she'd remained so naïve and innocent in the City That Never Sleeps.

There were monsters everywhere, and I was one of them.

I hadn't targeted her only for her luscious body and intriguing mind; I needed information from her. I'd been telling the truth when I said I hadn't planned to want her. She had likely given her own meaning to the words, but the truth was, I had initiated our little elevator encounter for a purpose, which had nothing to do with my dick. Had I just walked up to her on the street and tried to strike up a conversation, it would never have worked. She was entirely too wary for something like that. I had to come up with an in, a way to slip under her outer walls. There was something intimate about elevators. It had been the perfect way to freeze time and connect us in a shared moment.

I had needed a contact inside Triton, and Alessia had seemed perfect for the job. Then I hit snags, one after the other—the least of which was my growing need for the woman. She was an unholy seductress without the faintest clue of her effect on every heterosexual man who crossed her path. I wanted every ounce of that latent sexuality for myself, feeling the need to pluck the eyes from every other man who dared look at her.

I wanted her, but there was more to it than that. When she discovered I had ulterior motives, and she undoubtedly would, I'd have a fight on my hands. I was going to have to find a way to get what I needed without losing her in the process.

Just like I'd said, she complicated everything.

CHAPTER 12

Alessia

The morning after Luca came by my apartment, I had no idea what to expect. Our conversation had eased my mind somewhat, but I still didn't have any answers. He knew I was worried and had urged me to trust him. I knew he had secrets but had been soothed by his assurances.

Nothing had changed.

I was still uncertain about Luca, but I wasn't actively pushing him away. There was no deadline to make a decision, so until I had more information, I would try to guard myself and move cautiously forward.

We hadn't spoken since he'd left, which meant I wasn't sure if he was picking me up or where things stood between us. I carried on as if it were any other normal day, except for my choice of outfit. In the event I would see him, I wore a silk blouse that was more low-cut than I would ordinarily wear to work. My desire to appeal to Luca apparently outweighed my concerns about him, not to mention the risk of Roger putting on the moves.

Luca hadn't said anything about giving me a ride, so I kept my scheduled appointment with Leo to drive me. Instead of feeling despair over not hearing from him, I was relieved and reassured Luca had heard my request to slow down and was making an effort to give me space. His actions went a long way to ease my concerns about his domineering tendencies. Knowing I had a say in the relationship and he respected my wishes was just as attractive as his assertive, controlling nature. The only way for it to work was if the two were mutually inclusive. I wasn't sure a kind, respectful man with no backbone would stir my interest, just as an egotistical control freak would make me crazy. There had to be a delicate balance between the two, and it appeared Luca could walk that fine line.

My morning went smoothly, answering emails with few interruptions. Feeling a bit more at ease about the Luca situation, I was able to focus on my work and accomplished several tasks that had fallen to the wayside. I was so in the zone, I almost didn't notice when Roger stepped into my office. I was sitting at my desk, looking over printed drafts of a commercial storyboard when he approached, walking to my desk and standing over me, rather than taking one of the empty chairs.

"Hey, Roger. What's up?" I asked without the customary pep I might normally infuse in my voice.

His gaze lingered on my chest, making me realize he could see down my already revealing blouse from his vantage point above me. Embarrassment flooded me, my cheeks burning in frustration and outrage. I cleared my throat and leaned back in my chair, lifting my shirt to cover myself as I moved.

"I wanted to ask about the 'coming soon' signage on the DMV building," he said distractedly.

"It's scheduled to go up on the eighteenth."

He nodded, his eyes dropping back down to my chest. "You always put on a show for me, don't you? You like to tease—I know the type. One of these days, I'm going to fuck those tits, and you're going to love it." His thin lips lifted in a lecherous smile before he walked out of the room.

I couldn't move a muscle. I was in shock.

You'd think it wouldn't surprise me after dealing with the man for a year, but he'd never been so directly lewd. Roger's harassment was getting worse. Almost just as upsetting, I realized I'd completely forgotten to go down to HR and file a report.

How could I have forgotten?

I felt like I had been drenched in a bucket of ice water as a full-body shiver wracked me head-to-toe. He made me feel so fucking dirty and ashamed, even though I knew I'd done nothing wrong. Roger terrified me, and it made me so angry, I couldn't see straight. I could picture myself beating him relentlessly with a baseball bat, and I had never so much as harmed a fly—that was how deeply he upset me.

I wanted him out of my life so I could live in peace.

Taking a couple deep breaths, I stood on shaky legs, bracing myself against the desk until I felt steady enough to walk. With my chin held high, I walked down to the ninth floor to Human Resources. The door to their suite was locked, a sign taped to the window, "Out all day for training."

God damn it! Of all the fucking days.

Tears welled in my eyes, and the tightening grip of a sob clawed at my chest. I wanted this torture over. I didn't want to wait another day to get his ass kicked out of this building, but I had no choice. Of course, filing a complaint would only be the start of what could be a lengthy process. There was no telling how long I'd have to deal with an angry, vindictive boss who enjoyed sexually harassing me.

I escaped back into the stairwell and leaned against the wall. The fluorescent lights gave off a dim illumination, and it was eerily silent within the concrete walls, but it was precisely what I needed—the protective enclosure of my own private cave. I didn't think I could manage going back into my glass office to be stared at and scrutinized like jewelry in a display case.

It was all too much.

All morning I had put on a brave face and fooled myself into believing everything would be alright, and I knew deep down, eventually, it would, but at that moment, it felt like everything was a disaster. The constant pressure of my family, the stress of sorting out my relationship with Luca, and the strain of dealing with Roger—it was too much. Each added pressure had wound me tighter and tighter, and Roger's comment had been the final straw that had sprung my trigger.

I needed to get away.

I couldn't go back up to my office, not even for my purse. Instead, I took deep breaths as I slowly descended nine flights of stairs, exiting onto the ground floor and walking numbly through the lobby. One of the security guards I often conversed with asked if I was alright and made an attempt to have me sit down, but I assured him I was fine and slipped from the building.

I walked with no destination in mind. Far from my normal purposeful stride, I strolled aimlessly, blind to the people and activities around me. At one point, I noted Stern College, which was only a couple blocks from the Triton building. Other than that, my mind was a blank, as if my brain had overloaded and shut down.

I tried so hard all the time to be who my parents wanted me to be. There was no such thing as perfect, but by God, I had tried, and I felt like I'd come up unforgivably short. I didn't know who I was supposed to be. Maybe if I had a stronger sense of self, I'd have known how to handle Luca. He swept me away like a tiny leaf pulled out on the ocean current until I was surrounded by him, unable to see my way to shore. I thought I could manage him like I thought I was handling Roger, but I'd been a fool on both counts.

Luca couldn't be managed, any more than a tornado or an earthquake.

And as for Roger—I'd deluded myself that dressing conservatively and ignoring him was an effective strategy to address his behavior. Realizing how wrong I'd been made me feel weak and pathetic. The only thing I'd accomplished was allowing him to continue to prey on me. I should have reported him from the very first incident, but instead, I'd told myself dealing with him was necessary, not seeing the lie for what it was—cowardice.

I had been scared for others to know the things my boss had said and done, and the longer it lasted, the more impossible it felt to tell anyone. Each inappropriate comment and suggestive stare was a shovel full of dirt thrown on top of where I lay, down in a hole of my own making. The guilt and shame were unbearable.

In a thriving city of millions of people, I suddenly felt no larger than an ant.

Insignificant.

Worthless.

A tear dripped down my cheek, and my vision blurred just as my toe caught on an uneven sidewalk seam, and I lurched forward. Before I could stumble to the ground, a strong set of hands caught me. My head sprung up, and I gasped in surprise, sucking in a lungful of rancidly sweet air rank with cheap cologne. A large man with tattoos crawling up his neck and a shaved head leered down at me.

There was a cold madness to the gleam in his eyes, sending a bolt of electric adrenaline down my spine, all the way to my fingers and toes. The man was enormous and didn't look like he'd known a sane day in his life.

"Gotta watch where you're goin' lady," he said as his eyes traveled down my body, his hands still firmly clasped around my arms.

My eyes darted around in search of aid, but I quickly realized I had wandered too close to the river and was standing beneath the FDR overpass. There wasn't another soul around to help me, just the steady whooshing of cars above and the gentle coo of pigeons nesting under the bridge.

"Let go of me," I hissed, yanking myself free of his bruising grip. I stumbled backward only to walk straight into another body. Two more thugs stood at my back, clearly amused at my mounting fear. I jerked away from them, stepping aside until they flanked me on three sides, my back to a concrete pillar.

The first man took a small step forward. "There's no reason to panic, we just want your money."

"I … I don't have any money. I left everything back at the office."

"Don't fuckin' lie, lady," he ground out angrily. "No one lookin' as fine as you is gonna wander around the city with nothin' on them. Give us the fuckin' money, and you can walk away."

"I was upset when I left—I swear I don't have anything on me. Please, just let me go." My voice shook, and my eyes pricked with the threat of tears.

"Fine, you wanna do this the hard way, be my guest. We're gonna find it either way." He stepped forward and grabbed my hips, feeling for pockets in the seams of my slacks. "You got it stuffed in your bra? Where you hiding it?"

How was this happening?

All I could do was hope money was all he was after. The thought sent a wave of unadulterated panic through my veins, making me shove at the man's chest. "Get away from me. I told you, I don't have anything."

The man barely budged from my efforts, grabbing the neckline of my blouse along with the edge of my bra cup and pulled it away from my body to peer inside in search of hidden cash. It only took a matter of seconds, but it felt like an eternity. As fast as I could move after registering what was happening, I slapped at his hands. "Don't touch me," I hissed at his venomous glare.

"What the fuck?" came an enraged growl beside us. Fast approaching our little party, Luca descended like an avenging angel, lips in a snarl and eyes black with fury.

"This has nothing to do with you, man. Just walk away," warned the thug who had me cornered against the pillar. His two friends stepped closer to his back, helping to form a unified front.

Luca wasn't fazed in the slightest. If I didn't know better, I'd say the challenge excited him. He almost looked eager for the fight that was mounting. "That's where you're wrong. You see, that right there, she's mine, so this has everything to do with me."

Using the moment of distraction, I lunged away from my attacker and fled to a place of safety behind Luca. The dash had only been a matter of feet, but my heart pounded a furious rhythm in my chest, drumming its intense beat in my ears. "Let's go, please, Luca," I whispered with my hands curled tightly around his arm.

"This guy thinks he can take us," mocked one of the lackeys, curling his hands into fists.

"Three to one—not good odds," added the leader as the men lined up next to one another like a school of fish gathered to intimidate a hungry shark.

Luca's hand pulled at my clenched fingers, removing my hands from his arm. "Step back, Alessia," he murmured under his breath.

Was he going to fight these men? There were three of them—he was going to get himself killed! "Luca, *please*, let's just go."

"Yeah, *Luca*, you should probably do what the bitch says and scurry on out of here. Hate for that pretty face of yours to get rearranged."

The terror I'd felt for myself only seconds before quickly morphed into gut-clenching fear for Luca. The men facing him were ruthless and plenty large to land Luca on his ass … or worse.

In a matter of seconds, the scene descended into chaos.

The leader lifted his meaty fist and stepped forward, perhaps to take a swing or perhaps purely to intimidate—either way, I'd never know. Luca launched himself into action, delivering a punch to the man's face with a sickening crunch before unleashing equally devastating blows to the other two men in quick succession.

When the men recovered from their surprise, they attempted to attack, but Luca bobbed and weaved like Floyd Mayweather dancing around the ring. He rained down destruction with his fists, knees, feet, even his elbows. Every part of him was a weapon. It was like watching an action hero movie play out before me.

Luca was a thing possessed.

In a matter of minutes, one of the thugs dropped to the ground unconscious, and the other two clambered away into the shadows. Luca watched their retreating forms, running a hand through his disheveled hair, then spat on the unconscious man's motionless body. Aside from sweat dotting his forehead and tiny splatters of blood marring his white dress shirt, he appeared put together and unharmed.

He had seemed invincible.

Merciless.

He truly was an avenging angel. In the dusky shadows under the bridge, I wanted nothing more than for him to take me in his arms and never let go.

When he turned to find me, his blistering gaze locked on mine, and a sob of relief tore from my chest as I lunged for him. He pulled me snugly against him, holding me securely in the safe harbor of his embrace, allowing me the chance to process the shock of what had happened.

"Shhh, you're okay. I've got you," Luca murmured into my hair while his hand rubbed soothing circles against my back.

He didn't ask me questions or push for answers. Instead, he offered me the simple comfort of his presence and reassurance.

Eventually, my shuddered breathing calmed, and I lifted my tear-streaked face to his. "Thank you for saving me. If you hadn't … I don't know what would have …" My throat closed up with the thought, unable to utter the words.

"Let's get you home, then we can talk." He pulled back, giving my body a once over before gritting his teeth and taking my hand in his. Luca led me toward a cross street where he hailed a cab. He helped me inside, keeping a hand on me at all times. He gave the cabbie my address, and I numbly noted that my keys and purse were back at the office, so he rerouted the cab to Triton.

"I'm running up to get your things—you don't move, understood?" he instructed as he extracted himself from the backseat.

I nodded shakily, too disoriented to object. "My purse is in my bottom left drawer. I think I left my phone on the desk." They would wonder where I'd gone at work, but I didn't care. I would deal with the fallout of my disappearance later.

When Luca returned, he handed me my things and directed the cab to my place. I didn't know what his plan was, nor did I care. I was just relieved to have someone else run the show. I was too overwhelmed to make decisions—first the Roger incident, then the attempted mugging and watching Luca beat the men to a bloody pulp. My brain struggled to process it all, stuck in a feedback loop of images, unable to assign meaning to any of it.

Luca led me upstairs, using my keys to open the door and taking me straight back to my bathroom. He didn't turn on the light, opting to rely on the soft sunlight filtering in through the windows. Stepping into the glass shower stall, he turned on the water, then stood in front of me.

"Let's get you in the shower—it will help you feel better. Lift your arms," he ordered huskily.

I did as I was told.

I felt safe in Luca's care. Maybe it was a mistake, but at that moment, I needed to feel safe. I wasn't thinking about what I should do or the consequences of my actions. I was letting Luca make the calls because it felt right.

He felt right.

I was tired of overthinking. I just wanted to feel good, and Luca gave me that.

He lifted my blouse over my head. The silk trailing over my torso and arms was something I experienced every day, but under Luca's watchful eye, I felt each inch of my skin stir to life as the soft fabric drifted by. He discarded the blouse on the floor without taking his eyes from my body, then placed his wide hands on my hips and directed me to turn around before lowering the zipper on the back of my skirt and allowing the fabric to pool at my feet. I stepped out of my heels as Luca's hands glided from my lower back up to my bra strap. With a simple touch, the clasp sprung free. His hands came up to slip the straps over my shoulders, pausing on my upper arms.

"He marked you," Luca murmured, caressing the bruised skin. "I should have killed them."

I turned slowly to face him, totally exposed except for a scrap of silk covering my most private area. Luca's face was a study in harsh lines and turbulent emotions, and somehow, seeing him upset on my behalf made me feel better. Knowing he cared, that he was there to protect me, was exactly what I needed.

I lifted my hands under his jacket and swept the fabric down over his shoulders. His eyes flashed with guarded hunger as his fingers began to undo the buttons on his dress shirt. One article at a time, we undressed until we were fully exposed to one another.

Luca was the most beautiful man I'd ever seen.

My breathing became shallow as my eyes raked down his sculpted body. Every aspect was absolute perfection—tanned, olive skin with a smattering of black hair on his chest trailing down his taut stomach to where his thick shaft pointed eagerly toward me. Everything about him was solid and powerful—there wasn't a soft place on his body.

"Let's get you in the shower before I bend you over the sink." His voice was a guttural growl, a testament to his tenuous grip over his control.

I stepped inside the stall, reveling in the scalding water and warm cloud of steam as it helped heat my frozen body. Once my hair was wet, Luca poured shampoo into his hand and had me step out of the stream of water. His thick fingers scrubbed my scalp, lathering the soap through my long hair.

To keep myself steady, my hands came out to hold onto his sides, which flexed and twitched under my fingers. Fascinated with the movement of his body, my hands trailed over to his abs, fingertips grazing along the curves and dips of each muscle.

"Rinse," he barked, and my eyes snapped up to his face.

He was on the very edge of his control, dangling from a single thread.

I leaned my head back and rinsed the suds from my hair, feeling the water trail between my breasts and along my body where I sensed his piercing gaze. When I opened my eyes, Luca was fisting his cock, lazily stroking over the thick, red tip. Taking the bar of soap, he lathered his hands before bringing them up to massage my aching breasts, his thumbs swiping past my peaked nipples.

My body arched into his hands, the feel of his touch more consuming than I could have imagined. Abandoning his restraint, Luca let lose a savage growl and hefted me into his arms.

"I only meant to wash you, to help you get that asshole's touch off you, but I can't do it. I need to fuck you, Alessia." He moved us under the spray of water to rinse away the soap, then pressed my back against the cool tile, and I gasped, arching away from the cold. He used my movement to take my breast into his warm mouth, sucking angrily at the flesh. When he released me with an audible pop, the sensation sent a zing of pleasure straight to my core.

"Wait, Luca. I'm on the pill, but what about protection?" I asked breathlessly.

"I had myself checked after our ride in the elevator."

"Presumptuous."

"Confident."

"What about me? I haven't been checked since my last annual."

"Have you gone bare since then?" he asked, teeth clenched at the suggestion.

"No."

His lips pulled back in a predator's grin before he dropped his hips and impaled me against the wall. I gasped deeply, my head pushing back against the tile to help ease the pressure from his intrusion. Luca leaned in to nip and suck at my neck, easing out of me before pressing back inside in a slow but steady rhythm.

"I'm the only one who gets to mark you," he ground out as his thrusts picked up speed. "Anyone else fucking touches you, and I will bury them."

His words stoked the fire building inside me, and I clung to his shoulders to keep from incinerating. His scalding touch, the heat pulsing in my core—it was too much. I could feel the flames licking, burning my insides. I was going to ignite, and I wasn't sure I would survive the inferno. Not as the girl I'd been. The blaze between us was life-altering, but there was no way to back out now.

Luca pounded inside me, stoking the flames, and I could feel parts of me going molten and fusing to Luca, welding us together. I panted and clawed, overcome with the magnitude of sensation as the fire engulfed me, and I exploded into flame. My muscles seized, twitching and contracting as fiery pleasure coursed through my veins.

I only vaguely noticed when Luca grunted his release. Pulling me tightly against him, he trembled as his cock pulsed inside me, and my flames slowly burned themselves out. There was no fuel left for the fire, only rubble.

I lay against him, smoldering in the ashes of the girl I'd been only moments before.

Never in a million years would I have thought sex could be transformative, but that was before Luca. I knew deep in my bones, as I clung to his shoulders, water dripping from our quivering bodies, that my life would never be the same.

CHAPTER 13

Alessia

"**H**ow did you find me under the bridge?" I asked as we recovered in my bed some minutes later. Luca lay on his back with me draped over him, my head on his shoulder as I listened to his thudding heartbeat.

"One of the security guards told me you had left the building."

"You asked a security guard about me?"

"No, he called me to tell me you'd left."

"Why would he do that?"

"Because I paid him to."

"What? Why?" I lifted onto my elbow and stared down at Luca, his face impassive.

"Does it matter?" he asked somberly.

"Yes, I want to know what's going on here." I searched his face, trying to figure out what to make of his admission.

"I told you I'm not like most men. When I see something I want, I go after it, whether that means an unexpected elevator mishap or coincidental meetings on the street. I'm that way in all aspects of my life. If there is a business venture I want to take part in, I ensure it happens. I will never sit by and simply hope good fortune falls into my lap."

Was he telling me he'd set up the elevator malfunction just to talk with me? And he'd … what … paid the security guards to keep an eye on me? Holy shit. Was I horrified or flattered? My gaze dropped from his face down to where his hand rested against his chest, his knuckles raw and bloody. Luca had kept tabs on me, and that had saved me. My stomach clenched viciously to think of what would have happened had he not come after me.

Getting up from the bed, I retrieved a first aid kit in the bathroom and sat cross-legged on the bed next to him. "Let me clean up your hands," I said softly as I twisted the cap off a tube of ointment and took his hand in mine.

I glanced up, and our eyes met. His obsidian gaze flashed with lust so tangible, it stirred goosebumps across my skin. I offered a shy smile, and he smirked back.

"I take it that means I'm forgiven?"

"How about you tell me where you learned to fight like that." I still wasn't sure what to think of Luca, but condemning him for his actions was difficult when they had saved me from what could have been a horrible nightmare.

"Growing up, I was in my fair share of fights." His eyes turned up to the ceiling as he spoke about his past. "As I got older, hitting the heavy bag became a great stress reliever. I worked with a trainer for a few years, did some sparring, but never any actual matches. Now, I mostly hit the bag on my own. I like to stay fit—you never know when you'll need to defend yourself."

His eyes dropped back to me, but I avoided his gaze, repacking the items into the kit. I'd done a great job pushing thoughts of my attack to the back of my mind, but his reminder brought them back in frightening clarity. I could taste the fear I'd felt when I was backed against that cement column. I never wanted to experience that terror again.

"I think it's my turn to ask a question," Luca said, drawing my eyes back to his and my thoughts to the present. "Why were you out wandering the city in the middle of the day?"

I took a deep breath and dropped my eyes down to where my hands were folded in my lap. "My boss said something that upset me, and I've been under so much stress, I just needed to take a breather. I was so lost in my head, I didn't notice how far I'd wandered."

When he didn't respond, I peered up at him. Luca was unrecognizable. He looked like another man entirely—someone terrifying. Those dark eyes that normally devoured me with such heat were cut shards of glass, and his angular jaw was rigid with tension. He rose up to sit across from me, his eyes boring into mine.

"What did he say to you?" The words were a menacing rumble. His ire wasn't directed at me, but it was frightening, nonetheless.

"It doesn't matter what he said. I went to HR to file a complaint, so he'll be dealt with. I don't want to rehash what happened with him or think about the incident under the bridge. Can we talk about something else?" I had misled him by insinuating I had filed a complaint, but I was going to at the earliest opportunity, so a small white lie wouldn't matter.

His eyes narrowed, but he conceded. "You said you were under a lot of stress—what else has been bothering you?"

You. Us. "My parents always stress me out."

"How so?"

"Maybe it sounds childish, but I never feel like I measure up. I have two sisters—the younger one is an artist who can do no wrong, and the oldest was taken under my father's wing a long time ago, a few years after our brother died. I've always been stuck in the middle, the odd man out. I even went to school to work at my dad's company, and most of the time, I'm not sure he notices I'm there."

"I think it sounds perfectly reasonable to want their praise, but you can't let their opinions rule you forever."

"I know, and I'm finally starting to realize their opinions don't matter. It doesn't change anything if Dad is proud of me or not. I have to live my life in a way that makes me happy—it's *my* life." I was pleased with the conviction in my tone, recognizing there was truth in what I said. The sentiment had been building inside of me, and it felt good to put the thoughts into words.

Luca smiled softly at me before his lips fell. "How did your brother die?"

In a way, I appreciated that he had asked rather than proffering the token condolences that are customary. He didn't mince words or play games; he came right out and asked what he wanted to know.

"My dad took my brother and sister to a movie one night. On the way back home, they were mugged, and my brother was killed. He was eleven." It had been almost seventeen years since I'd lost my big brother, but it still hurt to talk about it.

"How old were you?"

"Seven. My older sister and I were at a school program dress rehearsal that night. We'd been dancing and singing while my brother was murdered. After that, my family changed. We have our moments, but for the most part, it tore us apart."

He nodded in understanding.

"How did you lose your mother?" I asked quietly.

"Drive-by shooting—wrong place at the wrong time. She had just stepped out of the house to run to the market and was gunned down on the sidewalk. I heard the shots and ran outside to find her in a puddle of her own blood. Some street thug with a target on his back had been walking by at the same time—a stray bullet hit her right in the heart." His voice was so devoid of emotion, it gave me chills.

"How old were you?"

"Seventeen. Arianna was only fourteen." His younger sister—she'd still been a young girl.

"Did you have to go into foster care?"

"Only for a couple months. The second I turned eighteen, I petitioned for custody of her."

"I can't imagine raising a teenage girl when you were only a kid yourself." I thought back to what a nightmare my sisters and I had been at that age and grimaced.

He huffed out a laugh. "Nothing about it was easy, but I did my best. You deal with what life hands you, but that's why I try to ensure in every way possible that life gives me a winning hand."

When he put it that way, and knowing what I now knew about him, his actions sounded perfectly reasonable. How could I fault him for being domineering and assertive when he was taking charge of his life, trying to give himself the best chance to be happy? He had seen his mother gunned down and been forced to raise his young sister; and despite those odds, he'd picked himself up and made a success of himself. His perseverance and honor were more than just admirable; they were incredible.

"Does the stalking mean you consider me a winning hand?" I asked coyly.

"Baby, you're a royal flush." He gave me a rakish grin that was so delectable on him, I jumped onto his lap and pressed my lips to his.

There was no longer any doubt. I was in way over my head.

CHAPTER 14

Luca

The first chance he had, my father walked away from us. There was something broken inside of him that made him weak. Made him incapable of understanding the concept of loyalty. Loyalty to his wife. Loyalty to his children. When times got hard, he turned his back on us for an easier path. A man who grasps loyalty and honor, not just the ability to recite the definition, but someone who truly understands the concepts, that man could never abandon his family. That was the conclusion I'd come to over the years when I'd wracked my brain, trying to figure out how my father could have left.

From what I could recall of him, he was a decent father, aside from his tendency to bail at the slightest struggle. He would take me to get ice cream and taught me how to shoot dice, but there were also plenty of times he wasn't around. I could only assume he'd been a shit husband. I was only five when he left, which meant I wasn't privy to the details of my parents' marriage, but I would never forget the screaming fights he'd *have with my mother. Their relationship must have been rough; there were countless nights I'd wake to the crash of glass breaking or my mother's raised voice chewing him out for coming home late.*

One Friday night, he never came home.

I worried endlessly about my father for the first few months, wondering if something awful had happened to him. My mother tried to reassure me he was fine, but I never could believe her. Not until I happened to see him walking into a restaurant years later with a woman on his arm did I accept he'd chosen a different life over us.

My dad walking out had been tough, but it meant no more late-night fights, and Ari and I still had Ma. The woman had been a saint— not the Mother Theresa type—she was too tough to be that angelic. My mother devoted her life to raising us kids. She kept a roof over our heads and food on our plates, but more than that, she taught us respect and self-discipline. Ma never let us get away with anything, but she was also our greatest ally.

She was our rock.

Never in my teenage brain could I have comprehended how quickly she'd be taken from us.

When I found my mother's lifeless body on the sidewalk, a part of me died there with her. I crossed the bridge to manhood that day, but it wasn't to become the man she'd been raising. I became something else. Something my mother had worked long and hard to eradicate from inside me.

She might have been disappointed, but I was glad. The man I'd become had enabled me to arrive at this single moment in time. Months of discretely asking questions, getting myself into unsavory places, and talking to dangerous people—all to get answers. Those answers had led me to a small rundown house in Jersey City.

Led me to vengeance.

It turned out my mother had been killed by a gangbanger upset at a rival for allegedly hitting on his woman. A petty argument over a girl who probably spread her legs for money had cost my mother her life.

I couldn't allow the crime to go unpunished.

I had tracked down the asshole responsible, learned everything I could about him, and now, I was there to dole out justice. I had wondered how I'd feel in this moment and was pleasantly surprised to find myself steady and determined as ever. I didn't think I'd turn chicken shit, but I had my father's blood in my veins, so there was always a chance.

I acquired a gun from a local pawn shop and had immediately taken it to a range to begin familiarizing myself with the weapon. I wasn't about to run headlong into a situation that would get me killed or locked away. Ari was counting on me to take care of her. I was the only family she had left, and I had no intention of leaving her alone in the world.

I watched the house for hours as I'd done on a number of other occasions. I watched as my target came home in his shitty grey Buick LeSabre, nearly lost his sagging pants as he exited the car, then walked inside the unlocked house. I wasn't sure if he thought there was nothing worth stealing inside or if he was so confident in his badass reputation, he assumed no one would intrude on his space, but he was in for the surprise of his life.

I waited until almost midnight. The lights were still on in the house, but the street had gone quiet, and my nerves were cool steel. I double-checked my weapon, taking the safety off and making certain the chamber was loaded, then stepped from the deep shadows and walked directly to the front door. As suspected, the door was unlocked.

I helped myself inside and found the worthless gangbanger asleep on the couch with the television blaring, a bag of chips resting on his chest. Not wanting to take anything for granted, I silently maneuvered through the small house and checked for any other occupants. Once I had verified he was alone, I walked to the couch, pointed the gun at him, and kicked his foot to wake him up.

He startled awake but quickly froze when his eyes landed on my gun, held perfectly steady in my firm grip. "Who are you, man?" His eyes darted around the room, searching for an answer.

"To you, I'm nobody, just another man on the street."

"Then why you holdin' a gun in my face?" he spat back, displaying forced bravado.

"Because you don't deserve to live. I've been watching you, Jacob Martinez, or should I call you Squeeze?" Night after night, I'd followed Squeeze to seedy bars and dark street corners where he did his business —sold drugs and pimped out girls, some that looked no older than Ari. As far as I could tell, he hadn't possessed a single redeeming quality.

Droplets of sweat beaded on his brow as Squeeze began to grasp the intensity in my gaze. "Yo, man, what d'you want? I got money, man, just put the gun down."

"Money's not going to fix this, Squeeze. I want something you can't possibly give me."

"Then what? You just gonna kill me?"

"Yes."

The night air rang out with a satisfying blast as a bullet buried itself deep into Squeeze's skull. Blood and brain matter splattered all over the sofa and nearby wall, just like my mother's had pooled on the cold winter sidewalk.

His life for hers.

It wasn't a fair trade, but it would have to do.

I took one more casual glance around the room, stuffed the gun in the back of my pants, and left the scene just as easily as I'd arrived. This time, I left from the back of the house, sticking to the shadows as I rounded to the front and made my way to the moonlit sidewalk.

I thought I'd feel different after the deed was done—either as a product of guilt from taking a life or relief from enacting the justice I'd sought for the last six months. I had been wrong. I felt no different now than I had an hour before. If anything, I felt somewhat lost. My attention had been so focused on identifying, locating, and killing Squeeze, I hadn't considered what I would do next.

Not that I had many options. I had secured a job at a local steel plant and petitioned for custody of Ari as soon as I turned eighteen. I'd *found unexpected help at the Attorney General's office—a kind older lady who had helped me get in touch with legal aid. Ari was now my sole purpose.*

I would be relieved to get her back, but the prospect was also daunting. How would I support both of us with my meager earnings? How the hell was I supposed to raise her? I had no idea what I was doing, but I was not my father—I would not run from my responsibilities. I clenched my fists in determination as I eased down the sidewalk when a voice called out behind me.

"Hey, kid. Wanna tell me why you did that?" The voice belonged to an older man and didn't sound particularly upset, but his words froze me in my tracks.

I slowly turned to find a man leaning against the car I'd just walked past. He was an average build and wearing a suit, but that was about all I could make out. Where the hell had he come from? Did he know I'd just killed a man? Or was he asking about something else entirely?

"You're gonna have to be more specific," I shot back, attempting to remain calm.

The corners of his lips pulled up with amusement as he stood and approached, signaling for us to continue walking. "I've been watching Mr. Martinez over the past few days."

My veins all turned to ice at the mention of Squeeze's name, but I kept my lips sealed.

"My associates and I had suspected he was stealing from us," he glanced over at me pointedly. "Which would have been rather unfortunate for Mr. Martinez. As things stand, you seem to have eradicated my problem for me. What I'd like to know is, who are you and who are you working for?"

My steps slowed to a stop, and I debated my answer. This man knew what I had done—if I told him who I was, he could go to the cops. On the other hand, it sounded like he had been working with Squeeze, and in that case, he was a criminal himself. Was I willing to kill him if he demanded my name and it came down to a fight? The answer was a resounding no, which left me with few options.

"Luca Romano."

His eyes narrowed. "Romano. As in Salvatore Romano?"

"Assuming there's not more than one, yes. My father is Salvatore Romano." My distaste at uttering those words was palpable, and the man's brows lifted in surprise.

"I wasn't aware he had any kids."

"That's because he left my ma when we were little, never came back."

"I see. He was never a particularly honorable man, so I'm not surprised." He peered at me more intently. I could see in the dim moonlight as a series of questions crossed his face. "What business did you have with Mr. Martinez?"

"He killed my mother."

He nodded sagely as if everything now made perfect sense. "So, this was a personal matter. Am I to understand you were working alone then?"

"Yes."

"It's no light thing, taking a life. You seem to be handling it rather well."

"He was scum—didn't deserve the air he was breathing. I did the world a service."

The man burst out laughing and patted his thick hand against my back. "You are a pip, you know that?"

"Thanks," I said wryly. "I appreciate the compliment, but I really should be going. The police could be here any minute, and it would probably be best if we both got lost."

"Why should they come? No one in this neighborhood is gonna call the cops. Even if they did, you're fine here with me." My newfound friend gazed at me questioningly, his eyes light with amusement. "You believe in fate, Luca?"

The question caught me off guard. Did I believe in fate? If I did, would that mean my mother was supposed to be killed? "I'm not sure I do."

"Well, I do. And you know what else I believe? I believe you and I have met here tonight for a reason." He held out his hand, and I hesi-

tantly clasped mine in his. "My name is Michael Abbatelli, and you and I are going to become very good friends."

CHAPTER 15
Alessia

"**A**lessia, wait up!"

I paused, turning around at Jackson's voice just outside the entrance at work. "Hey, Jackson. Twice in one week—you sure you're not following me?" I teased as he caught up to me.

"Nah, the judge says I'm not allowed to do that anymore." Those dimples. He was such a flirt. "Can you spare a minute to walk with me? Won't take long, promise."

What's this all about?

"Sure." I motioned him back toward the sidewalk. "What's up?"

He glanced behind us at the building, then peered back at me sheepishly. "I know I already said something, and I should probably keep my mouth shut, but I'm not good at doing what I should. I saw you yesterday … with the Italian."

I peered at him uneasily, my stomach starting to churn with

trepidation. "Yeah. I know you said he was dangerous, but I'm a big girl and can make my own decisions." Was he still trying to talk me out of dating Luca?

Jackson pulled me aside into an entryway alcove, glancing around as if he'd stolen something and expected to be busted any second. "I'm putting my neck on the line here, but you need to know," he said in a hushed whisper. "That man is in the mafia—you need to stay away from him." He stared at me, pleading earnestly with his eyes, but I just stared back blankly.

"That's absurd. Just because he's Italian doesn't mean he's in the mafia. My family is Italian, and we aren't in the mafia—that stuff doesn't exist anymore. You've been watching too much TV." I was incredulous. His allegations had come so far out of left field, all I could do was scoff at him.

Jackson pursed his lips and lowered his head, his face inches from mine. His chocolate eyes were no longer warm and inviting, instead, they were laden with shadows, dark and ominous. "That *stuff* is still very much alive. You know I'm Irish—some of my family is involved in a similar organization as the Italian."

"Organized crime?" I cut in. "Are you telling me your family is part of the Irish mob?"

He didn't answer my question, but I could see the truth in his cutting gaze. "I've heard things through the years. I know who key players are, especially in this area. That man is part of The Five Families."

"What's that?" I asked hesitantly.

"The five ruling families of the New York Mafia—Russo, Lucciano, Giordano, Gallo, and Moretti. They run the city."

"Luca's last name is Romano; he's not one of them."

"Alessia." He let out an exasperated sigh. "The family names are simply the organization names—it's not an actual family. For example, the Gallo family is run by a guy named Stefano Mariano with his underboss, Matteo DeLuca. I guess there may have been a Gallo way back when the families formed, but that's not how it works now."

"Oh. Well, that still doesn't mean he's a gangster," I insisted, not wanting to buy what Jackson was saying. Some of my incredulity was a natural defense mechanism to deny something I didn't want to hear, and some of it was well and truly disbelief. I'd lived in the city all my life and never heard even a whisper about the mafia.

"I don't know what I can do to convince you, but I'm not making this up. That man you're seeing, he's a made man—a mafioso. I tried to warn you, but you wouldn't listen. I'm telling you things I could get killed for talking about. You choose not to believe me, that's your call." He was clearly frustrated.

I wasn't trying to be ugly, but what he was saying was so absurd, I didn't know how to wrap my head around it. "I don't know what to say … this is all … Luca has money, but that's because he's a banker. He's not a mobster." My voice shook, confusion and uncertainty rattling my nerves.

"He's not a banker, Alessia, he's a loan shark. That's like saying a stay at Guantanamo prison is a beach vacation. *I'm* a banker—I don't charge people 150% interest, then break their kneecaps if they can't pay."

My hand flew to my mouth, my stomach roiling, and bile threatening to come up. It couldn't be. My Luca couldn't do what Jackson was describing. An unwanted image of his scarred, bloodied knuckles floated into my mind. He'd had a sound excuse for them, but now I had to wonder—did he use those fists for more than exercise?

I stepped away from Jackson, holding my hand out to keep him from coming closer. "I appreciate you trying to help me, but I need to go."

Jackson didn't fight me. He simply nodded before I tore off toward the building. When I walked through the front entry, my steps faltered when I spotted the security guards on duty. My eyes tracked from one to the other, wondering which of them Luca had paid. Could they tell what I had learned? Would they tell him they saw me?

Realizing how panicked I'd become, I berated myself for being overly dramatic. There was no proof Luca was in the mafia—I wasn't even sure it still existed. The mob hadn't been in the news since back in the 90s, outside of fictional tv shows and movies. Maybe Jackson was misinformed. Maybe he was just trying to get me to stop seeing Luca.

Before I jumped to any conclusions, I was going to do some research and look at the facts. Walking distractedly through security, I skipped my normal escalator ride and took the elevator to the tenth floor. Once I was in my office, I booted up my computer and pulled up Google, starting a search for the New York Mafia.

What I learned was mind-bogging.

For two long hours, I read articles about the rise and fall and recent resurgence of the American Mafia. I learned the federal RICO Act had strangled the life out of organized crime over a period of decades, but before a killing blow had been dished out, September 11th happened. When the terrorists launched their assault on our homeland, the crime-fighting resources previously concentrated on organized crime were redirected to fight terrorism.

Since the 2001 attacks, the mafia had seen a resurgence, adapting to modern-day technology and growing quietly underground. Just like Jackson had said, New York was ruled by The Five Families—five separate crime families who had split the city into sections, making money illegally in every fashion they could conceive.

I was stunned speechless.

I felt like I'd just learned there really were aliens secretly stashed away in Area 51. The mafia still existed—and not just small-scale thugs—billion-dollar operations, each with hundreds of men.

If mobsters still existed, could Luca be one of them?

He fit the mold, if there was a mold. He fought, had money, came from the streets, and he definitely had secrets. *After my mother died, I was adopted into a new family.* The words Luca had said to me came back now, and I had to wonder if he'd meant something far different than I had assumed. Had he meant he was taken into the mafia after his mother died? A young kid needing money, stuck raising his younger sister—I could see how turning to crime would feel like the only option.

And what about the mention of blood for blood—what had that been about? I didn't have to know the details to realize the caller hadn't been talking in code. He was talking about violence, maybe even people dying.

In my gut, I felt the truth.

I didn't want to face it, didn't want to believe it, but it was there, staring me in the face.

Luca was in the mafia.

Would I be in danger just by associating with him? Would he end up going to prison? Did he kill people? I could feel the panic welling up inside me, a wall of turbulent water threatening to drag me under. I had to stop seeing him—didn't I? Could I be with a mobster? Did I want that for myself? Absolutely not. But how did I break up with a criminal who had his sights set on me?

Run.

Not just run home. I would need to leave the city.

What about my job and my family? Money wasn't an issue, but there was a whole lot more to my life than money and possessions. Would I have to leave behind my entire life to get away from Luca? Was there a chance he would let me go if I tried to break things off?

Before my thoughts could devolve into all-out hysteria, my

phone vibrated with a call. Giada's face appeared on the screen, and a plan began to form.

"Hey, G. What's up?" I used my most practiced voice, the one I used with my parents when I wanted everyone to think everything was fine. There was no way I was telling Giada what a mess I'd gotten myself into. If needed, I'd bring my family into this, but if at all possible, I would handle it on my own. I had plenty of money, and I was a smart girl. I could manage this.

"Hey, I got tickets for the Pretty Woman musical on the 25th, you want to come with?"

"Um, yeah. I could probably do that. And if you're up for it, I was thinking about a sleepover tonight. I could come to your place, and we could catch up—unless you have plans."

Please be free. Please be free.

"No plans but you! We can watch the Pretty Woman movie in preparation—I even have popcorn on hand," Giada said excitedly.

"Sounds good. Mind if I come over straight from work? I'd have to bum pajamas from you."

"I gotcha covered. Come over whenever you can, and we'll get this party started."

"Thanks, G. I'll see you in a bit."

"Later, babe!"

I leaned back in my chair, exhaling with a small sense of relief. If I could avoid him for the rest of the day, that would give me a little time to figure out a more long-term plan. I was still reeling from what I had learned and the implications. Figuring out what to do about it would be an entirely different matter.

Part of me wanted to confront Luca and verify from him directly whether the allegations were true. I didn't want to run off half-cocked if I'd been fed false information, but I was scared to tell him what I'd heard. If Luca *was* in the mafia, would he hurt me for knowing more than I should? Would he hurt Jackson for telling me? I felt safe with Luca, but that didn't mean his obligations to his *family* didn't overrule his protective instincts toward me.

I went round and round, debating what I should do, unable to concentrate on anything else. By the time the clock read five, I was halfway out the door. Leo gave me a ride over to Giada's apartment where I hoped I could unwind enough to figure out the best course of action.

Giada had wine glasses on the counter and loungewear laid out for me. After I got out of my work clothes, we had wine and snacked as we watched Pretty Woman. When it approached time for bed, I was feeling more capable of handling my problems. Luca hadn't texted as I'd expected him to—in fact, I hadn't heard from him all day. Maybe he wouldn't be as persistent in his pursuit as I thought, and I had worried over nothing.

I said goodnight to my cousin and crawled into bed in her guest bedroom. Few of the city sounds filtered into the twentieth-story high-rise apartment, but the city lights were prolific enough to fill the room with a warm glow. I felt hidden away, safe from my boss and the looming threat of the mafia, but that sense of security was an illusion, shattered into the silent night air when my phone began to buzz.

I should have known there would be no hiding from him.

Luca's name displayed on my phone screen, and I considered not answering but decided it would behoove me to play along until I had a plan.

"Hey," I greeted him softly.

"How was your day?" His voice sounded worn out, and I wondered what he'd been up to all day. Despite what I'd learned, a part of me still wanted to soothe him—help ease his strain from the day.

"Good, just a standard workday. You?"

A long exhale came across the line. "I had a shit day, but hearing your sexy voice is doing wonders to improve my mood.

Work is important, but it fucking pisses me off it kept me from seeing you today."

I was helpless against him. Even knowing what he was and the dangers that presented, just a few words from him, and my heart soared. "I'm sorry your day was rough." As much as I wanted to tell him how much I had missed him, I didn't want to dig myself any deeper—I was already up to my neck in trouble.

"Have dinner with me tomorrow."

"Um … I have plans with my cousin," I sputtered, throwing out the first excuse that came to mind. My stomach twisted and clenched with a storm of emotions—fear, guilt, longing. I didn't want to lie to him, but I had no choice.

He was silent for a long, excruciating moment. "You aren't avoiding me, are you?" The tension in his voice was as much a threat as a question.

Would it matter if I was? "No. If I was hiding, I wouldn't have answered your call."

He huffed out a grunt. "It's getting late, and I've got another long day ahead of me, but I wanted to hear your voice."

"Get some rest, Luca. I'll talk to you tomorrow, okay?" My throat burned with the lie, and tears pooled in my eyes.

"After dinner with your cousin, you're mine. No excuses—you hear me?"

"Yeah," I whispered.

"That's my girl. I could have used some of that sweetness today, but I'll have to wait. You get some rest—you'll be up late tomorrow." The call ended, and Luca's honeyed voice was gone.

My heart lodged in my throat at the thought I might not ever hear his voice again. How did I reconcile Jackson's claim with the thoughtful man I'd just spoken to? I'd known Luca wasn't an average guy, but I never imagined anything so bad as the truth.

The Five Families.

The Mafia.

Criminal.

I was one-hundred percent Italian, living in the heart of the city, and I'd never once come across anyone in the mafia. That shit just didn't happen in real life. Of all the people, the one man who had the power to change me, to mark me as his own, was a criminal. A thug. The unfairness of it all only added to my hopelessness.

My heart blistered and tore.

My breathing stuttered, and I began to sob silently into my pillow. I gave myself over to the torrent of emotions, allowing the loss and frustration to crash over me like relentless waves on a rocky shore. Eventually, the tide let out, and I was left raw and exposed, slipping into a dreamless sleep.

I HAD to wake early in order to race home to shower and get ready for work. The bags under my eyes the next morning were the perfect complement to my swollen, bloodshot eyes. Forget foundation, I was going to need stage makeup to have any chance of looking quasi-normal. Unfortunately, I didn't keep anything stronger than concealer on hand, so I did the best I could with what I had.

I may have looked like hell, but I felt somewhat better equipped to handle my problems than I had the day before. I had come to the conclusion I needed to start addressing my problems head-on, instead of actively avoiding them.

First and most importantly was Luca. If I examined the facts logically, a relationship with him didn't make sense. He wasn't good for me, no matter how much that hurt. It would be best if I broke things off with Luca now, rather than letting it linger. More than likely, I was blowing things out of proportion anyway. I would tell him it was over, and he would move on. Men didn't get attached quickly like women did. It might zing his pride, but he wasn't going to chase after a girl who rejected him for long.

He surely had far too many willing options to spend much time pursuing me. As for me, the loss would hurt, but I would survive. It was hard to cause myself pain, but in the long run, I would be saving myself a world of heartache.

Burying myself in work, I pushed aside all thoughts of Luca. I even brought my lunch to avoid a chance encounter with him in the lobby. It may have been cowardice, but I didn't want to tell him in person—having him close to me would make the words that much more difficult. I waited to get out my phone until lunch when the office cleared out and only a few administrative personnel remained. Closing my office door, I began to type out my text to Luca.

I've thought about this a lot and decided this isn't going to work between us. This isn't a good time for me, and we are just too different. Please don't fight me on this. My finger hovered over the send button for long minutes while my inner voices warred over sending the message. It was the right thing to do, but that stupid organ inside my chest didn't agree.

When I finally amassed the fortitude to hit send, it felt like a monumental event, yet there was nothing to show for it. The gods didn't rain down their ire, and the Earth didn't tremor with the impact. I sat alone in an empty office, engulfed in silence.

Until my phone began to ring.

I dismissed the call, knowing it would be a mistake to speak to Luca. Instead, I texted him again. **Please, don't argue. I told you it's over.** I watched in breathless anticipation as the three conversation dots indicated he was typing a response.

You need to answer the fucking phone.

I'm not going to—there's nothing to say.

What happened in the time since I was in your bed two days ago?

He wasn't going to stop. He would keep arguing until I gave in and saw him or talked to him, then he'd have me. I wasn't strong enough to withstand him in person. I hated upsetting him, and breaking up over text was a shitty thing to do, but I didn't know how else to get the job done. I closed my eyes, my bottom lip trembling, and took a shaky breath. When I opened my eyes, I clicked to Luca in my contacts and blocked his number.

The silence in my office was suddenly suffocating. I couldn't breathe. The air was thick and heavy, too dense for my struggling lungs. I'd ended things with Luca, and it felt like I'd cut off a piece of myself. Tears pricked at my eyes, and I could feel a sob clawing to tear free of my chest.

Needing to find someplace safe to allow my heart to crumble, I hurried from my office and ran to the restroom. Hands on the sink, I lowered my head and cried, heaving, breathless sobs. I thought I'd purged all my tears the night before, but I'd been wrong. When would it be enough? How long would it take for my heart to be free of him? Was that even a possibility?

I feared that losing a man like Luca would wreck me— whether I'd been with him for a week, a month, or a year. He would set the bar so high, no other man could ever measure up. He'd be there with me always, the eternal presence of the one who got away.

Jostling me from my thoughts, the bathroom door creaked behind me. I hurriedly turned on the water and splashed my face a couple times before patting my flushed cheeks dry. When I opened my eyes, I startled at the reflection of the man standing behind me.

"Roger! What are you doing in here?" I spun around, my back pressed up against the sink. The office had been empty, except for a couple of assistants who had been eating at their desks. Where had he come from?

"I saw you run in here upset and wanted to make sure you were alright." He took a step closer, and my heart lurched in my chest.

"I'm fine, just had an upset stomach."

He took one more step, bringing us within inches of one

another. "You've been crying. You don't have to hide from me if you're upset. Let me help you." He reached out and pulled me into his arms. My body went rigid against his unwelcome touch.

"Roger, please don't," I said as I tried to push my way out of his hold.

"No one else is here—you don't have to pretend."

Pretend? What the hell was he talking about? "I'm not pretending anything." A flood of liquid fear rocketed through my veins as Roger maneuvered me against the cold tile wall. "Get away from me," I hissed as I tried to free my hands from between us.

"I see the way you're constantly flaunting yourself, trying to get my attention. You can't tease me forever." He thrust his erection against my belly and fumbled to lift my skirt to my hips. He wasn't a large man, but he had still managed to overpower me.

I sucked in a breath to scream for help, but his sweaty palm clamped over my mouth before I could get a sound out. I tried to shake my head, to deny his claims, to deny this could be happening right there in my own office, but it didn't help. Roger spun me around so that my stomach and the side of my face were plastered against the wall, his body pressed against mine, one hand still heavy over my mouth.

"You want me to have some of this, don't you?" his whispered close to my ear, making me wrench my head as far away as I could move it. "Yeah, you can pretend to play hard to get, but I know what you want." His hand snaked around between my stomach and the wall before inching down to cup my sex, his bony finger pressing against my opening through the thin barrier of my panties.

Rage leaked from my eyes in the form of helpless tears. Regret sat bitter on my tongue as I faced the fact I had allowed this to happen by not filing a complaint or telling my father. Fear shook my entire body, stealing the air from my lungs and making me weaker than I was already.

I grew up in this building, visiting my dad at his office. This was supposed to be a safe place. This was my other home. Now it was ruined, violated by this man who was about to do the same to me. My head swam from lack of oxygen, and I wondered if it might be better to pass out and not remember what was about to happen.

CHAPTER 16

Luca

"Get your fucking hands off her." The words were a savage growl, ripped from me as fury colored my vision.

I'd gone to Alessia's office, upset about her little attempt to walk away from me, planning to put her in her place. Her office had been empty, but her purse and phone were still there at her desk. She had to be nearby, so I prowled from room to room in search of her. When I peeked inside the bathroom, I never expected to find Alessia being assaulted by some dickhead in a cheap suit.

I thought I'd been mad when I arrived—that had been nothing.

Seeing his hands on her, the black tears streaking down her face, I rocketed past mad and went straight to blinding rage. I was doused in boiling anger so blistering, I was two seconds from going feral.

The only reason I didn't immediately launch myself onto the piece of shit and beat him to a bloody pulp was because Alessia ran into my arms the second he released her. It had given me pause just long enough to remember one of the fundamental lessons I'd learned long ago—never dish out payback when the insult was still fresh. It sounded lofty but had nothing to do with making rash decisions and everything to do with not getting caught. No threats, no evidence at the scene—then I would be free to do what I wanted later when the time was right.

Alessia needed me. I would get her out of there and deal with the asshole later, even though my head pounded with the need to rain down vengeance. The best I could do at the moment was glare at him with a promise of retribution. He seemed to get my meaning. The fucker looked about ready to piss himself.

I ushered Alessia out of the bathroom. "Let's get your things— we're leaving." My words were clipped, too much anger pulsing through my system to give her gentle and soothing like she deserved. Fortunately, she didn't argue, simply gathering her things and allowing me to lead her to my car outside.

Neither of us spoke for most of the ride. I tested the V10 engine, swerving in and out of traffic with the grace of a hummingbird weaving from one flower to the next. I was driving like a lunatic, but I didn't care. I needed the rush to help rid me of the excess adrenaline lighting my skin on fire.

"Luca, you're scaring me," Alessia said softly.

Exhaling the stale air trapped deep in my lungs, I made an effort to slow down. "That was your boss, wasn't it?"

"Yes." She bit down on her bottom lip and peered at me anxiously.

"He didn't just say something to upset you the other day, did he? When you wandered off and ended up under the overpass. He's been harassing you, hasn't he?"

"He didn't touch me—it was just something he said—but, yes,

he made a sexual comment that upset me." Her voice was so small, I wanted to scoop her into my lap and never let her go.

"How long?"

"How long what?"

"How long has it been going on?" I bit out.

"It was just little comments at first. Until a few days ago, the only time he's tried to touch me was at the company Christmas party," she explained in a rush.

"How. Long."

"A year," she breathed.

What. The. Fuck.

Just when I thought I was cooling down enough to talk, I was straight back to suffocating fury. My knuckles bled white as they clenched the steering wheel, my nostrils flaring as I tried to breathe through the pounding anger. That asshole had been making her life hell for a solid year, and she had been taking it. Why hadn't she put a stop to it? Wasn't her father the fucking CEO?

"Where are we going?"

"My place," I snapped. It was unfair to take out my anger on her, but my control was slipping. I felt powerless to have sat by while she had been suffering—it didn't matter that I hadn't known her—she was mine to protect, and I hadn't done my job.

I despised that feeling.

I could sense her eyes on me, but she didn't argue about my intended destination. Parking in the underground lot, I led her toward the elevator to my Park Avenue home. A short walk to Central Park, my apartment was ideally located in the heart of the city. I'd paid a pretty penny for that convenience, but it had been worth it. I loved everything about my place. I'd remodeled it when I bought it, so it was decorated in cool greys with black accents, exactly as I'd wanted. It was more space than I needed, but I liked knowing I had a little room between me and my neighbors.

I was unsettled at how good it felt bringing Alessia to my place. Normally, when I brought a girl over, I was itching to get rid of her as soon as she walked through the doors. I should have known Alessia would be different. She had crawled under my skin without even trying. Instead of getting rid of her, I puzzled out ways to make her stay. For now, I would rely on brute strength and manipulation; but soon, I'd need to convince her to stop running.

She came to a stop in the entry of my apartment, seemingly unsure as she took in her surroundings. I had noted how orderly everything was at her place, but I had no room to talk. My place bordered on institutional, but it wasn't because everything was in its place—there were no *things*. I'd never needed to buy crap just to own it and clutter up my living space. I'd grown up owning hardly anything and saw no reason to collect things now that I had money.

I had comfortable sofas with modern lines, the requisite number of end tables and lamps, and muted paintings on the walls. What I didn't have were shelves with worthless knick-knacks and fake plants cluttering every surface. It was the perfect escape from the chaos of life in the city.

Leading her into the living area, I motioned to a sofa. "Have a seat."

"I like your place," she offered as she sat down gingerly, taking off her heels and pulling her legs up to her chest.

I tipped my chin but didn't otherwise acknowledge her comment. "Why the fuck haven't you told anyone about your boss?" I stood at one of the large windows and stared outside as I waited for her response.

"I was trying to handle it on my own. Up until last week, there wasn't much to handle, just some inappropriate comments here and there. I didn't want to go running to daddy, not that he would have helped me anyway." The last part was muttered under her breath, not meant for my ears.

"Why the hell would you say that?" I turned back to her in astonishment.

"My dad's a big believer in handling your own problems. I've been messed with in the past, and he told me to figure it out—I wasn't going to run to him for help, just to have him embarrass me."

I couldn't imagine a father not wanting to murder anyone who had hurt his daughter. But then again, my dick of a father hadn't given two shits about me or my sister. Maybe Alessia had misunderstood her father, and maybe he was an asshole, there was no telling.

"You said you filed a complaint—why was he still working there?"

The color that had returned to her smooth olive skin drained away. "I tried to, but the HR office was out for training. I was going to do it the next day but got distracted."

I ran my finger back and forth over my bottom lip as I stared at my little songbird. "So, you lied to me."

She peered up at me through her lashes, regret and guilt leaking from her eyes. As if I'd had any question about my twisted proclivities, my dick roused at the sight of her small and broken. She was mine to protect, but also mine to do with as I pleased, and her current state gave me all kinds of depraved ideas.

"You can bat those eyes at me all you like, but it's not going to save you. I've warned you about lying to me … twice now. However, as much as I want to bend you over my knee this instant, we have other matters to discuss, so I'll just say this. If your boss makes lewd comments to you, you tell me. If the mailman catcalls you, you tell me. If any man ever puts a hand on you in a way that makes you uncomfortable, you tell me. Am I clear?" I waited until she nodded before I continued. "Now, what got in your head that made you think you needed to end things between us? And, I swear to God, woman, do not test my patience with a lie."

I leaned my back against the wall and crossed my arms over my chest. I was genuinely curious what her reasons would be, assuming she told me the truth. A part of me hoped she wouldn't. I would make her writhe until she begged, and still, I would deny her so she would understand what it felt like to be refused. It wouldn't help my cause to win her over, but seeing her tied up and panting would be worth it.

Alessia's eyes danced around the room, fear wafting off her in palpable waves. Eventually, her resolve solidified as her eyes met mine. "I know about you, Luca. I know who you are."

Every muscle in my body went rigid. "What do you mean?" I asked cautiously.

"I know you're in the mafia. I can't be with you—I'm not okay with that."

Wariness gave way to confusion. I'd been certain she was oblivious—decided the naivete wasn't just an act. She'd had no idea about my associations, which meant someone had fed her information. It had to have come from someone she knew, someone she was close to, someone willing to put their neck on the line to warn her.

We kept that shit locked down, not like the days of John Gotti, where press conferences and flashy mob killings were an everyday occurrence. The new American Mafia had gone back to its Sicilian roots. Omérta—our code of silence—was an absolute, punishable by death, and not just your death, the death of your loved ones. Too many made men had turned rat over the years; there had to be severe repercussions for turning on your family.

Whoever told her had to be in the life. I wondered if she knew or cared whether that person was connected, because she clearly resented my involvement. She was looking at me like I pushed the elderly in front of moving vehicles for fun. Alessia was the most complex, confusing woman I had ever met. Each word out of her mouth was more confusing than the last, and like a buffoon, I couldn't get enough.

"What I do for a living has nothing to do with you and me."

"So, it's true?" A glimmer of hope fizzled out in her eyes. She had hoped I'd deny her allegations. I hadn't denied them, but I also wasn't going to admit anything—another lesson I'd learned early on.

"I'm just an ordinary man, no different than the men in your family or anyone else. I'm a capitalist. I pursue lucrative business opportunities when they arise. I am the same man today as I was last week when those pretty eyes gazed at me like I hung the moon, begging me to kiss you."

"But you hurt people and break the law. I can't just ignore that —it changes things."

"You seem to have a very pretty picture painted of the world around you. We aren't so far off our less-civilized ancestors. This life is cutthroat—whether it's business opportunities, relation-ships, or anything in between. You think politicians and the wealthy play by the rules? That's a joke. They're more corrupt than the thugs on the street. I loan people money, just like any other banker. People don't have to accept my terms. They want a lower rate, go to a credit union—I'm not forcing anyone into anything. The law says, because I'm willing to take a risky bet and lend money to someone with shit credit, I'm a criminal. If a stockbroker makes a risky trade, would you call him a criminal? No. I'm not a saint, but I'm not the devil you're making me out to be."

CHAPTER 17

Alessia

H is eyes sparked with anger as he came off the wall, energized by his speech. What he said was true to an extent. I wasn't naïve enough to think corruption wasn't rife in the world, but charging an oppressive interest rate wasn't the same as breaking kneecaps to get your money. The more I thought about it, the more defensive I became.

"You tell me not to lie, but that's exactly what you're doing," I argued, sitting up straighter as anger infused steel into my spine. "You make it sound like you're purely a businessman, but I've seen you fight and shoot. You can't honestly tell me those are purely recreational hobbies—you *hurt* people."

"And what about your boss back there? He didn't have any qualms about hurting you, and you were innocent. At least the people I associate with know what they sign up for—your asshole boss and those men under the bridge are animals out looking to prey on the easiest victim to cross their paths. For each of them, there's a dozen more you never know about—they're everywhere. I don't go looking to hurt people, but I'm not going to let anyone walk all over me. Yes, I can defend myself, because it's just as necessary today as it was a thousand years ago."

His words resounded in a place deep inside me.

I didn't want him to make sense, but he did. It was easier when things were put in terms of right and wrong, good and bad, but life was far too complicated for such blanket characterizations. The vast majority of humanity fell somewhere on the spectrum—not purely good or bad. There was a small percentage of people who were downright evil, but I'd bet my life Luca wasn't one of them, but was that enough? Where was the cutoff on the spectrum to delineate allowable versus unacceptable?

I couldn't meet his eyes as I processed his argument. I was so confused and still reeling from my confrontation with Roger. Was he making sense, or was I just desperate to exonerate him from his wrongdoings?

"You told me your brother was killed," Luca said, bringing my attention back to him. "Did the police ever find the man responsible?"

I was surprised by his change in subjects, unsure where he was going, but I shook my head slowly.

"He could still be out there, living his life free as a bird. Would prison be adequate punishment, or would you want to see him dead for what he did? That would technically be murder, but wouldn't it be justifiable?" He stepped closer as he pled his case, seeing the indecision plain on my features.

He'd gone for the jugular by bringing up Marco.

My big brother was a sensitive topic. He'd been protective and loving, even when surrounded by three obnoxious little sisters. We were all devastated when we lost him. If I ever came across his murderer, I'd kill him myself. It would be no less than he deserved—gunning down an innocent child.

Some things were unforgivable.

Where Marco was concerned, my opinions were rigid and

harsh. What did that say about me? That I would kill a man, no questions asked? I've heard women say they could never pull a trigger, but I always knew I could, if only for that one purpose. Some people were unredeemable, and a man who kills a child is at the top of that list.

"Yes, it would be justifiable." My eyes slowly found his, and I knew the questions rife in his piercing gaze were mirrored on my face. His questions were doubtless very different than mine, but they were there, nonetheless.

"We live by a code, and we believe in honor and respect—that doesn't make us monsters. Laws are there to keep people in line when there is no other system of accountability. We have our own system—I can't go into the details but know that we are men of honor. I have sworn an oath to my family, and I will abide by that promise until the day I die. Those are the principles I live by, but that doesn't change the man I am. Until you knew about my family, you had no problems with me. Don't throw this thing between us away because of that."

Each word he said pulled me further to his side, and I wasn't sure if he was convincing or manipulating. I needed time away from his persuasive influence. "I hear what you're saying, but I need to think about it on my own. I think I should probably go." I rose from the couch, and Luca came to stand before me.

"Is that what you really want?" he asked quietly, his voice losing its demanding fervor.

Yes. No. "I don't know what I want—that's part of the problem. You're a criminal, but I have these feelings … I'm so confused, and I need to sort it out on my own."

"I know you want to go, but I can't let you leave, not after what happened." He held up his hand to stop my protests. "Let me finish. I have some things I need to go handle. I'll grab you something to change into—you can hang out here, and when I'm done with work, I'll take you to dinner. That gives you some time to think, and I'll feel better knowing you're here safe."

How could I argue with that?

With a warm hand splayed on my lower back, he directed me to his bedroom where he picked out an undershirt and boxers for me.

"These may be huge on you, but they'll work. I want you to relax while I'm gone—everything is going to be okay. You don't have to make any decisions this second." He placed a kiss to my forehead. "I'll be back in a few hours; make yourself comfortable." As he pulled away, his thumb swept across my lips, a soft, intimate gesture that made my chest constrict with conflicted longing.

Not only was his touch soothing, his reassurances were exactly what I needed to hear. How was it the very subject of my turmoil could also be my primary source of comfort? Luca was everything I wanted and the absolute worst thing for me. Logic and emotion warred inside me, and I had no idea which would win the battle.

After listening to the front door close, I went into his large master bathroom to change. The space was the perfect complement to the rest of the apartment—white cabinetry with beautiful grey marble counters and a large white free-standing porcelain tub near the far wall. Behind that, a walk-through shower extended the length of the back wall with a dozen shower heads for two occupants.

His closet door was open, which I took as an invitation to peer inside. One wall was lined with suits, which didn't surprise me since I'd seen him in a different suit each day we'd been together. As I walked along the row of clothes, I grazed my fingertips across the rich fabrics, and his spicy scent enveloped me in the confined space. My eyes briefly closed as I breathed him in, languishing in the illusion of having him near.

There were several pairs of sneakers, all worn but well cared for—an unwelcome reminder of his training activities. The closet boasted a collection of expensive ties of which Neimen Marcus would be proud—all nearly solid in powerful colors like red, black and royal blue. I wasn't brave enough to snoop in his drawers, even though I desperately wanted to.

Being left alone to peruse his personal belongings sent an excited tingle through all my nerve endings. I loved being in his space, and that was a dangerous prospect. My logical mind insisted I should walk out the door and never look back, but my body didn't comply. Despite what I'd said, I wasn't sure it made any difference if I had space from him or not—he was in my veins, with me always.

My body thrummed with need for him. Separation only made my awareness of him more acute, my mind plagued with thoughts of him, and my body heavy with a sense of loss. When he wasn't around, I felt empty. My need for him twisted my thoughts, and I rationalized reasons to keep him near me.

I was a junkie.

The realization hit me with the driving force of an arctic wind, and my entire body shivered. All it had taken was one hit—one fateful exchange in an elevator, and I was hooked. Could I break the habit? Did I want to? How could I consider staying with him when he was in the mafia?

The circular arguments and constant inner turmoil were exhausting. I hadn't even realized how tired I was until I stepped back into his bedroom. Sheer blinds covered the windows, casting a soft glow in the room, making it peaceful and inviting. The bed looked heavenly. It hadn't been made, but the covers weren't in disarray either. It was clear Luca slept on the near side where a clock and a glass sat on the nightstand. Leaning over, I sniffed the pillow—it smelled like him. The scent drew me closer as I crawled beneath the covers, surrounding myself in his safety and warmth. I wasn't sure I'd ever been so comfortable in my entire life, and my worries faded away as my eyes drifted shut.

A caress down the length of my arm roused me from my sleep.

"A man could get used to coming home to a sight like this." Luca sat next to where I lay in his bed, his eyes soft like warm milk chocolate. "Time to get up. I'm taking you out."

I glanced up at the clock. "Six! I slept longer than I expected." I sat up groggily, gently rubbing my eyes so as not to smear my makeup before I remembered all the crying I'd done. I was lucky if my eye makeup wasn't already spread all over my face.

"It was an eventful morning; you needed the rest."

I nodded blankly, and he chuckled.

"Get dressed, sleepyhead—although, I get an enormous amount of pleasure seeing you in my clothes." His voice deepened, and when I met his eyes, his gaze was hooded.

I set my feet on the ground and shook my head. "I'll get changed, but can we go somewhere casual? I'm not up for formal dining."

His face split in a wide grin. "I know just the place."

LUCA DROVE us along the Harlem River and over the George Washington Bridge into New Jersey. It was late enough in Spring that the sun still lit the sky, and I enjoyed watching the city go by as we rode in companionable silence. Rather than satellite radio or his phone, Luca had a local radio station playing, which I found intriguing but didn't ask about. It felt like we were in a bubble, removed from the expectations and responsibilities of life, and I didn't want to burst that moment.

We pulled into the parking lot of a hole-in-the-wall place called Hiram's. The small building had neon signs in each window and a faded wooden hotdog sign next to the name.

"You have a thing for hotdogs, don't you?" I teased, recalling our hot dog dinner at Coney Island.

"You can't beat a good hotdog. I grew up eating them, never been able to break the habit."

"I've heard of this place but never been," I noted as we got out of the car.

"Baby, if you haven't had Hiram's, you haven't really lived," he teased playfully, making me laugh.

The small restaurant must have been a house originally. The ceilings were low inside, and the far wall boasted a heavily decorated stone fireplace. It only fit about half a dozen small round tables, and there was a counter just inside the door where customers placed their orders.

"What do you want?" asked Luca.

"Just a plain dog."

"Plain? No chili or sauerkraut? You're at least going to put mustard on it, right?" He gaped at me incredulously.

"Nope," I replied firmly. "I'm a plain and dry kind of girl. Take it or leave it."

Luca leaned in to whisper in my ear. "I happen to know very intimately there is nothing plain or dry about you."

My cheeks flamed with heat, which must have shown because Luca grinned wickedly at my response.

The hotdogs were enormous—thick and almost twice as long as the bun—and they smelled delicious. We picked out a table in the corner of the room where we could watch the steady stream of people coming in for dinner.

"Sauerkraut is the best way to enjoy a Hiram's dog, but I have plans for you later that doesn't involve sauerkraut breath," he said as he slathered his hotdog in mustard.

I shook my head at his presumption, but I didn't argue. "This place is great."

"Yeah. It's been here since the thirties. Used to be a place called Callahan's right across the street—the hotdogs were almost identical, but Callahan's was my favorite because of their killer fries. They sold out a number of years ago—the land got too valuable. They opened another one in a different location, but it was never as good. This place stays busy all the time, especially at lunch. You think it's packed now; this is nothing compared to the lunch crowd."

We ate our food as a steady stream of firemen, construction workers, and other laborers came through the doors. Luca was in his element—laid-back and comfortable surrounded by the salt of the earth. Seeing him like that and thinking about him listening to the radio, I realized a good amount of his New Jersey youth had stuck with him. He may have had a gorgeous skyrise apartment right off Central Park, but the poor kid from Hoboken was still there in the shadows.

"You loved growing up here, didn't you?" I asked as we returned to the car under a sky painted in the soft colors of twilight.

"Absolutely. My friends and I had free rein of the neighborhood—it was great."

"Tell me about it."

He cut his eyes over to me mischievously before checking for cars in the rearview mirror. "Outside the buildings where I grew up, there were poles every so often to hang laundry lines. A block over from my place, one of the poles had a rope hanging from it. We could get to the rope from this ledge and swing to the next ledge over, but between was about a ten-foot drop off to the sunken lower level below. If you were gutsy enough to swing, it kept you from having to make the trip all the way around the lower level.

"For weeks after we discovered the rope, I would swing on it every time we'd walk past, but none of my friends would risk it. One night, my best friend and I were out late, tossing pebbles at front doors. Sounds idiotic, I know, but it seemed like fun at the time. At one point, I must have grabbed too big of a rock or thrown too hard, but I managed to bust a window at the top of one of the doors. I can still hear the glass shatter into thousands of pieces and crash to the concrete porch. The two of us took off like maniacs. When we came to the retaining wall ledge, I swung across without a thought. At first, my friend didn't want to do it, but sirens blared to life behind us, so he grabbed the rope and swung. Damn if that rope didn't break and send him careening to the concrete below."

"Oh my God, was he okay?"

"Broke his ankle and the cops found him while I hid in the shadows. He never gave me up, but he was pissed at me for weeks," he chuckled to himself.

"You just left him there alone?"

"He would have done the same. No sense in us both getting caught."

I rolled my eyes and shook my head. "Did he get arrested?"

"Nah. They took him to the hospital and called his mom. She worked in a diner and knew one of the cops who found him. They figured his broken ankle was punishment enough, although, his parents still made him work off the money it cost to replace the window as soon as his ankle was healed."

"You really were a little shit," I teased.

"Baby, you have no idea. What about you? You ever get yourself into any trouble?"

"Nothing compared to you, I'm sure, but I managed a little mischief here and there," I said coyly.

"Spill. I want to hear what you consider *mischief.*"

I took a deep breath, laying my head back on the headrest. "Back in high school, my sister, Sofia, and I almost got arrested for being on the roof of my high school."

"Not bad. What were you doing up there?"

"One night she was upset about something—she never would tell me what. We went for a walk and ended up near the school. It wasn't all that late, but since it was January, it was already dark. There were a few people at the school, working on preparations for the winter dance, and they had propped open a side door. We decided to check it out, and when we didn't see anyone right away, she led me upstairs to an exit onto the roof. I hadn't even known the thing existed, but her gifted and talented class had done some egg drop project where the teacher had taken them onto the roof. Sofia wanted to go out and look at the stars, which was what we did until security showed up. They questioned us, asking if we were smoking cigarettes and crap like that. They couldn't accept that we didn't have some nefarious purpose—it wasn't long after a big school shooting, so they were overly cautious. I was terrified they were going to call my dad or arrest us, but eventually, they let us go with a warning."

"Aren't you the little juvenile delinquent," he said playfully.

I smacked his arm, and he let out a full-blown laugh that made my chest flutter with happiness. There was a lighter, care-free side to Luca that was just as captivating as the intense, stoic man I originally met in that elevator—the two together were the perfect complement.

When we arrived at my apartment building, I was reluctant for our evening to end. "Come up with me?" The words were out of my mouth before I'd had a chance to think about them.

Luca didn't comment; he simply turned off the engine and came around to help me from the car. It only took the short walk to the elevator for worry to set in. What was I doing inviting this man upstairs? Hadn't it been bad enough I spent the evening with him? My mind launched into a never-ending cycle of longing and self-loathing.

When the elevator doors closed behind us, Luca caged me in against the wall. He didn't touch me, yet I could feel his body all over mine. "No more thinking. Let your guard down and just feel." His rumbled words close to my ear sent an electric shock of lust straight to my belly.

As if obeying his command, my mind blanked—fear and worry evaporated until there was only me and Luca and the insatiable lust that pulsed between us. My lungs forgot how to function as my breathing stuttered and my head swam with his intoxicating closeness.

The elevator dinged our arrival, and Luca pulled away from the wall, taking my hand in his and tugging me toward my apartment. The moment the door closed, he had me pressed against it, his mouth seizing mine. My hands wound behind his neck, pulling him closer, raking through his thick hair. Luca's deft hands pulled up my skirt, then lifted me against him with his hands on my ass. My legs wrapped naturally around his waist as he carried me back to the bedroom.

The moment he set me down, his hands were all over me, tearing at my clothes, his mouth searing against my heated skin. In no time, I was bare before him, his hungry gaze raking over my exposed body.

"On the bed," he ordered softly.

I eased back onto the soft linens, my eyes glancing to the sheet as I contemplated pulling it over me.

"Don't even think about it. I want you where I can see you—all of you." His hands pulled at my legs, yanking me closer to him, then pressed my knees open, exposing me fully to his view.

Never taking his eyes from me, he lifted his shirt over his head, and my self-conscious thoughts were forgotten as I devoured the breathtaking sight of his naked chest. The sound of his zipper drew me back to the moment, and my stomach surged to my throat as I realized I was about to cross a threshold with this man. This criminal. My breathing went shallow and shaky as he lowered himself above me.

"It's just you and me. Don't think about anything else." His eyes stayed locked on mine, now just inches away, and I lost myself in their black depths. His darkness was all-consuming, and it called to me. When everything else dropped away, and it was truly just us, I felt free—like all was right in the world, and I could breathe.

"That's my girl," he cooed as he eased inside me with gentle thrusts, sweat beading on his brow from his measured restraint. My back arched into the pressure, and his mouth claimed my breasts. As his pace increased, strained moans left my mouth, and he hungrily devoured them with his kiss. Before long, he was pounding into me as if I held the key to his survival deep within me. He was merciless, relentless in his pursuit.

I had never been fucked the way he fucked me.

He didn't just have sex with me, he owned me.

He took possession of my body, branded my flesh with his touch until my soul itself bent to his will.

He snaked an arm between us to press against my swollen clit, rubbing in perfect rhythm with his thrusts. My skin began to tingle with the building pressure of what would be a mind-bending orgasm. My body stiffened as muscles contracted and tensed in preparation, whimpers and moans pouring from my lips.

"Come for me, Alessia. Milk my cock with that tight, wet pussy."

His course, dirty words were all it took. Pleasure exploded from my core and pulsed through my body in powerful waves. Eyes shut, I screamed my release, its intensity overpowering my every inhibition. My convulsions triggered his guttural release, and I could feel his cock swell and pulse inside me as he slowed his thrusts.

My body lay limp beneath him, utterly spent.

Ruined.

I'd read before that a man could ruin a woman for all others, but it always sounded absurd. Now, I knew there was truth to it. A release with Luca was unlike any I had experienced—gourmet wedding cake when all I'd had before were Twinkies. I couldn't imagine how I'd lived before without the taste of him.

He sat up and pulled out of me, then watched as our juices slipped from my entrance. His eyes sparked with possession as he gazed at his work.

"You like that?" I asked quietly into the sudden stillness.

He didn't answer. Instead, he swiped at the moisture and

spread it up to my clit. I jerk at the sensation on my oversensitive nerves, but he didn't stop. "Stay still," he commanded.

"It's too much—I can't."

"You can, and you will." His eyes bore into mine, and before long, the sensation became pleasurable, and I was again a puddle of wanton need. I moaned and ground my hips, undulating against his touch in search of my next fix.

He knew just where to touch and when to change his movements to build the pleasure to its maximum potency. His mouth came down on my breast, and he grazed his teeth against my nipple, sending a stroke of pain shooting through my nerve endings until a second wave of pleasure crashed over me. He barely milked the sensation from me before he was back inside me.

This time it was different.

He hovered over me, and I could feel his warm breath ghost across my skin as he moaned into the crook of my neck. His movements were slow and measured, gliding against me in an intimate caress. Weaving my fingers through his hair, I held him tightly against me as he trailed kisses along my collarbone. His breathing became shaky as he trailed the bridge of his nose along my jawline in a motion that was achingly tender.

"Lessia," he whispered against my chest. The single word was so heartfelt, so reverent, I couldn't breathe.

The beauty of that moment eclipsed all else.

When he lifted himself up to look into my face, tears streaked from my eyes at the raw vulnerability written across his features. He finished inside me, eyes never leaving mine, and I reveled in the look of triumph that passed across his face. Luca made me feel like the most precious treasure in the world—something priceless and cherished. It was a feeling I never wanted to lose, and it scared me to think how far I'd go to keep it.

CHAPTER 18

Alessia

The next morning, I woke in my bed alone. The pattering of rain sounded on the windows, and the cloudy sky cast my room in a melancholy shadow, making me want to sleep for a week. I thought about giving in to the tug of lethargy but decided to drag myself out of bed. When I sat up, I noticed a note on the nightstand.

Had shit to do. I'll call you later. PS—you're fucking beautiful when you sleep.

As usual, Luca made me smile, not just a casual everyday smile—a fifteen-year-old-girl-gets-noticed-by-her-crush smile. Why couldn't Brad, the grocery store manager, make me smile like that? Would it be so much to ask that I could fall for an upstanding citizen—someone who pays their taxes and doesn't hurt people for a living?

I groaned out a long sigh and flopped back onto the bed, taking my phone with me. Thank God, it was Saturday—I didn't have to face work for two full days. Considering everything that had gone on and the maudlin weather, I had no plans of leaving my apartment all day. I needed some time to think about my life and get my shit in order, and there was only one person I trusted enough to help me do that. I texted Giada, asking her to come over, then flipped to Luca in my contacts and made certain to unblock his number. I had no idea where things would end up between us, but for now, he was still a part of my life. After that, I commenced staring at the ceiling, which is where Giada found me an hour later.

"Al ... you okay?" she sung in a wary but playful voice.

"You might want to come sit down for this." I scooted toward the middle of the bed, and she crawled over to sit cross-legged next to me.

"Did something happen with that guy?"

"Yes, but it's so much bigger than that. G, if I tell you this, you have to promise never to tell another living soul."

"You're starting to freak me out."

"Say it, Giada—I need to know you won't discuss this with anyone."

"You know you're my one and only."

Anxiety made my heart flutter in my chest as I held her eyes. "Luca's in the mafia." The room fell into an awkward silence as Giada processed the news.

"Sooooo, you stopped seeing him, right?" she asked, confused.

"Sort of ... I mean, I tried to…"

"You're still seeing him?" Her voice rose a series of octaves with the question.

"He's insanely persuasive! And I really like him—G, don't look at me like that! I need your help." I sat up facing her, placing my hands on her knees. "He's everything I never knew I wanted, but now that I know what it's like to be with him, I can't imagine it any other way—he even saved me from Roger and from being mugged."

"Your boss?"

"Yes, he attacked me in the bathroom yesterday."

"*That fucker,*" she hissed.

"But it's okay because Luca busted in and saved me. I know I should probably end it, but I can't seem to do it. It's like telling myself not to sleep or breathe."

"What if being with him puts you in danger? Plus, he could go to prison! Are you okay being with a convict?"

No, absolutely not, and yet... "The thought of losing him makes me feel like I'm drowning—it's terrifying," I admitted in a whisper.

"Damn," she breathed, pulling me into a hug. "I leave you alone for one day..." she teased, making me laugh.

"I know—I'm a hot mess. Thank you for loving me anyway."

"Always. Plus, I'm sure I'll have my turn one of these days."

"Good Lord, let's hope not. I think I've got myself in enough mess for the both of us."

Giada forced me out of bed, and we spent the rest of the morning talking through my Luca troubles. I told her about the three thugs attempting to mug me and about being assaulted by Roger. She threatened to throat punch me if I ever let someone treat me like Roger had again. I promised to let her if I did.

By the time she left just after lunch, I was feeling noticeably better. I still had no idea what I was going to do, but I felt better about being undecided. It wasn't like I'd agreed to marry Luca—I just hadn't stopped dating him. That didn't mean I was going to stay with him forever.

Bluster, bluster, bluster.

The manipulative mind of an addict is a terrible thing.

When the phone rang that evening, my heart danced in my chest as Luca's name flashed on the screen. Damn heart was a traitor. It had declared mutiny over my mind and was now campaigning for a total overthrow.

"Hey, Luca," I greeted softly.

"How was your day?" His voice was a sexy rasp that conjured pictures of his naked body.

"It was quiet, relaxing—perfect for a rainy day. You?"

"I wish. I was out running around in that rain like a schmuck, and it's not over yet. I still have dinner plans with a friend before I can call it a day."

A friend? Was that code for another woman?

I'd been so wrapped up in the mafia bombshell, I hadn't even considered if Luca and I were exclusive. The thought of him with someone else didn't just hurt, it made me irrationally angry— massacre his closet and key his car angry. His dinner date wasn't necessarily a woman, but logic failed my brain where Luca was concerned.

"Oh."

He was quiet for several beats. "There a problem?"

"No."

"What did I say about lying to me?"

Fuck. If I told him what I was thinking, I'd look like a crazy woman, jealous when we'd only just started dating. But then again, I was trying to end the relationship days earlier. If he thought I was too possessive and left me, that would solve my problems.

"Are you seeing someone else?" I blurted.

"That's my girl," he purred, a smile implicit in his voice. "I want to know exactly what you're thinking—no games. As for my dinner plans, I'm meeting an associate. He's sixty years old, bald, and weighs close to three hundred pounds. No, I'm not seeing anyone else, and I expect the same courtesy in return. Does that work for you?"

"Yeah, that works," I whispered breathlessly. As if hearing Luca call me his girl wasn't enough to do me in, his speech had me melting into a puddle of female hormones.

"Good. When can I see you tomorrow?"

"Not sure. I've got to get some chores done, then I've got dinner at my parent's house."

"I'm free in the evening; I could come with you."

What? No, no, and hell no. "I don't think that's a good idea, not yet, anyway." Most guys avoided meeting the parents like the plague, but Luca wasn't most guys. He threw me for a loop in every way.

"I understand. Whenever you're ready. In the meantime, why don't you tell me more about them."

Everything he said shocked me—I never knew what was going to come out of that man's mouth next. Curling up on the couch, I dove in. "Well, I have two sisters. Sofia is the baby, eighteen months younger than me, and we have a decent relationship. She's an artist, marches to her own beat. Maria is two years older than me and has always been too cool for me or Sofia. She's intensely private—I know where she lives, and that's about it. Mom is a pretty traditional Stepford wife. She doesn't actually cook or clean, but she organizes fundraisers and is always busy with friends or family. As you know, my dad runs Triton, so that's the center of his universe. When we were little, before Marco was killed, he used to play with us. He would get on his hands and knees, and we would ride his back like a bucking bronco until we laughed so hard, we couldn't stay on."

"Sounds like a good dad," commented Luca.

"He was, and he still is, just not the same as he was before."

"So, you're close to your sister?"

"Yeah, but I'm even closer to my cousin, Giada—you saw her that day at my place."

"Right. How is she related?"

"She's my dad's brother's daughter. We grew up together and have always been inseparable."

"You have many aunts and uncles?"

"You drawing my family tree?" I teased.

"Maybe. There a problem with me wanting to know more

about you?"

"I suppose not; it's just unusual. Most guys don't want anything to do with my crazy family."

"I think we both know I'm not most guys."

No joke. "My dad has the one brother and a sister, who is bat-shit crazy. My mom was an only child—her mom was never able to conceive again. She's super close to Giada's mom, and dad is best friends with my Uncle Sal."

"That his brother?"

"No, he's not actually related—it's an honorary title. They've known each other since they were kids."

He paused as he considered. "Makes sense. None of my family, except for Ari, are related to me by blood."

"Different kind of family."

"Is it?"

I contemplated his question. I'd always been of the opinion family didn't have to mean blood relations, but mafia associates didn't seem to fit the bill. The people you work with weren't necessarily family. I couldn't imagine how being sworn into a club would automatically make each of the members feel like family.

When I didn't answer, Luca continued. "Our loyalty is always to family. I trust them with my life—isn't that what you would consider family?"

"I guess so," I muttered.

"It's not what you're envisioning, I promise. Just try to keep an open mind."

"Okay."

"I have to head out. I'll come by your place after dinner."

"'kay"

"Night, baby."

"Night, Luca."

I wasn't just sinking; I had removed my lifejacket and was doing a cannonball into the deep end.

CHAPTER 19
Alessia

To snowball: to grow or become larger, greater, more intense, etc., at an accelerating rate.

The term is not innately good or bad. Sometimes, 'snowball' can be used to describe a series of fortunate events, such as 'the young actor's career snowballed after his appearance in an Oscar-winning film.' Other times, the term can imply a much more catastrophic unraveling of events. In these instances, the term might conjure the image of an avalanche, rather than the friendly snowman it might otherwise invoke. The tiny bits of snow at the top of a mountain peaceably tumble until they gather enough steam and become an unstoppable force of nature.

For the innocent victim in its path, there is no escape.

The only hope for survival is luck.

As the ground shakes and the massive white cloud comes barreling down the mountainside, those in its path can only brace themselves and hope it will be enough. The tricky thing about an avalanche—you never know when one might strike.

One minute, you're sampling the fresh mountain air, enjoying the view, and the next, you're buried six feet under, unable to breathe from the suffocating weight of all the tiny snowflakes.

If ever there was a perfect day for an avalanche, it would be a Monday.

I had dreaded that first day back at work but was armed with a plan, so my nerves were contained within reason. Before I went to my office, I rode the elevator directly to the ninth floor and marched to the HR suite. The receptionist wasn't at her desk, but a peek around the corner told me the employees were gathered in a circle in a small breakroom, raptly discussing something.

"I'm sorry to interrupt—I was hoping someone could help me with a private matter."

"Not a problem, dear," said the older woman who worked at the front desk. "We were just talking about what happened over the weekend—so tragic!"

"What happened?" Had I missed a terrorist attack or some other news event? I'd been too busy wrapped in my problems to notice the world around me.

"Roger Coleman was—"

"Beth, he was her boss," cut in one of the others.

"Oh," she gasped, her eyes going soft. "I'm so sorry to break this to you, dear, but Mr. Coleman was killed on Saturday. It was on all the local news stations; I'm surprised you didn't see." All six pairs of pitying eyes fixed on me, waiting intently for my reaction.

Roger was dead.

Not just dead, killed.

I was in shock—unable to react because I couldn't process the unexpected news. Instead, I nodded and stumbled from the office. I couldn't go upstairs; I needed somewhere private to think. I found myself back at the elevator, next to which was a maintenance room. Hurrying inside, I closed the door behind me and dropped down to sit on a large cardboard box.

The source of my torment for a solid year was dead.

I was free.

The relief I experienced was so great, I felt physically lighter, almost dizzy. For a fleeting moment, I wondered if it was wrong that I was glad a man had died. Trailing behind that thought was image after image of Roger's snide face as he commented about my legs or ogled my chest. I could still feel his unwelcome hardness pressed against my backside from days earlier when he very likely would have raped me had Luca not arrived.

No, I had every right to rejoice.

Roger was a disgusting human being, and the world was a better place without him.

How had he died? I hadn't even thought to ask. They said he was killed—did that mean he was murdered? Or had they meant he died in a car crash or other accident? I pulled out my phone and Googled Roger Coleman.

New York businessman, Roger Coleman, found dead early Sunday morning. Coleman received numerous stab wounds in what appears to be a surprisingly brutal attack of gang violence.

Gang violence? *Holy shit*!

Aside from being a pervert, Roger seemed strait-laced, as far as I could tell. My reeling mind focused as confusion set in. How on Earth had he wound up being murdered by a gang? It could have been a chance encounter, but a stabbing with numerous wounds sounded rather intentional—not like the stray bullet that had killed Luca's mom.

Luca—could he have had something to do with this? Looking back, I was somewhat surprised he never lifted a finger when he caught Roger assaulting me. He wasn't exactly the type to turn the other cheek. He hardly even spoke about the incident when we got to his place. I knew it had affected him; he'd been practically vibrating with anger.

An ominous chill settled over me, causing goosebumps to

perch on my arms and legs. Had Luca used his mafia connections to have Roger killed? What were the chances Roger's death was a coincidence? Rolling waves of nausea caused my stomach to surge into my throat as I faced what was most likely the ugly truth.

Luca had Roger killed.

Or had it been even worse? Had Luca done it himself?

Fighting off the insistent need to vomit, I lowered my head to my knees and took shaky, deep breaths. Luca wasn't the type of man to let Roger's crimes go unpunished. The simplest solution was most likely the right one.

Luca was a criminal. Luca was angry at Roger. Roger was killed. Luca killed Roger.

I should have known Luca let the incident go too easily. I should have followed my gut instinct and ended it the minute I discovered his mafia connection. I hated Roger, but I didn't want him dead because of me. Beating up someone was one thing—murder was entirely different.

A cloud of emotions swarmed me like angry wasps. Attempting to free myself from their suffocating grasp, I stood and began to pace the small room. I needed help, but I was more scared than ever to bring anyone else into this mess. Before I fell into a total panic, I needed to know the truth. I needed to confront Luca. As much as I wanted to run and never look back, I'd promised him I'd come to him with my problems, and he was the only one who could confirm my suspicions.

Not giving myself a chance to chicken out, I dialed Luca's number with shaky fingers. I was petrified and furious at the same time, perched on the precipice of a point of no return.

"Alessia, is everything okay?"

I took in a shaky breath to calm my nerves. "Did you kill my boss?" Jerky and no louder than a whisper, the words punctuated the deafening silence in my small hideout.

"I'll be at your building in ten. Meet me outside."

The line clicked dead, and with it, a stabbing pain wrenched through my chest.

He didn't deny it.

He knew exactly what I was talking about and didn't deny it.

I could feel myself falling apart like a sheet of glass splintering until it was webbed with cracks. All it would take was the right touch, and I would come apart, a jigsaw of pieces scattered across the floor.

I tried to take a deep, calming breath, but my lungs wouldn't cooperate. They convulsed with each attempt, making the air draw in and out in shaky puffs. Tears burned in the back of my throat, and I felt the intense pressure of the walls closing in around me. Unable to bear the crushing strain any longer, I burst from the room and came face-to-face with two coworkers.

They gaped at me, eyes rounded as they both took in my disheveled appearance and tear-filled eyes. The moment it registered who I was and that I was likely upset after finding out my boss had been killed, their brows lifted in pity, and their lips thinned in awkward smiles. If only they knew—my problems were far more extensive than mourning my deceased boss.

I jumped when the elevator dinged behind me, glancing back as the doors opened.

"You go ahead, hun. We can catch the next one."

I wasn't sure which one of them had spoken; I couldn't even recall any of their names. I nodded wordlessly and drifted into the waiting car. The elevator ride and walk through the lobby were a blur. The possibility Luca might harm me never even entered my mind. All I could think was I needed to hear him say the words, then I was done.

I would walk away for good.

Whether it was the distress of suspecting he was a killer or the apprehension of leaving him, I wasn't sure, but something had caused my brain to overheat and shut down. I walked numbly past the security desk and outside where I found a seat on one of the raised flowerbeds and waited.

The new spring leaves in the trees above me fluttered in the wind, and the constant stream of people on the sidewalk coasted past me. Life went on, even when I felt like my world was crumbling down around me. The reminder helped me pull back the reins of my chaotic emotions, so I was somewhat coherent by the time Luca arrived.

My eyes stared directly ahead, unseeing as he approached and joined me where I sat.

"I don't suppose you'd be willing to take a drive with me so we can discuss this more privately."

I shook my head, just a hint of movement, but it was enough.

He exhaled a resigned sigh. "Alessia, he hurt you. I couldn't stand by and let that go." He spoke softly, an attempt to keep our conversation private on the busy sidewalk.

"People will hurt me—that's just life. It happens. You can't go killing someone just for upsetting me."

"I can and will if I decide it's necessary—if someone touches what's mine. Plus, that man was scum. He deserved what he got and worse. You think you were the only woman he assaulted?" he spat angrily.

That was true. I highly doubted I'd been Roger's only victim, but that didn't justify killing him. Sending him to prison would have kept other women safe just as effectively. Of course, that had been my job—to report him to the authorities. But what was I supposed to tell them? My boss told me I have great lips? The cops would have laughed me out of the station.

My thoughts were digressing on a tangent of self-imposed guilt. I had plenty of time later to dwell on my role in what happened. For now, I needed to deal with Luca. He had given me the admission I was after; it was time for me to find my backbone.

"I can't do this; I can't be with you. I thought I could ignore your situation, pretend you were an ordinary man with an ordinary job, but I can't." I forced as much calm certainty as I could muster into my voice.

"You don't know what you're saying. You're upset—"

"Don't treat me like a child," I hissed, turning to glare at him. "Whether I'm upset or not, I'm not okay with you killing people. Me being upset changes *nothing.*"

"We can't discuss these things in public. We need to go somewhere private." He stood up, towering over me.

"I'm not going anywhere with you."

He leaned down, and I froze as he spoke quietly next to my ear. "Either you come with me willingly, or I throw you over my goddamned shoulder and carry you out of here. We are going to talk about this, and I'm not doing it where half of New York can listen in." When he pulled back, his black eyes bore into me with ice-cold fury.

He wasn't the only one battling indignant rage. I experienced anger so violent, it pulsed at my temples. He was the one who had brought on this situation, not me. He was the one responsible for a man's death. His actions had pushed me away. His anger toward me was completely unfounded, and it made me furious.

I shot to my feet, giving him an equally cutting glare. "*Fine.* There's a family restroom in the lobby. We can go there, but I'm not leaving this building." Not allowing him a response, I whipped around and stomped back to the Triton entrance.

Once we were inside the single-stall restroom, Luca locked the door, and I folded my arms defensively across my chest. When he turned to face me, I had to fortify myself against his dominating presence. He was a giant in the tiny space, and I had to force myself not to cower.

"I don't know why we're here—there's nothing more to say," I snapped at him.

"There's a hell of a lot more to say. I couldn't figure it out at first. You seemed so naïve and rule-bound, but then I realized you had no idea. He's done such a flawless job secreting himself away, not even his children know who he is."

"What are you talking about?" My arms came down to my sides, my austere resolve faltering.

"You think I'm a monster, but you live with the biggest bad of them all," Luca sneered.

"Stop playing games and just tell me what you're talking about!"

"Your father, the boss of the Lucciano crime family."

"Don't be absurd! My family isn't in the mafia—I would know." I stepped forward, pointing my finger at him angrily.

He met my advance head-on, closing the small distance between us. "You think you would have had any idea what I did if I didn't want you to? I told you I would never lie to you, and I haven't. I didn't lie then, and I'm not lying now. Your Uncle Sal is your father's underboss and acts as the face of the outfit—to keep him and his family safe, your father's identity has been kept confidential. His own soldiers don't know who runs the outfit. Your mention of Sal is what confirmed my suspicions that your father was the boss."

"So, you don't even know for sure—you're just guessing. You think just because my dad is friends with Sal and because we're Italian, we're in the mafia? That's just crazy!"

"You think what I've done is bad, your father is ten times worse. If you don't believe me, *ask* him. You think I'm full of shit, fine, but go talk to Daddy and see for yourself."

His insistence was absolute.

He was wholly confident he was right, and his resolve shook me. What if he was telling the truth? I suddenly felt like I'd walked into the movie *Inception* where the constructs of our reality no longer applied—as if at any moment, the walls of the room might turn, and I'd be walking on the ceiling rather than the floor. Could my father be a mafia boss? Had my entire world been a thing of fiction?

The possibility was more than unsettling—it rocked me to my core.

"Get out," I whispered, not meeting his eyes.

"Lessia—" he started, but I never let him finish.

"Get out. Get out. *Get out!*" Each of my commands grew in strength until I was nearly shouting. If someone heard me in the lobby, I didn't care. I was done caring. My world turned upside down, and the only thing I could focus on was survival.

Luca stood motionless and silent for a long moment as I stared at the dirty grout lines on the floor. "I'm going to give you time to cool down, then we're going to talk this through like adults. Go talk to your father. I'll be in touch." He let himself out of the bathroom, and I dropped my head in relief that the moment was over.

Stepping toward the small vanity, I stared vacantly at my reflection. Who was the woman staring back at me? I never thought the answer to that question would be so elusive. Was I the daughter of a criminal? Had my entire life been a lie?

My father was imposing, but so are plenty of men. Could he have had a secret life hidden away from us all these years? If so, had my mother known? I felt sick with betrayal. I needed to know the truth, and there was only one way to do that.

I stepped out of the bathroom, scanning the active lobby as I'd done so many times before. The place I'd been so proud of only hours ago now looked tainted. If my father was in the mafia, it was doubtless my family wasn't the only casualty of his activities. The company I loved so dearly likely bore the sticky fingerprints of his criminal ties.

I walked straight to the elevator, eyes directly ahead. Looking at the lively animation of the people who called this place their home away from home made me sick to my stomach. My lifelong dream had been dipped in tar and was now irrevocably spoiled—corrupted and dirty.

Avoiding eye contact with my coworkers, I walked numbly to my father's office. I wasn't sure how he would have managed a second life when he spent so many hours inside these walls. Everything about Triton had felt legitimate. How could something so real, so tangible, be a sham?

I didn't knock when I walked into his inner sanctum. His was the only office with rich wood paneling on the walls. He said it made the space feel more inviting, but it would also help soundproof his office. It was amazing how, in a matter of minutes, one piece of information forced you to look at the world from a different perspective.

I approached his ornate wooden executive desk, standing awkwardly, feeling suddenly like a child again. "Is any of this real? Has it all been a lie?" My words had been cryptic, but it was the first thing that popped into my head.

My father looked up in surprise, unaware I had entered the room. His eyes narrowed as he took in my pallor and my bloodshot eyes. Without saying a word, he went to close the office door before slowly returning to his desk chair.

"I'm not sure I understand—can you explain what you're asking?" His words were the epitome of caution and diplomacy. Just like Luca, everything I needed to know was there, written between the lines.

"You're in the mafia, aren't you? Our lives have been one giant lie."

He inhaled a deep breath, then leaned back in his chair, lips pursed tightly. "Who gave you this information?"

It was unsettling how calm I felt when my world was crumbling around me, piece-by-piece. I slowly lowered myself into one of the guest chairs, perching on the edge of the cushion. Who was this man who sat across from me? I glanced up, searching in vain for a hint of familiarity. Only the contours of his face and his outer appearance bore any significance—the man beneath the surface was a mystery.

He stared at me expectantly, a dangerous glint in his eyes, still waiting for an answer to his question. Would Luca become a target for sharing the truth with me? Regardless of my torn feelings for him, I didn't want him hurt because of me. "A friend."

"A man," he concluded.

I kept my lips sealed, not confirming or denying.

"I take it someone from one of the other families. No one in my outfit would have dared."

"I guess I appreciate that you aren't trying to deny it. I can't imagine it's been easy lying to everyone for so long." My words were clipped, an undercurrent of anger infiltrating my numbness.

He lifted a brow in warning. Normally, I'd never be allowed to speak to my father with attitude, but he was giving me a small amount of leniency, considering the circumstances. "I did it to keep you and your sisters safe. After Marco was killed, I wasn't going to put you all at risk."

Then it clicked—Marco's killing wasn't a random mugging. His death had been a byproduct of my father's mafia dealings. "It was you. You're the reason he died," I breathed the words more to myself than him.

My father went inhumanly still.

What I'd said had been hurtful, but I didn't care. He'd brought it on himself—and for what? Power? Money? I'd rather we had been poor and still had my brother alive.

"None of this is any of your concern," he said coolly. "You've lived all your life in the dark; there's no reason this has to change anything. Find a nice young man to marry, have children, and join the PTA."

"Not my concern? This is my *family*—of course, it's my concern! What happens when you go to prison or get killed?

What happens when Triton is shut down by the feds? Everything about your actions affects my life."

"Why do you think I've kept my identity a secret?" he shot back at me, his anger finally getting the better of him. "To ensure I'm never touched and neither are any of you. No one, outside of a select few, knows who I am—that now includes whoever fed you the information. You're going to tell me who that is, for all our safety."

"And Mom, does she know?" I asked, ignoring his last comment.

"Of course, she knows."

The more I learned, the clearer it all became. "Maria too—she knows, doesn't she? That's why you two have always been so close—she's always known." That realization was surprisingly painful. Was I not trustworthy enough to be brought into the fold? Why had she been included in their secrets but not me? "Am I the only one who didn't know?"

"We've never told Sofia. Giada and her sisters, none of them know. La cosa nostra, this thing of ours, it's not discussed. There's no reason for the children to know—it's safer for all of us."

"Giada? Uncle Edoardo—he's in this too?"

He dropped his chin in affirmation.

Holy shit. How had I not known my entire family was part of the mob? What rock had I been living under?

"The man who told you this information—is he the man you've been seeing?"

I was steadfast in my vow of silence. I would not give up Luca's identity.

"Don't protect him, Alessia. The only reason he's seeing you is to get information about our family. Our business in the last year has been booming, and the other families are jealous, looking for ways to bring us down. He's using you."

Could he be right? How could I trust anything my father said when he'd lied to me for so long? Sure, I believed he wanted the best for me, but maybe he thought that meant keeping Luca away at all costs. Luca claimed to be honest with me and gained nothing by telling me about my father, but he was just as morally corrupt. He knew who I was the whole time, setting up ways to get close to me, then worked his way under my skin. Had it all been a tactic to get close to my father?

I couldn't trust either of them, but I still didn't have it in me to rat out Luca. I didn't want to be near him, but I didn't want my father to hurt him either. "I'm not seeing him any longer, so you don't have to worry about him, but I'm also not telling you his name. I need to go home now—just being here makes me sick." I stood without meeting his eyes and walked toward the door. Each step was heavier than the last under the crushing weight of heartbreak.

"I'm going to let Leo know to be on the lookout for this man —I don't want him anywhere near you," he called out behind me.

I paused and turned back, unable to summon any more surprise. "My driver? He's one of yours then?"

"One of our best soldiers. Just because you never knew, didn't mean I haven't provided protection for you."

I could sense the pride in his voice, but it didn't sway me like he may have hoped. "Silly me, I should have known Leo was never just a driver."

"How do you think I've been able to give you all this?" He lifted his hands to indicate Triton and all the advantages we'd grown up with. "Before you go back to your pretty high-rise apartment and condemn me, think about all the opportunities this life has given you."

"I see nothing but blood money."

"Well, you're a part of the family now, so you better get used to it."

I walked away from him, tears welling in my eyes. He was right. No matter how I felt or what I did, I was a part of the life.

My knowledge alone could get me killed. I never wanted any of it, but fighting would be futile. So, where did that leave me?

Leo was waiting for me outside, his black Cadillac double-parked on the busy street. Instead of slipping into the back seat as I usually did, I joined him up front in the passenger seat.

"Well, hello," he offered with a surprised raise of his blond brows.

"You work for my father?" I asked without any greeting.

"Uhhh … what's this all about?"

"You don't have to play dumb; I know about my father now. I know he's in the mafia."

"Shit, Alessia, watch your mouth." He gaped at me as if I'd called in a bomb threat to the White House. "You don't go spouting that shit—you'll get yourself killed."

"I'm not going to tell anyone. He said you were one of his soldiers, whatever that means, so I knew that you knew. You don't even work for a service, do you?"

"I work for your father. You are my one and only priority."

"Do you report back to him on where I go and what I do?"

He cut his eyes over to me in answer.

All these years, while my father had acted indifferent about my life, he'd been watching over me. It was somewhat reassuring to know he had cared, but it didn't totally make up for the feeling of betrayal. I felt like my life was a reality TV show, and everyone knew but me. I had been living a pretend life, blithefully unaware nothing around me was real.

My lifestyle had been supported by dirty money—my clothes to my education—nothing was clean. The man I'd called father all my life was a stranger. Even my life's purpose to run our family business was now tainted. The question remained—who was I in the wake of so many lies? Could I be the same person I'd been hours ago? If I could still be that girl, did I even want to be her any longer?

CHAPTER 20

Alessia

I spent the rest of the day hiding in my apartment. Luca and my father both did me the courtesy of leaving me alone. I called in sick at work, letting my staff know that I wouldn't be in the rest of the week. I was too upset to handle life. I needed time to decide what my next move would be.

My emotions acted like a carousel with different horses rising up and down on poles. I'd left Leo in a haze of despair and hurt, but by the next morning, anger had trumped all the other emotions, taking the lead. I was furious that any semblance of control I had over my life had been taken from me, manipulated in ways I'd never even known.

So many lies.

My life had been built on them.

Midway through the morning, Maria called me. I debated not answering. I was pissed at her for being included by my father and for not telling me herself about our family, but Maria never called me, and my curiosity won out.

"Hello?" My curt greeting was lukewarm at best.

"You need to stop acting like a child."

"Excuse me?"

"Everything Dad's done was to keep you and Sofia safe. You find out and throw an unholy tantrum, pissed you weren't included in the secret like it's some game." That was Maria, always telling it exactly as she saw it.

"I know this is no game, Maria. That's exactly why I'm so upset. This is my life, and now I'm inextricably bound to a family of criminals without any say in the matter."

"You could always leave."

Her words stunned me. "Is that what you want? You want me to leave?"

"I didn't say that—don't put words in my mouth," she shot back, a touch of anger in her voice. "You don't want to be a part of this, leaving is always an option. Don't say you don't have a choice. If you stay, then yes, to some degree, you will always be connected, especially now that you know."

"Why did he tell you and not us?" My question was rife with hurt, and I hated myself for showing her that vulnerability.

"You and Sof were always too good for the life. Dad wanted to give you two the chance to be free of the family."

"And you?"

"I was a different story. Surely you remember what a terror I was as a kid. Dad knew I would get myself into trouble if he didn't guide me and give me an outlet for all my raging emotions. Hell, I broke Billie Tomlinson's nose when I was only ten—I wasn't like you two. Never was, never will be."

My heart hurt for her. Why had she been so tormented as a kid? Could I have done something differently to help? She had been the closest in age to Marco, and her discipline problems had started around the time of his death. I could only assume she had taken his loss harder than the rest of us.

"I wasn't trying to throw a tantrum," I attempted to explain.

"You have to try to understand that my life was just turned upside down. Everything I thought I knew was wrong, and now, I'm struggling to sort it all out."

"I get it. You've led a charmed life, though, and you need to understand there are all sorts of ugly out there. Just because you grew up thinking life was sunshine and rainbows, doesn't mean it is. You may think we're monsters, but we are far from the worst things out there. It's time for you to accept that life has its darker side."

"So, I've heard. I'm surprised you're even talking to me about this over the phone. Aren't you worried about wiretaps or crap like that?"

She choked on a laugh. "It's not like the movies—don't let your imagination run away from you. We're very cautious—we only use iPhones because they're encrypted, and not even the feds can get in. We don't have regular meetings, and the bosses are rarely ever seen at all. Business is often done online and always very discreetly."

"The movies are the only thing I have to go by. This is all new to me."

"To some extent, everything can stay exactly as its been. You don't have to be involved. I know you're hurt and upset, but it's not the end of the world."

She wasn't entirely wrong. What I'd learned felt life-altering, but it didn't necessarily have to be. "Alright," I conceded. "I'll try to calm down, but I'm still not happy about this."

"I know, but if it's any consolation, I'm glad you know now, and I don't want you to leave."

"Thanks, Maria," I could barely get the words out over the lump that formed in my throat. Those had been the nicest words she'd ever spoken to me. Maybe our relationship might be the one silver lining to this whole nasty mess.

We said goodbye, and I went back to moping but feeling far less alone than I had minutes before. I laid down on the couch to lose myself in some mindless television, and the next thing I knew, I was woken by a knock at my door.

Shaking off the confusion of sleep, I rubbed my eyes and stumbled to the door. A glance through the peephole told me Luca had decided my time away was over and had come to talk.

"Go away, I don't want to see you," I called through the door.

"I'm not leaving until we talk. You can open the door, or I can break it down." His deep voice resonated through the thick wood and twisted my insides.

I opened the door a crack, tears of frustration pricking at my eyes. "Please, stop. I don't want to do this right now."

Seeing him unruffled was unexpected. His normally perfectly styled hair shot up in all directions. His suit had been abandoned for a wrinkled t-shirt and jeans, and if I didn't know better, I'd say he had bags under his eyes. Why was he so upset? I was just a means to an end for him.

"I was right, wasn't I? I was right about your dad."

My momentary sympathy was dashed away. His mention of my father reminded me of my dad's warning about Luca using me. Like a metal garage door slamming down into place, I erected a wall between us.

"I don't know what you're talking about. You need to leave." I started to close the door, but he shot his foot out just in time.

Pushing with all his weight, he thrust the door open and forced his way inside. "Don't play that fucking game with me. I've been nothing but honest with you—telling the truth when no one else in your own family offered you the same courtesy. The least you can do is talk to me."

"Telling me the truth? Does that include using me for information about my family? All you ever wanted was to get close to my father, so don't pretend to be some white knight," I shot back at him.

He ran a hand through his ruffled hair, eyes darting around in frustration. "That was it at first, but then it became more."

I huffed out a bitter laugh. "And why should I believe you now?"

"Because not one thing I've said has been a lie. Yes, I sought you out to get information, but my interest in you has been real. Why else do you think I'm here?"

"To hurt my family?"

"No, I'm trying to save your family. Telling you about your father put my life at risk—why would I do that if I didn't care about you? You deserve to know the truth, and you need to know because you're in danger."

I wrapped my arms around my middle protectively, unsure where this was going. "What are you talking about?"

"For months, tensions have been rising because your family has been double-crossing the other families. Three weeks ago, a made man was killed the day after he met with your father. It was unsanctioned by the Commission, which is comprised of the heads of each of the New York families, along with the families of the Chicago Outfit. Used to be every family in the country had a seat on the Commission, but the feds hit organized crime so hard in the eighties and nineties, the Commission shrunk. Anyway, an unauthorized killing of a made man in our world gives the right to blood for blood—it keeps order among the families. You don't kill a made man or his family because you or someone you love can be killed as payback. This man was killed on the orders of someone in your family, the Luccianos. Your father is the boss. Therefore, if he gave the order, his family would be vulnerable to retribution—not just his mafia family, his blood family. That means you, Alessia. You and your sisters or your mother could be a target."

"I thought the mafia didn't go after women and children?"

"Normally, we don't, but the guy who was killed was the Gallo family Consigliere's son. The Gallos have a number of men who are fresh from Sicily—they're called Zips—their code far more stringent than ours. They want blood, and they want one of the boss's children to make up for their loss."

"Are you in the Gallo family?"

"I'm a part of the Russo outfit."

"So, how does any of this involve you?"

"The Commission had reason to believe your father, the boss, wasn't behind the Lucciano actions. They chose me to infiltrate the Lucciano outfit and find out what was going on. I have somewhat of a portfolio of investigative work, making me ideal for these kinds of operations."

"If you weren't sure who the boss was, how did you know to target me?"

"Some investigative work and a little luck. I followed Sal to Triton one day, and I knew your dad had met with the Gallo man before his death. It was too big of a coincidence—if your father wasn't the boss, he was at least someone high up. I spent a couple days studying who went in and out of Triton and decided to see if you could get me the info I needed." His lips pulled up in a smirk. "I decided mixing business with pleasure would make the job less cumbersome."

He picked me because he'd wanted me. "You didn't know I was Enzo's daughter?"

He slowly shook his head. "Just got lucky." His eyes heated, and my heart skipped a beat. "Not until you told me about your Uncle Sal did the pieces fall into place. You're in danger, Alessia. The things that have gone on have made the other families bloodthirsty. If we aren't careful, we'll have an all-out war on our hands."

"I don't understand. I just talked to Maria earlier, and she said it's not like that anymore."

"Most of the time it's not, but trouble's brewing. I can't guarantee what will happen. I've turned over the information I uncovered to the Commission—they call the shots, not me." He stepped closer, making a move to reach for me, but I pulled away.

"No, Luca," I insisted firmly, holding up my hand. "I'm not ready, and I don't know that I'll ever be. None of this is what I wanted for myself. I'm still trying to figure out how I feel and where to go from here."

His jaw twitched and flexed as he mulled over my words. "I won't push you for now, but you better not block my number, and you *will* answer if I text or call. Those are my conditions—take it or leave it."

"And if I don't agree?" I asked with a touch of sass.

"I could always kidnap you and keep you at my place. I know you'll be safe there." His eyes danced with challenge, begging me to try him.

"Fine," I said insolently.

Before I could argue, he yanked me to him and placed a warm kiss on my forehead. "I know you're pissed, and this is a lot to take in, so I'm giving you some space. Don't mistake that for me walking away. This thing between us—it's not over." With those parting words, he let himself out and disappeared down the hall.

I locked the door, then leaned back against it, wondering at the twists and turns of life. One minute, life is black and white, and the next thing you know, there are only shades of grey. Sometimes, that change occurs slowly—the death of one stage in your life setting in like an insidious virus. Other times, change comes about dizzyingly quick like the sudden drop of a guillotine —blinding and altering reality until life is unrecognizable.

At least when change is a slow progression, the memories of where you started are grainy and distorted, your new reality the only clear picture remaining. When change is sudden and violent, it creates an open wound that is a glaring reminder of how things were, the images still fresh in your mind.

The other problem with sudden change is there's no undoing it.

Once it's done, there's no going back.

I couldn't undo the knowledge my father was a criminal any

more than I could rid the stars from the sky. Not just the knowledge of what he did, but his actions themselves. The fact that he was a mobster would never change. I could pack up and leave, but they would still be my family, and my dad would still be a criminal.

Not just my dad—nearly my entire family.

The most upsetting part about starting a new life would be the searing pain of losing Luca. His relentless campaign had worn me down, and not even the fact he had used me for information could douse my desire for him. I didn't think there was one defining moment when he'd stolen my heart, but piece-by-piece, with each stolen kiss and whispered caress, the criminal had absconded with a part of my soul.

I had known from the beginning he would leave me in shreds, but there'd been no stopping it. He'd battered my defenses like the blowing desert winds softening the edges of sandstone towers—my own pieces swept off in his punishing winds until there was no telling where one of us began, and the other ended.

Making the decision to leave my family would be hard enough, but adding Luca into the mix was gut-wrenching. If I rejected my family's way of life, he would be lost to me, and that hurt more than any of the lies I'd been forced to swallow. If I chose to accept him, and therefore, my family, my life would be forever lies.

CHAPTER 21

Luca

I followed Alessia to her parent's house on Sunday to learn where they lived but had yet to approach her father. I hadn't been certain I was going to tell her about her father's position, but she had forced the issue. Once she had confronted him about his mafia affiliation, I knew it was time to talk to him myself. That had never been a part of the plan, but I'd dug myself in a hole and needed to find a way out.

I was about ninety-five percent sure the information I had to offer Enzo would be news to him, which meant there was a five percent chance I was about to get myself killed. Enzo Genovese was most likely pissed I had unmasked him to his daughter, but hopefully, my crime would be forgiven if what I was about to tell him was accurate.

It was a Wednesday evening, and the affluent neighborhood was quiet. I had watched Enzo's car pull up an hour earlier and had been procrastinating ever since. It wasn't like me, but I was about to do one of the most reckless things I'd ever done. Wiping my sweaty palms on my slacks, I exited the car to confront Don Genovese about his corrupt underboss.

I rang the bell, looking straight into the security camera. It was crucial I conveyed nothing but the utmost confidence. In my world, fear would get a man killed as fast as any bullet.

Enzo himself opened the door in black slacks and a white dress shirt, the sleeves rolled up to his elbows. He had short salt-and-pepper hair with a neatly trimmed matching beard. Seeing him on the street, you would think nothing of him—just a man like any other—but you would be dead wrong. Enzo Genovese held a fifth of New York City in the palm of his hand. He was no one to be trifled with.

"I suppose you're the man my daughter's been seeing?" He was astute and direct, both qualities I appreciated.

"Yes, my name is Luca Romano. I work for Michael Abbatelli."

"A Russo. Come in—it's time you and I had a chat." He stepped back to make room for me, and I willingly entered the lion's den.

"You have a beautiful home," I offered respectfully. At that point, formalities wouldn't get me far, but I figured it couldn't hurt either.

"You got some balls coming here after you told my daughter about the family. I can't decide if you're an idiot or just suicidal." He led me into the living area, taking a seat and gesturing for me to sit in an adjacent chair.

"I understand you're upset, but I came here to explain. She needed to know the truth because she's in danger."

"No one even knew who she was until you showed up."

"You did an excellent job of falling off the radar after your son was killed. You were just a capo at the time, I believe. Two years of family warfare, some rumors about you leaving the life, and suddenly, you're sitting in the captain's chair without anyone the wiser."

"I worked very hard to protect myself and my family by keeping us hidden," he said, glaring at me. "Between the loss of men and renewed levels of secrecy, I was able to disappear. It's hard to be killed when you're already a ghost. In the matter of one afternoon, you've taken all that away."

"Yes, but if I could figure it out, others could too. Up until recently, there wasn't reason for anyone to go digging, but things have changed."

"What is it you need to tell me that you've worked so hard to flesh me out?"

"A month ago, the Commission confronted Sal about a number of shady business deals made by the Lucciano family."

Enzo narrowed his eyes, his posture stiffening. "What the fuck are you talking about?"

Instant relief flooded me at his response. Enzo was clearly shocked by my accusations. Had he been guarded and dismissive, it would have indicated he knew what had been going on, and I wouldn't be leaving his house alive.

"The Luccianos have been stealing jobs from other families, crossing district lines and bypassing the Commission. The other families are pissed. They decided they needed to figure out who was calling the shots so the problem could be eliminated. At a recent meeting, they demanded Sal call the boss and ask for remuneration. They hacked the cell towers and had tech guys ready to triangulate the signal in order to figure out who was running the show. When they got the number, guys were immediately sent over to the location, only to discover it was Sal's home number, and no one was there. He'd faked his call to the boss and lied to the Commission."

Worry lines creased Enzo's forehead, but his eyes still held a glint of defiance. "That doesn't necessarily mean anything—maybe he knew I was busy and was trying to placate the Commission."

I appreciated his attempt to defend his second in command,

but his trust was misplaced. "You saying you were behind the shipment of guns that disappeared off the Giordano docks? Or maybe you gave the order to branch into trucking and undercut the Russos?"

He glared at me. "Continue."

"They started to suspect Sal was two-timing his boss. They needed to figure out who Sal was working for and get proof he was crooked, so they called me in. I followed Sal, and eventually, he led me to the Triton building. Three weeks ago, you met with Gio Venturi, son of the Gallo family Consigliere, Diego Venturi."

"Yeah, and the next day he hung himself—what's that got to do with me?"

"His family didn't believe it was suicide. They hired a handwriting expert who determined the note he'd left behind hadn't been his writing. You were the last person seen with Gio, and you'd been arguing over cement prices. Put two and two together —it looks like you're running the Lucciano family, or at the very least, working with Sal. So, the question is, what is your role in all this? The other bosses are all very interested, so answer carefully." My words were somewhat confrontational, but I needed him to hear the confidence in my voice and know I had the Commission's backing. It was a whole lot easier to kill a lone wolf asking questions than the voice of The Five Families.

Fortunately, he was too stunned about what had been going on under his nose to focus on my manner of delivery. "I don't understand," he murmured. "Sal has been my best friend since we were kids."

"It looks like he's been maneuvering to get you in trouble for months, maybe even years. You sure your friend doesn't have his sights set on your job?" I gave a second for that to sink in before I continued. "The hit on Venturi was easy to pick off—you were the last one seen with him, and the note was a dead giveaway it wasn't suicide. Someone wanted us to know it was a hit, and they wanted you to take the blame."

"I knew the guy had died, but I didn't know anything about the note," he said absently. "We have too much bad blood with the Gallos; they'd want my head for this."

"Exactly. It was an unsanctioned hit—the Gallo family is out for blood. They have a load of Zips in from the old country just itching for revenge. Your family isn't safe."

Enzo ran his fingers along his bearded jawline, his eyes distant as he processed the news. "I never had anything to do with the kid's death or any of the shady dealings. I've been through war before when my son was killed; I have no desire to see the families come to that again."

"I believe you, and I've reported as much to the Commission, but that doesn't mean the Gallos won't move against you. It's time to come out of hiding."

Enzo's dark gaze met mine, and I could see the reluctant acceptance on his face. He knew it was the only way, even if it meant putting his family out in the open. "I suppose you're hoping I'll be so grateful for this information, I'll overlook the little stunt you pulled telling my daughter about the family."

Fuck. Heat seared the back of my neck, but I refrained from adjusting my collar to relieve the pressure. "She's in danger. Keeping her in the dark was only going to make things worse."

"That wasn't your call to make." His eyes were steel-coated daggers, boring holes straight through me.

My chin lowered a fraction, but I didn't say a word. He was right, and we both knew it. I had done something that was potentially unforgivable with hardly a thought as to the consequences. At that moment, the only thing that had mattered was not letting Alessia slip through my fingers. I could claim her safety had been my top priority, but that was a lie.

Lucky for me, I was able to fall back on the excuse, but it hadn't been the true motivation behind my actions. There was fear involved, but it was fear she'd never speak to me again, rather than fear for her safety. What I'd done to her boss had pushed her over the edge—it was written plainly in the hollow depths of her glassy eyes.

The only viable way to get her to change her perspective was to shred the rose-colored veil her parents had erected around her. Once she saw I wasn't so unlike the people she called family, maybe she'd let me in. At the very least, it would keep her from slamming the door in my face.

Regardless of my reasons, Enzo had every right to have me gutted.

I had betrayed a sacred oath and jeopardized his relationship with his daughter. Like the man said, it was total insanity for me to walk straight up to his front door. All I could do now was hope he was a forgiving man and saw courage in my actions.

"My daughter appears to have developed feelings for you. I can't imagine having you killed would improve my already strained relationship with her. If I let you walk out of here, understand I would not be so generous a second time." The threat implicit in his words was mirrored on his stony features. This was not a get-out-of-jail-free card—I had been warned.

I LEFT the Genovese home without any missing or broken body parts, so I considered the trip a raging success. Enzo was now clued into Sal's actions and the mounting danger surrounding his family. The concern I'd expressed for Alessia had been legitimate. There was no guarantee someone wouldn't seek revenge, even without the Commission's approval.

The more I thought about it, the more I needed to check on her. I told her I'd give her space, but I needed to see her for myself to know she was alright. The unused adrenaline from my meeting was still coursing through my system, so I decided to hit the gym first before I paid Alessia a visit. If I went over this keyed up and she raged at me like she had before, I might do something

I'd regret. Tying her to her bed and fucking her into submission might seem like a good idea at the time, but it would come back to bite me in the ass. I was walking a fine line with her, and I knew it.

I drove straight from Enzo's house to the gym. I always kept a set of gym clothes in my trunk, which had proven handy on more than one occasion. When I walked into the old, musty warehouse building, Rafi was already geared up and hitting the heavy bag. I gave him a nod and went back to the locker room to change before returning to spar with him.

"I take it the hunt isn't going well?" asked Rafi when I joined him at the bag.

"It's over, actually," I said smoothly as I wrapped my hands.

"What do you mean? You found him?"

"Yeah, I was right—it was her father. Had a meet with him just now."

"God damn, you got balls." He punched my shoulder, sticking his unusually long tongue out at me. "Glad you're still alive."

"He wasn't thrilled I was there, but he didn't know anything about Sal's bullshit, so he was glad I spoke up."

"That two-timing asswipe better run—he's gonna have all five families gunnin' for him." He held up his fist, fingers out like a gun, and pretended to shoot. Crap like that would keep Rafi from ever becoming more than a soldier. He was a good kid, but street smarts didn't come naturally to him.

"The Commission meets on Thursday. Until then, we wait. No unsanctioned hits, even for revenge—you know that," I warned him with a leveling stare.

"Yeah, yeah. That doesn't mean we can't beat the shit outta this bag instead."

"Exactly." Finished with my wrap, I shot out my fist and pounded the bag with the first of what would be hundreds of brutal strikes.

CHAPTER 22

Alessia

I hadn't heard from Luca since he'd forced his way into my apartment the day before. I'd spent all evening thinking, but the only decision I'd made was that it was time to bring Giada into the fold. It wasn't an easy call to make. Telling her might endanger her, and I didn't want to get myself into trouble for spreading information. However, there were any number of counter-arguments. I could count on her to keep her mouth shut, plus, she deserved to know what was happening in our family. In a much more selfish vein, I needed to tell her so she could help me figure out what the hell I was supposed to do. She had helped me through every major life decision until that point, and I floundered at the idea of forging ahead without her on this front.

Telling Giada was one thing, my sister Sofia was entirely different. She had been so insistent on paving her own path; I hated to disrupt her progress by throwing our family secrets at her feet. Hypocritical, I know, but she was my little sister, and I felt protective. This type of information changed things.

Once you knew, there was no going back.

Giada and I decided to meet for lunch at a small pizza place near her apartment. I normally tried to eat healthy, but the stress of my current situation called for carbs. Lots of carbs. When Giada arrived, we ordered our oversized slices of pizza, then found a table on the patio outside for privacy.

"What's the latest news?" she asked, completely oblivious to the bomb I was about to drop in her lap.

"This talk is going to call for another warning."

"I got it—you, me, no one else. Spill," she said as she waved her hand at me passively.

"Jeeze, alright. So, I decided it would be best to break up with Luca. We fought—it was ugly. Then he told me something that changed everything, and the only reason I'm telling you is because it involves you too."

"Me?" she balked.

I glanced around, ensuring there were no prying ears nearby. "Yes. Luca isn't the only one who's in the mafia—practically our entire family is ... connected. Giada, my dad is the boss—a bonafide godfather."

She lowered her pizza to her paper plate, her brows drawn tightly together. "What the hell are you talking about?"

"I know it sounds crazy. I didn't believe it at first either, but I confronted my dad, and he admitted it. Mom knows, Maria's one of them, and Uncle Edoardo—your dad—he's mafia too." I let the information sink in, taking a bite of pizza as Giada stared at hers.

Her eyes slowly rose to meet mine, none of the horror I thought I might see present. "Well, I'll be damned," she whispered. "We're like the real-life *Sopranos*." Her voice was awed as if she had just learned Jason Mamoa was her long-lost brother.

"You're taking this awfully well."

"Are you kidding me?" she blurted. "This is fucking amazing! Do you know how many times I've watched the Godfather? Scarface? Carlito's Way? Pretty much any mob show ever made. You know I love that shit."

"G, our lives could be in danger because of this—it's not some movie."

"I figure it's been this way since we were born. If it were dangerous, we would have seen some of that by now."

"Like my brother getting killed?" Every ounce of levity vanished from my voice.

Giada's eyes rounded in surprise. "Holy shit."

"Yeah. Our lives are a lot more dangerous than we ever realized. This isn't TV, and it's not a game."

"I'm sorry, honey. I didn't mean to make light of it."

"You don't have to be sorry. I get why it sounds exciting, but there's a much darker side to mob life. I don't want that to touch either of us."

"What about a sexy mafia man?" she teased with a questioning smile. "Can one of those touch us? Cause that guy of yours is sexy as fuck."

I shook my head, rolling my eyes as I took another bite of pizza. "You're crazy, you know that?"

"Don't judge."

"Whatever. Just keep your mouth shut about it. You promise?" I gave her a piercing stare, hoping she'd understand the severity of the situation.

"Trust me, if I have learned anything from all the shows, it's that talking gets you dead. I'm not saying a word." She dug into her pizza as if I hadn't just rocked her world. Giada always did roll with the punches, but her nonchalant attitude toward our mafia connections had surprised me.

As we finished eating and our conversation wound down to evening plans and pedicure appointments, I noticed that feeling of being watched had come back. I lifted my eyes, and they were drawn straight to Luca. He stood across the street, two storefronts down, leaning against the building and watching us—watching me.

"G, I have to go. I'll text you later, okay?" I murmured distractedly as I stood from the table.

"Sounds good." Head down, she scrolled through her phone, hardly noticing my departure.

I charged straight for Luca, fists clenched at my sides. "Are you stalking me?" I hissed at him once I was close enough not to be overheard.

"I'm making sure you're safe. Things are dangerous right now —I don't want you going out without an escort."

Oh. My anger ebbed as I glanced around, wondering just how much danger I might be in. "I'll call Leo for a ride home, but I don't want you following me around like a creeper." I got out my phone and immediately texted Leo, not wanting Luca to have any reason to stick around. "There, all set. You can be on your way now." I turned my back and stalked over to the curb, intent on ignoring his presence.

I should have known my actions were irrelevant. I could no more ignore Luca than I could will myself to stop breathing. I didn't even have to look behind me to sense him approaching— the electrical charge between us alerted me to his presence, heating the skin along my back where he now stood just inches away.

"You think that attitude pushes me away," he rumbled from behind me, so close to my ear that the little hairs on my neck stood on edge. "But all it does is make me want to see those sassy lips wrapped tight around my cock." His mouth came closer before he clamped down gently on my earlobe with his teeth, then sucked on the flesh as he pulled away.

My breathing shuddered, and my head swam with a rush of dizziness. My nipples were hard enough, every man, woman, and child on the street would be able to see them, but I was too disoriented to care. Thankfully, Leo must have been nearby. His black SUV pulled in front of me, drawing me from my lust-filled haze. Jumping into action, I opened the backseat door and leapt inside. When I glanced at Leo, he was scowling over his shoulder to where Luca stood with a smirk.

"Just go," I muttered.

Leo begrudgingly followed my instructions, dropping me at my apartment building and walking me to the elevator.

"I got it from here, thanks."

"Your father wants to make sure you have someone with you whenever you're out—just a temporary thing. You let me know whenever you need to leave your apartment, okay?"

"Yeah, I got the memo." I gave him a tight smile, wondering just how long this increased supervision would last.

When I got off on the fourteenth floor, I found my Uncle Sal waiting for me outside my apartment. It was strange to look at him and know he wasn't just my father's best friend, he was in the mafia. I wasn't sure if my father had told him I knew, so I decided not to broach the subject.

"Hey, Uncle Sal! This is a surprise—I hope you weren't waiting long." I gave him a hug and began to fish my keys out of my purse.

"Not at all. It's my fault for not calling before I came up. I was nearby and needed to get a gift for my upcoming anniversary, so I thought I'd drop by and you could help me with some ideas. Us men are no good at these things," he said with a chuckle.

"Sure, I'm happy to help. Come on in." I held the door open for him, then set down my purse. "Can I get you a water or soda?"

"Nah, just come have a seat." He walked toward the sofa and gestured for me to sit.

The entire situation was irregular. I couldn't shake the feeling something was off—he was my uncle, and older people were strange sometimes, but his surprise visit notably coincided with my discovery about my family's mob involvement. Did he know that I knew? Was he trying to uncover how much I knew? I suspected he had an ulterior motive, but I had no idea what it might be.

"You know," he started in, hands in his pockets as he gazed out the window. "You've always been my favorite—so ambitious and eager to please. When you were little, you used to tickle my beard, your little fingers on my chin."

"And you would call me a scamp and chase me away, making me laugh until I couldn't breathe."

"You remember," he said with surprise.

"Yeah, we've had a lot of good memories together. Remember the time you took me and Sofia to see the Rockettes? Looking back, I think maybe that was a little for your own benefit," I teased, remembering the gorgeous dancers and their long, beautiful legs.

He smiled at me, but there was a deep sadness behind those grey eyes. "That's why this pains me so much. It wasn't supposed to be this way, but plans change, and sometimes, we have to make sacrifices."

Before I could ask what he was talking about, Sal pulled out a handkerchief from his pocket and pressed the wet cloth against my face. Unable to help a gasp of surprise, my lungs filled with a sickly-sweet smell. Almost instantly, my vision blurred, and my flailing arms failed to respond to my muddled commands. Not even terror-induced panic could overcome the numbing effects of whatever chemical soaked the cloth. All I could do was plead in the silent recesses of my mind as I slipped deep into unconsciousness.

THE FIRST THING I noticed as I woke was the rank odor of stale cigarettes and the biting cold of metal against my back. When I tried to rub at my aching head, I discovered my hands were bound with leather cuffs to the hard surface below me. The restraints triggered a cascade of memories, ramping up my heartrate and flooding my system with adrenaline.

I tried to open my eyes, but the glaring light sent a stabbing pain deep into my skull. All I could do was squint, my lids blinking rapidly as I tried to survey my surroundings. I still wore my clothes, which was a relief, but that was the only shred of good news.

I was strapped to a metal examining table as best I could tell, and two brilliant pendant lights hung down over me like the lights in an operating room. The implications weren't lost on me. Choppy, shallow breaths puffed from my chest as I continued to look around the small concrete cell.

An evil laugh, low and malicious sounded from behind my head.

"Stop, Rico, you're scaring her."

It's amazing how the brain can cling to hope. The instant I heard Uncle Sal's voice, hope surged inside me. It didn't matter that he had been the one to abduct me. He was family, and therefore, my mind insisted he might help save me.

"But it's so fun to watch her squirm and panic," said the man with the evil laugh. His words bore the heavy drawl of a thick Italian accent.

"Uncle Sal?" I whimpered. "Please, help me." My voice was scratchy and horse, sending me into a coughing fit.

"I'm sorry, little Lessi, but I can't do that. Rico here wants revenge for some very bad things your father has done. Those are our rules—blood for blood." He was silent for a moment, then slowly approached the table until I could finally see him above me. "You're not surprised by any of this, are you? I see you must have known more than I gave you credit for." His head tilted to the side, more intrigued than bothered.

"Why would you do this?"

Sal's lips thinned as he thought. "Rico, leave us," he ordered the other man.

I had yet to see the other man, but I could hear the clicking of a door open and close. It sounded like a heavy metal door, and I wondered where on Earth they'd taken me and how they'd removed me unseen from my apartment.

My uncle lifted his hand and swept at a tear that had leaked out of the corner of my eye. "If you have to die for this, it seems only fair you know why. Your father has grown weak in recent years, soft and complacent. It's no longer in the best interest of the family to be led by him. Unfortunately, in our world, there are no letters of resignation or peaceful takeovers. There is only one way a don can be removed from power. I tried to set up your father, have the Commission take him out on my behalf, but it hasn't played out according to my plans. Now, it looks as though war may be the only way I can take over his position. Your death would ignite already explosive tensions between the families. It works out for everyone—Rico here gets his revenge, and I get my war."

"Everyone except me. Please, don't do this, Uncle Sal. Please, I'm begging you." I hated how my jaw quivered as I plead with him but not enough to overrule my desperation.

He peered down at me with a look akin to remorse, but I knew better. This monster I had called family was incapable of something so human as remorse or empathy. Before I could curse him and spew insults, he walked to a table on the side of the room I hadn't noticed before. He picked up a roll of duct tape and tore off a section with his teeth.

"What are you doing?" I blurted.

"I'm afraid I can't have you telling all my secrets." With both hands, he stretched the tape over my mouth and pressed down to seal my mouth shut.

I wailed and raged against the tape and my constraints, but it did no good.

"I'm sorry again, sweet Alessia. I hope you understand, it's nothing personal." If there'd been any question the man was evil, it was dashed away when he winked before leaving the room.

My chest puffed up and down with unfettered rage until Rico came back into view, and my breathless pants turned into sobs of terror. The middle-aged man was so thin, his sallow cheeks indented below the bone. His mousy brown hair flopped to the side, just long enough for the greasy strands to cover his eyes. Those pale blue eyes were the worst part of all—soulless and empty. I could feel their filthy touch as they roved over my body, hungry for blood.

"It's important when someone wrongs you to not only get your pound of flesh but to ensure a lesson is taught. Those filthy Luccianos must learn to never, ever fuck with the Gallos. Luca did an excellent job leading me straight to you. I watched you for days, but I wasn't allowed to touch, not until Sal here made his offer. Now, we make things right."

His eyes glowed with depravity, and when he lifted a knife where I could see it, warmth spread beneath me where I lost control of my bladder. He sniffed the air, then laughed at my fear, but embarrassment was the farthest thing from my mind. Humility was nonexistent when one was lost in abject terror.

My nostrils flared angrily as I tried to pull in the oxygen my lungs desperately needed to keep pace with my racing heart. My eyes stayed fixed on the small switchblade he gripped in his hand. Taking the hem of my shirt, he sliced through the fabric from my navel to my throat, cutting the blouse in half.

"Your skin is beautiful, such a perfect canvas," he mused to himself as he trailed the knife down my chest and belly without so much as a single scratch. When he got to my slacks, he popped the button off and lowered the zipper.

I began to thrust my hips and squirm, fear taking control of my body.

"You know, this knife is very sharp. I wouldn't want to do that if I were you. One slip of my hand, and this could all be over very quickly." His words were spoken with an eerie calm that chilled me to my core.

Every muscle in my body clenched, locked down motionless —too scared to move, too terrified to relax. A twisted, vile grin spread across his face as he returned to his work.

I wished to God this was the moment where help came for me —that Luca or my father came bursting through the door and put a bullet between Rico's eyes. I would have even celebrated if Uncle Sal had experienced a change of heart and had come back to save me, but that wasn't the case.

This was the moment in the movie when the camera pans back, and everything fades to black. No one wants to see the details of what happens—the innuendo is enough. For me, there was no escape. I was forced to experience first-hand each sadistic detail, memories that would haunt me forever.

CHAPTER 23
Luca

After Alessia took off with her driver, I jumped in my car and started to make the trek into Jersey to check on Arianna. I'd been so consumed with all things Alessia, I hadn't provided adequate supervision of my little sister. A few weeks' time on her own and there was no telling what kind of trouble she could get into.

Before I crossed over the GW bridge, I texted Alessia. **Did you make it home?**

Setting my phone back on its charger, I waited for a response. The tires passing over each section of bridge made a clicking sound that counted off the seconds as my text went unanswered. She swore she would answer me, and I was fairly certain she hadn't been lying to appease me. With growing agitation, I grabbed the phone and dialed her number. Ring after ring came across the line before her voicemail picked up.

It was entirely possible she had jumped in the shower or had some other valid reason for not answering, but I couldn't shake the feeling in my gut that something wasn't right. As soon as I made it to the other side of the bridge, I flipped a U-turn and started back toward her Manhattan apartment.

By the time I reached the building over a half-hour later, she still hadn't returned my text or answered my calls. My head filled with gruesome images as I went from concern to worry to all-out fear. I wasn't normally the type to succumb to the emotion, but in this instance, I was drenched in the sticky substance.

I double-parked and tore off toward the entrance. The concierge attempted to stop me, but I blew past him and caught an elevator already waiting on the ground floor. Each agonizing rise between floors felt like a lifetime. When the elevator finally opened, I ran to her apartment and pounded on the door.

"Alessia, it's me. Open up!" Hand flat against the door, I stood motionless and waited, listening for sound on the other side.

Nothing.

Pulling out my pocketknife, I jimmied the lock, and her door popped open, the deadbolt not in use. I scanned the room, instantly zeroing in on her purse set on the counter. Inside were her keys, phone, and wallet.

Shit! Fuck!

I didn't have my gun with me, so I took a knife from the kitchen and slowly scoped out the apartment. It was empty, no signs of a struggle, nothing out of place. If I'd gone to the cops, which was never going to happen, they'd probably tell me she'd gone for a walk, but I knew that wasn't the case.

Alessia had been taken.

Grabbing my phone, I dialed Enzo, thanking God her father had given me his number before I'd left his house.

"Yeah."

"Enzo, this is Luca. We got a real problem—Alessia's been taken."

Silence. "How do you know?" His voice had gone steely. I was about to see a side of Enzo Genovese that had been dormant for a long time.

"She didn't answer my texts or calls, so I came to her place. Her purse is here with everything in it—phone, keys—but she's not here. She knows the dangers; I'd just told her she wasn't to go anywhere without an escort. Her driver brought her home, but someone must have taken her as soon as she got here."

He was silent for a moment, and I waited for his instruction. He far outranked me, even if he was from a different outfit.

"Let me make some calls. You check out the security office at her building and see what the cameras show."

"Got it." The phone clicked dead, and I resisted the urge to launch the device against the wall. How could I have fucked this up so badly? I'd been watching her, warned her and her father, got information to the Commission as fast as I could, and it hadn't been enough. Alessia was gone, and all I could do was hope she was still alive.

AFTER THREATENING to cut off his balls, I was finally able to get the concierge to take me back to the security office. The surveillance film for the lobby over the previous hour showed only residents coming and going. When we pulled up the footage for the fourteenth floor, the recording started just thirty minutes earlier. Everything prior to that had been erased.

"Is there another way up, aside from the front lobby?" I asked the older man who was clearly shaken.

"There's a service elevator and emergency exit out the back."

"Are there cameras in those locations?"

"No. The backdoor stays locked, and the service elevator requires a keycard."

Whoever had done this had been savvy enough to cover their tracks. I thanked the man for his help and called Enzo to give him an update. He instructed me to call my underboss and have him meet us at Tedesco's, a small Italian joint in Little Italy. The old-timers used to base their operations in that area, but things didn't work that way anymore. With modern technology, there was no reason to be so predictable. Little Italy existed for tourists, that was about it.

When I arrived, I was escorted to a basement where an ancient table and chairs were set up in the middle of the room. The scene was straight out of an old gangster movie—empty cellar with a single dangling light over a rectangular table, highlighting the angles of each severe face below. Enzo was there with his brother, Edoardo, who had been acting as his Consigliere. The two brothers had relied too heavily on Sal for information, both completely ignorant to what had been going on. Next to them sat my underboss, Michael Abbatelli, who nodded as I entered the room. Along with them, the Moretti underboss sat at the table, face stoic as he waited to hear why everyone had been gathered.

"What's the plan?" I asked, not allowing any of my wariness to enter my voice.

"We're waiting on the Giordano and Gallo representatives to show up, then we talk," said Enzo, his features devoid of emotion. I was impressed. He'd managed to call together an impromptu meeting of The Five Families. The only seats missing from the Commission were those occupied by the Chicago Outfit, but this was too short of notice to get them here.

I went to stand on the back wall, knowing it was not my place to sit at the table with the underbosses, when Enzo spoke up.

"Have a seat," he motioned to a chair across from him. "You're just as much a part of this as the rest of us."

I followed his instructions and sat at the table next to Abbetelli. Moments later, steps sounded on the wooden stairs. I tensed as Matteo De Luca, underboss of the Gallo family, came into view. He was an intimidating bastard—tattoos inked on each finger and snaking up from the collar of his dress shirt. There was nothing subtle or demure about him. He made no attempt to hide who he was or mask the nature of his dealings. He didn't draw unnecessary attention, but he also didn't try to fit in with civilized society.

"De Luca, I appreciate you joining us. I know this is rather unorthodox." Enzo stood, an offering of respect to the rival family. He had to be fuming inside—his calm exterior was truly impressive.

De Luca was in his late thirties, young for an underboss, but he was good at commanding respect. He too had his game face on, making it impossible to tell if we were about to have a civil discussion or unleash a bloody war.

"Unorthodox, yes, but also reminiscent of the old days." Matteo gazed around the musty basement. "You appear to have a nostalgic side. I remember sitting upstairs as a kid while my father had meets down here."

"From what I've learned recently, I knew trust would be hard to come by. I figured old Gallo stomping grounds would give me a better shot of getting you to show up."

Matteo gave a nod with a tight smirk that held no humor. "There's been some very bad blood between our families, and recent months have not made things any better."

The door above creaked open, and all eyes turned to the stairs as the Giordano underboss joined the party. Each man had come with one or two soldiers who now stood lined against the walls, eyeing the room cautiously.

"Excellent," Enzo said, drawing everyone's attention. "Now that we're all here, we can get started. Edoardo has our Chicago associates on speakerphone, so we don't leave them out of the discussion. I understand this was very unexpected, and I appreciate everyone giving me their time today. It's been a long time since I've seen all of you, some I've never had the pleasure of meeting. From here on out, that changes. It's been brought to my attention my absence from the scene has enabled my underboss to commit some unforgivable acts in my name. I want to assure each of you, I in no way sanctioned his actions." As he spoke, Enzo held the eyes of each man at the table, one-by-one, professing his veracity. "We've all gone back to the old ways—silent in our operations and demanding absolute adherence to our code. I thought if I remained a ghost, invisible to even my own outfit, it would protect me and my family. If you ever have the misfortune of losing a child, you would know there is no greater pain. In trying to protect myself from outsiders, I made myself vulnerable to an attack from the inside."

"I appreciate your efforts to smooth things over," cut in Matteo. "But how are we supposed to trust you aren't just throwing Sal under the bus?" His point had been valid, and everyone in the room seemed interested in the answer.

"Because my daughter is missing. I never, ever would have intentionally set in motion events that would so clearly lead to retaliation against my own. Certainly not without taking the proper precautions first. Do you think I'd be fucking stupid enough to have a Gallo man killed the day after I'd met with him?" Enzo's fervor let slip the first signs of just how deeply he was affected.

Every man in the room shifted at his announcement, and the tension thickened more than I'd thought possible. The room had already been stifling; now, it was downright oppressive.

"How long has she been missing?" asked Abbatelli.

"About two hours, give or take." He turned to Matteo and addressed him directly. "I fear this is a retaliation hit for the Venturi death, which would mean a Gallo was behind her disappearance. I know it can't be easy to trust me, but I will be in your debt if you will help me get her back."

Matteo remained unmoved, only the slightest lift of his chin gave any indication that he'd heard Enzo at all. "There must be blood for blood—how do you propose that's handled?"

"Sal." There was no hesitation in Enzo's response. "The moment I get him into my custody, he's yours."

The room sat in excruciating silence for long seconds before Matteo nodded and stood. "I'll take this to my boss and let you know his decision." He exited the basement, followed by his two soldiers, and the room seemed to fill with fresh oxygen.

"Holy shit, Enzo, you know how to make an entrance," came the Moretti underboss, wiping beads of sweat from his forehead. Postures relaxed, and the room filled with the shuffling of sound.

"Trust me, this isn't how I'd have preferred to show back up. If I'd have known this would happen, I never would have taken a back seat." His tone was morose, and the room got quiet again.

Enzo visited with the remaining underbosses, renewing his connections and assuring them things were going to change in the Lucciano family. Unable to sit still any longer, I started to make my way back upstairs when Enzo called out to me.

"Luca, wait for me outside." His tone was casual, but the unknown reason for his request coiled my already tense muscles even further.

I waited under the old red awning out front as each of the men slowly dispersed. Eventually, Enzo and his brother stepped outside, Enzo placing a grateful hand on his brother's back. They exchanged a few quiet words before parting ways, and Enzo turned his hard gaze my direction.

"I want you to promise me you won't go after her."

I wasn't sure what I expected, but that hadn't been it.

Enzo strolled over, hands in his pockets, his face a map of worry lines that hadn't been visible at our first encounter.

"What am I supposed to do—go home and watch television? I can't sit by while she's missing." No fucking way. I'd never forgive myself if something happened to her while I was sipping a beer, pretending everything was peachy.

"You don't think I want to do the same damn thing?" he spat back, renewed spark giving heat to his words. "That's my daughter out there, in the hands of God knows who. However, there are protocols that must be followed. We go in with guns blazing, nothing good will come of it. You kill someone getting her back, only to end up with a price on your head, isn't going to help. If anything can be done to get her back, Matteo will make it happen. He knows how huge it would be for me to owe him. The only thing we can do now is wait."

He was right, and I fucking hated it.

I whirled and kicked one of the small metal dinette chairs on the sidewalk patio, sending the thing clattering onto its side. Pain blossomed in my foot but did little to ease the suffocating frustration sitting like a heavy boulder on my chest.

"Get it out—go to the gym or do whatever you need to but keep your nose out of trouble. I'll call you when I hear something."

I offered him a nod and stomped back to my car, unable to unclench my teeth long enough to say a word in response. I had no idea what I'd planned on doing to look for her, but having the option taken from me made me feel even more helpless.

I sat in my car, boxed in by the deafening silence. I couldn't remember ever feeling so fucking powerless. What was I supposed to do—go home and pretend Alessia wasn't out there in trouble? I slammed my hands on the steering wheel. The only thing that would remotely help was the gym, so I started the car and drove like an asshole to the one place where I could get out the rage eating me alive.

CHAPTER 24

Alessia

I wasn't sure how long he worked on me.

The minutes when I was under his knife felt like hours, and the time between sessions seemed like mere seconds. He had drawn out removing my clothes, taking pleasure in my fear, milking every ounce of terror from my quivering body without even harming me.

Only after I was naked before him did Rico begin his real work. He explained that back in his homeland, he was called 'the Surgeon' for his skill with a knife. His technique was something akin to the Chinese death by a thousand cuts. Slowly and methodically, he sliced his knife across my delicate flesh countless times, turning me inside out, one cut at a time.

My arms. My stomach. My legs.

Cut after excruciating cut, I bled and silently wept.

He was precise and meticulous, moving at a torturously slow pace. No single cut was deep enough to endanger me nor give me substantial enough pain to allow me the mercy of passing out. I was forced to lie there awake, listening to him hum as he mutilated my body.

I was glad I couldn't see his work. The feel of warm blood dripping down my cool skin was nauseating enough. How long could someone survive this brand of depraved torture? How much blood could a body lose before the organs gave up and shut down? I didn't want to die. I was utterly terrified, and there was no escape from the fear.

The pain was intense, but it was the fear that was crippling.

I prayed in my head, over and over, that I would live to see my family again.

I swore vengeance if I could get free.

I cursed Sal and Rico a thousand awful deaths and struggled with blame and guilt.

The one thing I didn't do was beg to die.

Soaked in my own blood and urine, drifting in agony and lost in a sea of fear, I was steadfast in my desire to live.

We were alone for the entire duration. I had no idea if Sal remained nearby, or if I'd been left entirely alone with Rico, which is why it startled me when the door clicked open. I couldn't see who had entered, but I could see Rico when his chin lifted, and his spine went rigid. His response sent a new surge of panic racing through my veins.

"Frederico, tell me if I'm wrong, but I don't believe the boss gave orders for retribution just yet." The voice was confident, steeped in power and control.

Rico paled, but his rigid stance remained unyielding. "They took the life of my cousin—there must be blood taken in return."

The newcomer strolled closer until I could see his penetrating eyes holding Rico captive. He was older than me, perhaps late thirties, and much more refined than my torturer. Aside from swirls of ink against his skin, he could have been a powerful politician or business mogul in his expensive suit with a neatly groomed beard. Each calculated step he took was a measured warning.

He never dropped his gaze to my flayed, bloody flesh as if this was something he'd seen before and was unbothered by the image. "An arrangement has been worked out—the girl was not part of the bargain." Finally, the man's eyes drifted down to me, and a whimper forced its way past the tape still glued to my lips. "You're fortunate, however. She's still alive, which means you'll survive this ordeal, but there will be consequences." His eyes flitted back up to Rico, who dropped his chin to his chest, finally conceding submission.

"Thank you, Matteo. I didn't know there was an arrangement," he muttered in broken English.

"That's because you never asked. This will be your only warning—step out of line again, and it will be the last move you make."

Rico nodded and scurried from the room like the sewer rat he was. My chest shuddered with the force of a restrained sob, overcome with emotion. It sounded like I was going to be freed, but perhaps I had only heard what I'd wanted to hear. When Matteo peered back down at me, the space between his brows lightly creased, and his lips thinned as he studied me.

He took out his phone, hitting a number on autodial. "Get Jacobs here immediately and bring a woman's robe, something soft." He hung up as soon as the words were out and slipped his phone back in his pocket. "We're going to get you cleaned up before I return you to your father."

He took hold of the corner of the tape over my mouth and pulled it free in a single yank. The sudden pain and immense relief I would be going home brought on a deluge of uncontrollable sobs. One-by-one, Matteo freed my arms and legs from their restraints, but when I tried to sit up, he pressed my shoulder back down.

"I've got a doctor coming. I know you want to get out of here and aren't crazy about being naked, but you have to wait a little longer." His words were clinical, emotionless—he may have been freeing me, but it was not out of the kindness of his heart.

This was business.

I wasn't going to argue. Matteo appeared to be running the show and claimed he was going to take me home—if that meant walking there naked, I'd do it.

He took out his phone again, and this time, I recognized the curt greeting on the other end, and the sound brought on a new wave of silent tears.

"I've got her. She's a little worse for wear but otherwise okay. I'll get her to you as soon as the doctor has looked her over." Matteo glanced down at me. "Yeah, here she is." He held the phone out, and I took it in my shaking hands.

"Daddy?" I rasped.

"Lessi, thank God. Are you okay?" The relief in his voice and the use of my old nickname did me in. My aching chest swelled with warmth as tear after tear cascaded down my blotchy cheeks.

"I'm okay. I want to go home," I whispered shakily.

"I know, sweetie. You'll be home soon—now give the phone back to Matteo." I did as he instructed, a sense of calm settling over me after hearing my father's voice.

The doctor showed up not long after and tended to my wounds. Some were shallow enough to have stopped bleeding on their own, others required sutures and butterfly bandages. The process took at least an hour. As each cut was doctored, he gently wiped the excess blood from my skin and moved to the next. Only when every square inch of me had been treated did he help me into the ivory robe that had arrived with him.

Another thirty minutes later, Matteo was pulling up to my parent's house. My father met us at the car while my mother watched from an inside window, most likely instructed by my father to stay safely inside. Each movement I made was painful, but it was infinitely more bearable knowing I was going home.

My father opened my door and gingerly helped me out of the car. Matteo came around to the passenger side, and the two men eyed each other like big cats caged next to one another at the zoo.

"Thank you, Matteo. Your cooperation will not be forgotten," offered my father.

Matteo's lips curved up just a fraction. "You owe me a marker —and for the record, we still want Sal."

My father clenched his teeth, his lips thinning. "You and me both. I sent men to his house to collect him, and he managed to slip through our fingers. He's on the run now—it won't be easy to find him."

"Sal escaped?" I blurted, a trickle of fear dancing down my spine.

Both men stared at me in surprise.

Sensing their unasked questions, I explained. "Sal was waiting for me at my apartment. I didn't know I shouldn't trust him, so I let him in. He started acting weird, talking about the past, then he jumped me and held a cloth with some chemical to my face, making me pass out. He was the one who turned me over to Rico —said he wanted to start a war."

Matteo dropped his chin in a nod. "We'll all be on the hunt for him. In the meantime, I'll be in touch."

My father held out his hand, and the two shook hands uneasily. When the moment was over, Matteo sped off in his flashy car, and dad ushered me inside.

I spent the next hour being fussed over until I was finally able to escape to my old bedroom. Dad had called Luca to let him know I was home safe. Luca wanted to come by, but I told my dad I didn't want to see him. I wasn't ready yet for a number of reasons. My dad assured me he would take care of informing work and keeping Luca at bay. With that settled, I curled up in bed and lost myself in sleep.

I dreamed I was alone somewhere in the arctic north, lost with nothing but the clothes on my back. There was enough light cast from somewhere behind the horizon that I could see the endless white landscape where not even trees dared to grow. I spun around in fear, clueless how I would survive in such harsh conditions.

The biting wind tore at my body, creating blinding pain where numbness had not yet set in. Even breathing was painful, the frozen air like razor blades against my sensitive lungs. How would I ever survive? My hand came to the strap on my backpack, and I knew innately I had a blanket tucked inside the bag, but I couldn't touch it. Why? The heavy cloth would give me the protection I needed from the brutal outdoors. Why couldn't I wrap its soft warmth around me?

A particularly violent gust threw me to my hands and knees, the icy ground brutal and unforgiving. Sitting back on my knees, I glanced at my bloody palms, fear allowing the cold to further penetrate my bones.

I would not survive, not like this.

Tears froze against my burning cheeks as I curled into myself and cried. I didn't want to die. I was so young, how could life end so quickly? There was so much I wanted to see and do, but the cold had sapped every ounce of energy I had—there was none left for survival. All I could do was curl into myself and hope the frozen wilderness took me quickly.

I woke on a gasp, starting to sit up in bed before a bite of pain reminded me of the very real nightmare I'd endured. Lying back down, I reoriented myself to my surroundings. I'd been under my covers, but I could still feel the icy chill from my dream. The moonlight in my room lit the space enough for me to see my father sitting in a chair in the far corner. Had he been watching me sleep?

"Dad?" I asked dazedly, still groggy from the dream.

He rose from his seat and came over to sit next to me on the bed, lifting a hand to smooth my hair back behind my ear. "I'm so sorry, Alessia. I tried so hard to protect you and Sofia—to protect all of us—but it wasn't enough. I hid us away, kept men posted to guard you, and made sure your work never touched the uglier side of my business." He paused, his moonlit eyes heavy with remorse. "You expressed your desire to stay out of the life, and I respect that, but sometimes we're born into our circumstances. The poor don't want to be poor, and you may not want to be a part of this life, especially after what's happened, but as my daughter, you will never be completely free unless you started over. It wouldn't be my preference, but I'll help you disappear, if that's what you want. With a new name and a new life, you could live how you see fit." He glanced down at his hands in an uncharacteristically vulnerable gesture. "Think about it; there's no rush to decide." He leaned in and kissed my head, lingering for an achingly sweet moment.

My father hadn't been so openly affectionate to me since I'd been a child. I wanted to capture the feeling and seal it away so I would have it always.

"You know, you'd have to be blind not to see how much Luca cares for you. Leaving is always an option, but so is staying. With a man like him, I'd feel confident you'd be protected and well cared for. I won't push any more than that, but please keep an open mind." He gave me a sad smile and got up to leave.

The red display of the digital clock on my nightstand read eleven at night. I'd slept through the evening, and now that my dad started me thinking, I wasn't sure I'd be able to go back to sleep anytime soon. He was one-hundred percent right. The only way to truly remove myself from the mafia was to uproot my life and start over somewhere else as a different person. Was that what I wanted? Was I prepared to make that kind of change?

I thought about my sisters and my parents, Giada, and my other family—I may not have been close to all of them, but they were my family. Walking away forever felt like losing a part of myself. All I'd wanted since I was a kid was to help my dad run Triton. I wasn't sure how much dad's mafia operations had touched the company, but there was still a legitimate business in place. If I could still run it, wouldn't that be a satisfying life?

I loved my apartment and the city—I loved my life. Now that Roger was gone, there wasn't one thing I would want to change, aside from my father's connections. Maria had said things could be the same, that I could continue my life as it was. Could she have been right? It wouldn't be exactly the same, but could there be enough similarity that it would still be my life, my choices? What if I threw Luca into that mix? Would being with him make my mafia ties that much stronger? I'd already had a mob boss for a father—would dating a made man be any different?

I noticed someone had placed my phone next to the bedside clock while I'd been asleep. I had three missed messages from Giada and a slew of missed calls and messages from Luca. Most of his were from earlier in the day when Sal had first taken me, but there was one from just an hour ago.

I don't think I can sleep until I know you're alright. I've never been so scared in my whole life. You've changed me, Alessia, and I don't think I can go back. Please talk to me.

Tears pricked in my eyes, and my chest ached to be near him. Just the thought of Luca comforted me. Before I had a chance to second-guess myself, I texted back. **I'm doing okay. Please get some rest.**

The conversation bubble immediately popped up as he typed a response. He'd been waiting by his phone to some degree, and I hated to think of him worrying.

Are you in pain?

I'd been avoiding thinking about my wounds as much as was possible when I hurt every time I moved. Since waking up, I'd needed to go to the bathroom but had resisted because I didn't want to see the damage. Would I be horribly scarred? Would Luca—or any man for that matter—still want me if they saw how I looked now? My face and breasts weren't damaged, but my stomach, arms, and legs were a crisscross of jagged wounds. At some point, I would have to face the reality of what Rico had done to me, but it could wait. **Some, but it's not too bad.**

I wish I had you in my arms—I want to make you feel safe.

~~You do. I want that too. I miss you.~~ I didn't want to lead him on when I was still so confused. Yes, I wanted him to hold me and assure me no one would ever hurt me again, but was that what I'd want a week from now when I felt more like myself? **I need some time, please understand.**

I'm not going anywhere. Sweet dreams, my beautiful girl.

Night, Luca.

No decisions had been made, my body was still mangled, and Sal was still at large, but just a few texted words from Luca, and peace settled over me. I made a quick trip to the restroom—careful not to look in the mirror or down at my arms and legs—then crawled back into bed and drifted easily back to sleep.

CHAPTER 25

Luca

It was two days after Alessia's ordeal, and I was close to losing my mind. I learned she'd gone back to her apartment but not much else. She had only texted a few words here and there, and I'd tried not to push her, but my patience was wearing thin.

I never claimed to be a good man.

I wasn't even necessarily the best man for her, but I didn't care.

She was mine. Period.

I would do whatever it took to make her understand, and that included asking her father for help. I wasn't normally the type to ask for any sort of help, let alone with a woman, but for her, there wasn't much I wouldn't do.

Attempting to be respectful, I set up a time to meet with Enzo at his office. It was a Friday afternoon, but the place was still bustling with activity. When I entered his office, I realized I was already feeling more comfortable around the man.

"Have a seat," he offered in a formal tone. "What can I do for you?"

"I want to talk to you about Alessia."

He didn't look surprised. "I know you're very interested in her, but you need to accept she may not be cut out for this life."

"There's nothing to be cut out for—I'll protect her," I argued in return.

"Like you did this week?" His eyes were stone cold, but the rest of his features were impassive.

"I'd do a hell of a lot better than you. At least I didn't turn a blind eye as my daughter was sexually harassed in an office down the hall." My temper was flaring, and it wasn't going to help me win his support, but I'd be damned if he questioned my abilities when he had been just as negligent if not more so.

"What the hell are you talking about?"

"Her boss, Coleman was his name. He'd been harassing her, making passes at her, even groping her right here at Triton from the day she started working for you."

Worry lines creased his forehead, and his eyes fell to his desk. "Why didn't she tell me? Or report him to HR?"

"She said you'd want her to handle it herself, so that's what she was trying to do, but her methods were ineffective. I caught him forcing himself on her in the bathroom a week ago."

"Coleman died about a week ago, he was…" His eyes found mine, silent communication passing between us. The tension in his shoulders eased as realization dawned that my devotion to Alessia knew no limits.

I would keep her safe at all costs.

Enzo gave a single nod. "I did the best I could with my girls. This world is a dangerous place, and it's hard to know how best to protect your children."

"You kept them uninformed and weak."

"Be careful how harshly you judge me," he warned with a bite in his tone. "God willing, someday you will have children of your own, and I think you'll find the task much more challenging than you could ever imagine."

"You're right," I conceded, lowering my head with a sigh. "I get emotional where she's concerned—something I'm not used to. I haven't seen her since before she was taken, and it's making me rather unbearable. I nearly decapitated one of my best friends when he suggested I needed to get laid. I want your daughter. I know I can make her happy, but I need help making her see that —getting her to accept our way of life and to accept me."

He stared at me for a long moment, his expression detached. "I appreciate your persistence—it's an important quality in a young man. I also believe you'll keep my daughter safe, which is of the utmost importance to me. For those reasons, I'll see what I can do, but I can't promise anything. Alessia is her own woman, and she has the freedom to choose who she sees."

"I understand," I replied, dizzy with relief. "All I ask is you talk with her." I stood and reached out my hand, which he accepted with a firm grasp. "Thank you, Mr. Genovese."

"Call me Enzo. I have a feeling I'll be seeing a lot more of you." He glared at me sardonically, and for the first time, I saw a touch of humor in the old man's eyes. He'd not said it in so many words, but I'd just received Enzo Genovese's blessing to date his daughter.

CHAPTER 26
Alessia

I t was amazing how much better I felt just being back in my own apartment. My father's doctor had tended to me before I left their house, something my parents had insisted on before they'd allow me to leave. The doctor assured me the wounds would heal nicely, leaving minimal scarring, but I would believe it when I saw for myself.

As he removed my bandages, I got a front-row view of just how much damage Rico had done. I had eighteen cuts on the underside of my left forearm alone, almost all perpendicular to my arm. He must have seen his work as a form of art because there were patterns to the lines.

I tried to remind myself I was fortunate he liked to play with his victims—had he gone straight for the kill, I would have been long dead when Matteo had come for me. The few scars that remained would forever be a reminder of just how close I'd come to death.

And a reminder of Sal's betrayal.

How had a man I'd known all my life offered me up to be sacrificed like so much garbage? Ever since that day, my brain had struggled to grasp how such evil could have hidden among us without detection. All I could surmise was the sheer depths of his depravity enabled him to hide in plain sight. He bore no guilt or doubt about his actions, and that meant he could do whatever it took to protect himself and achieve his goals.

He was a sociopath.

There was no other viable explanation.

Unfortunately, that meant there had been little we could do to protect ourselves. Someone like that is absolute in their ruthlessness. Like a terrorist bent on bombing a building, his blind conviction and depraved lack of empathy made him enormously dangerous.

The most frightening part was how well he hid it. I shuddered to think what else he could have been capable of through the years. It was good his true nature had been revealed, but he was still on the loose. A part of me wouldn't be able to breathe easily until Sal was caught. I knew what my father would likely do to him once he was captured, and I couldn't summon an ounce of sympathy—not as long as that wink played over and over in my mind.

Whatever Sal received, he'd brought it on himself.

Giada came over not long after I went home to my apartment. I explained what had happened, and we cried together. She spent the evening with me, watching movies and helping me keep my mind off everything that had happened; but when night fell, and I was all alone, there was no escaping my thoughts and memories. By Saturday, I was sick of thinking.

When my mother texted, asking to come by for a visit, I welcomed the distraction. She rarely came into the city—I could count the number of times she'd been to my apartment on one hand—but considering the events of the week, I wasn't surprised when she asked to stop by.

Having company over was the perfect excuse to shower. The doctor had told me not to bathe for a couple days to allow the wounds time to close. It had been Tuesday since I'd had a good shower, so by Saturday morning, I felt wretched. As far as I was concerned, the wounds had been given enough time. If I went another day without a shower, I was going to lose my ever-loving mind.

My first step into the warm spray was the delicious feeling of waking up on a Monday morning only to realize it was still Sunday. I kept the normally blazing temperature of my shower down to a comfortable warmth so as not to burn the tender skin. I washed my hair twice, shaved what could be accessed, and simply enjoyed the cleansing feel of the water.

By the time my mom stopped by, I was feeling almost human again. She gave me a gentle hug, careful not to press too hard against my wounds, and made herself comfortable.

"I'm so glad to see you looking so much better. I've been worried sick," she said as she put her things down on the table.

"I know, Mom, but I needed to get back here to my own space. I feel much better, so hopefully, now you can stop worrying."

"I brought some deli meat for sandwiches—it'd help to see you eat."

"I was kidnapped, not starved," I teased.

"I know, but something about eating says everything will be fine." She waved her hands in the air in a grand sweeping gesture.

"It's the Italian way—it's a miracle we're not all obese."

"From your lips to God's ears," she said as she crossed herself. "On that note, let's eat—I'm starved."

I grabbed plates and condiments while she opened the deli bags and filled the silence with updates on the upcoming graduation party. I listened half-heartedly, part of my brain still stuck on an endless loop of worry about my life.

"Are you even listening?" she chided. I must not have been paying as much attention as I'd thought.

"Sorry, Mom. I've been distracted lately thinking about things."

She set down her sandwich and took a deep breath. "Actually, that's the other reason I wanted to come by." She gave me a look that said, please try to understand, and it made my spine stiffen. "Growing up, my father was a soldier in the family. Things were very different then—keeping something like that a secret from your children was nearly impossible. I knew from a young age that my dad was a family man, so when I met your father, his role in the organization never fazed me."

"Did you ever consider separating yourself from that life?" I asked. Not only was I interested in getting her take, I was fascinated to hear this part of my mother's history. It was a side to her I'd never known existed.

"Not really. That was just life; it never occurred to me that there was anything wrong with it."

"What about the dangers?"

"I know this is going to be hard to believe after what you've just gone through, but there isn't much more threat being in the family than there is driving at rush hour. Sometimes, things happen. It's an unfortunate part of life—there's never any way to be totally risk-free."

"Yeah, but it seems like it would be best to minimize that risk if at all possible."

Mom's head listed to the side, and she gave me a sad smile. "Sometimes, risk is the only way you get to the most beautiful parts of life. Your father was worth whatever risk came with him. I don't regret one day I've spent with him, even when he leaves his dirty dishes on the counter."

My mom hounded my dad incessantly about cleaning up after himself, and it never stuck. Maybe it was some kind of bizarre game between them. I had no idea, but it was an endearing part of their relationship that made them my parents. The reminder made me smile, but it quickly fell from my face when I thought of what I needed to ask next.

"What about Marco?" The words were nothing but a frightened whisper. I didn't want to hurt her, but I needed to know how she reconciled Dad's role in my brother's death.

She physically recoiled at the reminder. "I think a parent always shoulders an unbearable amount of guilt when their child dies, no matter the cause. Your father and I will always regret not keeping Marco safe, but we can't take responsibility for the actions of monsters. When a school is shot up, a parent can't blame themselves for not homeschooling their kids. Drunk drivers and terrorists, murderers and rapists—bad people are everywhere, in every walk of life."

I stared at my mom, my eyes searching hers and finding the strength and compassion I'd always known from her. "I'm scared, Momma," I admitted softly.

"I know, baby. But your father and I don't want you to miss an opportunity just because you're scared. We know how you like to walk the straight and narrow, but sometimes, you have to step out of your comfort zone."

"You and Dad?" I narrowed my eyes at her. "Did Dad send you over here?"

She huffed out a breath and squirmed in her seat. "I would have come over to check on you anyway, but Luca came to talk to your father, and this killed two birds with one stone."

"Luca went to talk to Dad? About me?" I was stunned. Luca wasn't the type of man to cower, but I also couldn't imagine him approaching my dad about dating me. Maybe it had been about business matters, and I was just being presumptive.

"That man has it bad for you, honey. You should give him a chance."

"Mom! You should be on my side!"

"He's cute," she shrugged. "You could do a lot worse."

I shook my head, fighting the pull of a smile. We finished our lunch without any further heavy conversation. When it came time for her to leave, I was almost sad to see her go. We weren't best friends like some mother/daughter combos I knew, but I preferred the way things were. She was my mother, not my friend. I could count on her to give me hard truths and to love me with her whole heart.

I SPENT the afternoon growing more and more bored, making me realize it was time to go back to work come Monday. Being a stay-at-home wife had worked for my mom, but I wasn't sure that was in the cards for me. I loved my job and the feeling of accomplishment that came with it. Pacing in my apartment as the city moved on without me was excruciating.

I had just wiped down my countertops for the third time when a knock sounded at my door. I wasn't expecting anyone, which never would have bothered me before, but now, an unannounced visitor gave me reason for pause. I quietly approached the door and peeked through the peephole.

Luca.

The tension in my neck eased, and my cheeks warmed in anticipation of talking with him. I'd told myself I didn't want to see him until I'd decided what I wanted, but the temptation was too great. It had been days since I'd laid eyes on him, and the draw of knowing he was just a few steps away had my hand undoing the lock.

When I opened the door, the unobstructed sight of him stole the air from my lungs. He was more beautiful than I remembered, and the magnetism between us was impossibly strong after our brief separation. He was dressed casually, t-shirt and jeans, but his hair was neatly styled, and his face was unreadable, making my stomach clench with unease.

"Hey," I offered softly. "Come in." I stepped back, making room for him, sure to lock the door behind him.

He didn't off a greeting, not with words. Luca was a man of action, and he let his body do the talking. Stepping close, his eyes devoured my face, searching, learning, memorizing every detail. I would never be more revered than I was in this man's eyes. He cupped either side of my face, and I stared into those black eyes, twin vortexes sucking me deeper into the depths of his darkness.

He had become the air I breathed, and only now that I was with him again did I feel alive.

My lips tingled with the urge to kiss him. His hands ran up my back, pulling me closer until I was pressed flush against him. I could feel his length hardening, pressing against the confines of his pants, and I reveled in the knowledge that he was just as addicted to me as I was him.

My hands found their way to his belt, fumbling at the buckle before he took over and made quick work of it. I slid my hands up under his shirt to the delicious warmth of his hard stomach. As his pants dropped to the ground, I slid my hands lower and cupped his solid length. The warmth of his stomach was nothing compared to the searing heat of his cock. Our lips devoured one another as each article of clothing was discarded to the floor.

He stood back for a moment and took in my bandages and the exposed wounds that were small enough to heal on their own. His face went feral with the promise of revenge. Uncomfortable under his gaze, I maneuvered my arms to hide some of the uncovered wounds, but he grabbed my hands and pulled them away.

"Don't cover yourself. I want to see you, all of you."

"Luca, there are going to be scars—I won't look like I did before." My eyes fell as worry set in.

"Look at me," he commanded, waiting to continue until my eyes met his. "There's nothing that man did or could ever have done that would make you any less beautiful to me. Understand?"

He paused, waiting for my agreement. "Now, I know you're still hurt, but I need to be inside you, feel you, know that you're mine."

His guttural demand roused an aching need in my core, making my breaths shaky and shallow. "I'm okay, you won't hurt me."

Luca lifted me into his arms gingerly and walked us back to my bed where he lay me down, hovering over me. For long minutes, he worshipped every inch of my body, kissing, sucking, licking until I was writhing with need. Not waiting for permission, Luca lined up his cock with my entrance and pressed inside me in one long motion.

My eyes went wide at the delicious pressure of my body adjusting to his size, and his eyes held mine as his fingers entwined with my own.

Allowing me an unguarded view into his soul, Luca made love to me. He flayed me open, bare for him, the swell of electric pressure building inside me, threatening to shatter me.

"I love you, Alessia. You're mine, and I can't let you go. Not now, not ever," he rasped as he pumped inside me.

His words ignited my fuse, sending me careening over the edge into a place without rules or boundaries—a place where it was only the two of us and infinite serenity. As he rocked into me languidly, allowing me to coast on the waves of pleasure he'd given me, I was swallowed by a swell of emotion. An emotion so blinding and pure, there was no mistaking it.

Love.

I was in love with Luca Romano.

Regardless of what he did for a living or who he associated with, I loved this man. My eyes drifted open, and I met his gaze, knowing every bit of my revelation was being broadcasted on my face. He stilled, his body going eerily motionless above me, and I wondered if I had done something wrong. There could have been no misunderstanding his words, but his reaction to my confession was unsettling—such disturbing intensity, I squirmed under his scrutiny.

Whatever had come over him only lasted a matter of seconds. His eyes blazed with triumph and determination before he pulled out and slammed back into me. I gasped at the blinding stab of sensation his assault created in my sensitive core. Over and over, he pummeled into my body with the ferocity of a man possessed, as if he were trying to force his way inside me until we were one body.

Still stimulated from my orgasm, my body was instantly back on the precipice, but this time, the building pressure was too much. I panted and flexed, trying to control the feeling that threatened to annihilate me.

Without pausing for breath, Luca demanded my submission. "Don't fight it, Alessia. Don't fight me. Give it to me, give me everything."

My body detonated, limbs convulsing, and an inhuman cry tore from my throat. At the same time, Luca roared his release, dropping his head down like a man kneeling at an altar.

He was just as much a prisoner to this thing between us as I was.

The realization struck me as I coasted down from my orgasmic high. Luca lowered himself and nuzzled my neck, placing reverent kisses against my sweat-lined skin. Our bodies heaved with exertion, intertwined as we recovered together silently.

I was at peace when I was with Luca. I didn't feel the need to prove myself or strive for acceptance. With him, I wasn't just enough—I was everything. He accepted me just as I was, and I owed him nothing less.

Love was unconditional, and I felt that when I was with him.

I never wanted to lose that feeling.

"I love you, too," I whispered in the dimly lit room, and the words hung in the air. I didn't feel as nervous voicing them as I thought I would. They were a natural part of this thing that had grown between us.

Luca stared at my face until I gave in and met his gaze. "Say you're mine. I want to hear the words."

I didn't hesitate. "I'm yours." I wanted to say the words—I wanted to be his.

Neither of us said another word. There was no reason for any other sentiment. As complex as everything else was, what existed between us was simple, and there was no need to sully it. He rolled to his side and pulled me back against his chest where I fit perfectly into the curve of his body.

I never imagined myself with a man like Luca, but now that I had him, I couldn't imagine my life without him. Plans and aspirations were great, but sometimes, life threw a curveball, and you simply had to adjust your swing.

My family was in the mafia, as was the man I loved.

It wasn't the life I'd seen for myself, but it was the life I was choosing—my new path, which promised to be every bit an adventure.

EPILOGUE

"I can't believe you're doing this," I muttered with my eyes cast outside the car window, watching the city blocks whiz by.

"It shouldn't be such a shock. You go to family dinners every Sunday—we're together now, so I'm going with you." Luca's voice was light with amusement, clearly enjoying my discomfort.

"It hasn't even been a full week, and you're already inviting yourself to my parents' place for dinner? Yeah, I'm a little shocked—shocked and anxious."

"Baby, you have nothing to worry about. Your dad and I have an understanding."

My head whipped to the side where he smirked in the driver's seat, one arm draped lazily over the steering wheel. "What do you mean 'an understanding?'"

"He knows I'm not letting you out of my sight, not when things are still so turbulent. Plus, he gave me his blessing to date you, so it's not a problem," he explained as if describing his favorite dessert rather than the status of our relationship.

"When did this happen?" I gaped at him. Why hadn't my father mentioned they'd had a conversation about our relationship?

"It was while you were … gone." His voice deepened, and he took hold of the steering wheel with a white-knuckle grip. "It wasn't something he said in so many words, but he gave his approval. Trust me."

Well, this should be interesting. "Glad you two sorted everything out. Maybe next time, you'll want to fill me in when it's my love life you're arranging." I gingerly crossed my arms over my chest, more interested in broadcasting my annoyance than avoiding the discomfort of my healing wounds.

Luca's eyes glanced my direction, and his lips pulled back in a broad grin. "Try and be annoyed all you want. You know that sass just makes me hard."

I tried not to smile, I really did, but that damn playboy charm of his got me every time. I shook my head, and instead of arguing, opted to enjoy the scenery as we finished the drive to my parents' house. We pulled up at the same time as Sofia, so I exited the car with a deep breath and prepared for the introductions.

"Hey, Sof."

"Lessi, oh my God, it's so good to see you!" She pulled me in for a gentle hug, then searched my eyes for confirmation I was alright. We'd spoken over the phone since my kidnapping but hadn't seen each other in person.

My father had suggested we tell her that my abduction had been a freak kidnapping and I'd managed to escape my captors by sheer luck. The lie about what had happened to me was not too far off the truth, but it still felt eerie how easily it had slipped off my tongue. She didn't ask many questions, and those she did ask had been centered around my current welfare rather than the circumstances of my abduction. She knew that Sal and our father had parted ways, but she didn't know he was in any way connected to my kidnapping. Looking at her golden hair glistening in the sun, I hoped none of that ugliness ever touched her.

I smiled at her warmly, then stepped back toward Luca. "I'm doing great, Sof, I promise. I suppose I have some introductions to make. Luca, this is my little sister, Sofia. Sof, this is Luca, my ... um ..."

"Boyfriend," he filled in, taking Sofia's hand in his.

Holy crap, Luca called himself my boyfriend!

Warmth filled my chest, easing some of the tension that had coiled on the way over.

"It's wonderful to meet you," she offered shyly but smiling ear-to-ear.

"Alright, let's get this over with," I murmured, pulling a smiling Luca toward the front door. I pushed down on the lever to find the door locked, so I pressed the bell. Within seconds, the door swung wide, and my father welcomed us inside.

"Alessia, Sofia," he said as he kissed each of our cheeks, then turned to Luca with a hand outstretched. "Luca, I'm glad you could make it."

The two men shook as I stared on in astonishment. I wasn't sure I'd ever get used to seeing my dad welcome a man I'd brought home. There'd only been a couple in the past, and each time, my father had been positively brutish.

Dad turned to me with a questioning raise of his brow. "You two go help your mother. I need to have a word with Luca." Without waiting for a response, Dad ushered Luca toward his office.

I turned to Sofia, who gaped at me with a mirrored look of surprise. "I feel like I've walked into a funhouse full of mirrors and illusions. Who was that man?" I asked as I looked back to where my father had disappeared down the hall.

"No idea. They've both been acting odd. Mom took me shopping with her yesterday to get a dress for my party. She hasn't asked to shop with me in years—we never agree on anything."

"Did you find a dress?"

"Eventually, but it wasn't easy. Everything she liked had rhinestones or tulle." She did an exaggerated full-body shiver. "And that wasn't the worst of it! She tried to set me up with a guy —the worst possible guy she could have picked."

My eyes bulged wide. "Nico?"

"The one and only," she confirmed, her lips pursed firmly together. "I have no idea what she was thinking." Sofia shook her head in exasperation and led the way back toward the kitchen. My mother didn't know everything that had gone on between Sofia and Nico, nor did I for that matter, but she should have known enough not to try to set them up on a date. I was just as confused as Sofia.

We joined Mom in the kitchen, the men meeting us in the dining room just as we placed the food on the table. The new addition to our family dinner helped give a new flow to the conversation, which was far less awkward than expected. My dad was unusually engaging, and Luca was the perfect gentleman. I couldn't have asked for a better outcome.

By the time we said our goodbyes and made our way to the car, I was exhausted. The night had gone well, but my overactive nerves and still-healing body had drained every ounce of energy. I laid my head back against the headrest and took a deep breath as Luca made his way to the driver's side.

"Let's go home," I said softy, my head turning to take in his stunning features in the dim light of the car.

He reached out and traced his knuckles down the line of my jaw. "And where would that be?" he rumbled in a voice I felt deep in my belly.

"Wherever you are." It was a little cheesy, but it was how I felt. I didn't care if he took me to my place or his, as long as he was with me.

"My girl's tired. I enjoy the sass, but there's always room for soft and sweet as well. We'll head to your place—I want you to get a good night's sleep." He pulled the car out of the driveway and started the thirty-minute drive home.

"Thanks for making dinner go so smoothly."

"I told you there was nothing to worry about."

"Easy for you to say, it wasn't your parents. Speaking of, what did my dad say to you in his office?" I peered at him curiously, a small surge of energy giving me life as I remembered their private conversation.

"It looks like Sal was doing more than lighting fires among the families—he's done something to piss off the Russians. Your father is amping up security for you girls until we can get it all sorted out. I don't want you to worry, though. We're going to get it all sorted and find that bastard, Sal. In the meantime …" he said, his voice growing warm and honeyed. "I'm going to take excellent care of you, all day and all night." He glanced at me, and our eyes locked for a long second full of promise.

The passion glinting in his eyes vanquished all other thought. It was the same thing he'd done since he cornered me in that elevator—his presence eclipsed all else.

He was my world, and I was his.

I was still coming to terms with the mafia element of the equation, but as for Luca, there was no longer any doubt in my mind. He was the one for me, and there was no running from that. I believed he would never hurt anyone unjustly, and he would never let anyone lay a finger on me. I trusted him to always give me the truth, his truth, no matter how ugly that might be; and I would give him my light to guide him through the darkness.

Head to the back of the book for a sneak peek at *Never Truth*, book 2 in *The Five Families Series*.

A NOTE FROM JILL

I'd like to offer a sincere thank you for purchasing *Forever Lies*. If you enjoyed reading the book as much as I enjoyed writing it, please take a moment to leave a review. Leaving a review is the easiest way to say **Thank You** to an author. Reviews do not need to be long or involved, just a sentence or two that tells people what you liked about the book in order to help readers know why they might like it too.

The next book in the series, *Never Truth*, is about Alessia's little sister, Sofia, and it's going to give you all the feels! It releases January 21, 2020 and is available for pre-order, so get your today!

ACKNOWLEDGEMENTS

My dad was born into an Armenian immigrant family in New York City. He didn't speak English until he started school and was primarily raised by his grandparents, who owned a small sandwich shop in Hell's Kitchen. (The picture is my dad with his mom and grandma in front of the shop.)

While my dad was an only child, he had a cousin who was like an older brother. This cousin grew up friends with the kids who became key players in the Irish Westies and the Italian Mafia. He started robbing trains at the age of ten with his friends and became well-liked by both factions—he was one of the few people who successfully associated with both groups. My father's cousin had a long career as a bookie, working with people like Fat Tony and Louie the Count—names and characters you would swear had to have come from a movie.

My dad is a phenomenal storyteller, and I grew up hearing about his cousin's antics and the insanity that was life in Hell's Kitchen in the 1950s. This fostered in me a mildly unhealthy fascination with all things mafia. I want to thank my dad for inspiring my imagination and giving me an appreciation for a lifestyle otherwise foreign to this Texas girl.

I'd also like to thank the amazing authors, such as L.P. Lovell,

Cora Reilly, J.M. Darhower, London Miller, Sarah Brianne, Cora Reilly, and Ashleigh Zavarelli, who fed my mafia obsession with the most harrowing, passionate stories of romance in the dark underworld. Not only are these ladies incredible storytellers, they are also fellow indie authors and trailblazers in their trade. Each of them has inspired me on a daily basis, and I am eternally grateful.

ABOUT THE AUTHOR

Jill Ramsower is a life-long Texan—born in Houston, raised in Austin, and currently residing in West Texas. She attended Baylor University and subsequently Baylor Law School to obtain her BA and JD degrees. She spent the next fourteen years practicing law and raising her three children until one fateful day, she strayed from the well-trod path she had been walking and sat down to write a book. An addict with a pen, she set to writing like a woman possessed and discovered that telling stories is her passion in life.

Social Media & Website
Official Website: www.jillramsower.com
Jill's Facebook Page: www.facebook.com/jillramsowerauthor
Facebook Reader Group: Jill's Ravenous Readers
Instagram: @jillramsowerauthor
Twitter: @JRamsower

Interested in a sneak peek at the next book in the series?

Never Truth
By
Jill Ramsower

Pre-order now, and here's a taste of the Sofia's emotional journey…

CHAPTER 1
Sofia

THEN

"Please, Daddy, can I go with you? I don't wanna go with Mama. I want to go with you and Marco to the movies. I swear I'm big enough to sit quiet. *Pleeeeeease!*" I infused my voice with as much earnest pleading as a five-year-old girl could muster and looked up at my father with Oscar-worthy puppy-dog eyes.

My dad had said he was taking Marco to the movies while Mama was at the school play rehearsal with Lessi and Maria. I was supposed to go with the girls, but that wasn't my choice. Given the opportunity, I was always at my brother's side. He was eleven, the oldest of us kids, and I idolized everything about him. If he thought it was cool to wear ankle socks, I wanted to wear ankle socks. If he went out to ride his bike, I would run along behind him as long as he would let me. As far as I was concerned, my big brother hung the moon.

"Sweet girl, we're going to see a spy movie. I'm not sure you'd like it," explained my dad, trying to let me down gently.

"Yeah!" Marco said as he entered the room. "You'd be pretty

scared, Sof. This one's got guns and lots of action. It's not really a girl movie."

My face immediately pinched with annoyance. "I watch lots of movies with you, Marco. I'm not scared!"

My father chuckled as he patted my head. "Alright, Sof, you win. Grab your jacket, and we'll head out. We have one quick stop to make before the movie starts."

It might have only been early November, but I felt like it was Christmas morning. I bolted up to my room to grab my yellow jacket and put on my red sneakers. As I was headed out of my room, I caught sight of Maria in her room with one of Mama's candles. Stunned, I watched as she burned a small piece of paper, then lifted one of Lessi's dolls and held its beautiful golden hair to the flame.

"I'm gonna tell!" I called out from the doorway, knowing Maria would be in *big* trouble. She might be nine already, but she still wasn't allowed to play with Mama's candles, and she certainly wasn't allowed to burn Alessia's doll.

She didn't balk or chase after me. Maria just looked up and curled her finger at me. "Come here, Sofia. I want to tell you something."

Cautiously curious, I stepped inside her room. She was the oldest of us girls and claimed to be too old to play with Alessia and I. It didn't bother us too much because she could be a little mean. Maria mostly kept to herself or Marco, so she was a mystery to me. When she called me over to talk to her, I was unable to resist hearing what she had to say.

"Have you ever heard anyone say 'snitches get stitches'?" she asked coolly.

I shook my head, eyes wide as I gaped at my oldest sister.

"It means when you tell on someone, that person will hurt you for getting them in trouble. What do you think I'm going to do if you tell on me?" She lifted her brows, giving me a chance to imagine all the nasty things she was capable of. "And it's even worse when you tell on family, then you're a rat, a traitor. You see something you're not supposed to, you keep your mouth shut or bad things are gonna happen to you. Understand?" She glared at me, making tears burn at the back of my throat.

Maria could be all kinds of mean when she wanted to be. I didn't want her angry with me, so I nodded, unable to speak.

"Good, I'd hate for your paints to accidentally get thrown away or your pretty golden hair to get chopped off in the night." Her cold gray stare gave me no doubt she'd do it. I didn't know why my older sister didn't seem to like us—that was just the way she was—and I had no desire to make it worse.

I ran straight for Marco and the safety of his company, my lips sealed about what I'd seen. "I'm ready for the movies!" I said, giving him a big hug and trying to forget what Maria had said.

He chuckled, then ruffled my hair. "Alright, let's get in the car."

When Mama drove, she made Marco sit in the back seat with us girls, but Daddy let him sit up front. That meant I sat by myself in the back seat. It didn't bother me at all, as long as I got to go with them. Daddy drove us to one of his friend's houses not too far from ours. I couldn't recall ever visiting the place before, but I wasn't great at paying attention.

When we stepped out of the car, Daddy's lips pursed together just like they did when Maria got in trouble at school or when Lessi cried about something silly. I glanced around, wondering what had bothered him, but saw nothing out of the ordinary. Coming over to where I stood in the grass, he squatted down until we were eye to eye.

"I have a little business to handle, but it shouldn't take long. You run around to the backyard and play for a few minutes. I'll grab you when I'm done."

"Is Marco coming with me?" I asked with more quiver in my voice that I had wanted. I liked to be brave in front of Marco but going off by myself made me nervous.

"Marco's going to come with me, but you're not old enough. I need for you to play in the backyard for a bit while we're inside."

I could feel tears building in my eyes at the frustration of being left behind. As the youngest, it felt like I was always being left out. "I don't want to go in the backyard. I want to stay with you two."

Marco stepped forward and placed his hands on my shoulders, bending low to look me in the eye. "Hey, Sof, don't get upset," he said softly. "It's only a few minutes, and you're gonna love the yard. I've been back there, and there's tons of flowerbeds. I bet you can find a whole army of ladybugs." He gave me a warm smile, and his words were just what I needed to hear. I adored hunting for ladybugs with him. In the blink of an eye, the backyard became a grand adventure rather than a punishment for being too young.

"Okay, Marco! And maybe I can find one of the yellow ones just for you."

"Sounds good. You can tell me all about it as soon as we're done."

"And Sof," said my dad, "make sure you stay in the backyard until we get you, understand?"

"I will!" I tore off around the side of the house, completely absorbed in my new mission to capture as many ladybugs as possible. Daddy had been right—the yard was huge. Our house sat on the edge of the water, so we didn't have much of a backyard, but this yard was lined around the edges with trees that soared high into the sky, just like an impenetrable barrier protecting a beautiful castle. At the base of the trees were winding flower beds full of all kinds of plants and flowers. I ran directly toward the nearest bed. Ladybugs loved flowers. Dropping to my knees, I started to scour the leaves and dirt for any trace of red or yellow polka-dotted bugs.

"Whatcha lookin' for?" a voice from behind me said, startling me from my task. A boy about my age peered over my shoulder, shaggy blond hair curling into his narrowed eyes.

I'd never seen the boy before, but I was always happy to make new friends. "Ladybugs. Wanna look with me?"

"I thought girls didn't like bugs."

"They're *lady*bugs," I explained in exasperation. *Clearly, this boy didn't know anything about girls.* Of course, we liked ladybugs—it was right there in the name. I returned to my search, sensing the boy join me when he dropped to his knees beside me. "You live here?" I asked him without taking my eyes from the miniature jungle of vegetation.

"Nah, this place is way nicer than my house. My dad's inside talking. He made me come out here." He grumbled the last part, his displeasure obvious.

"Same here. They said I wasn't old enough to come inside, but this is way better than listening to grown-ups talk."

"You're probably right," he admitted reluctantly. "How old are you?"

"Five and a half. How old are you?"

"Six, almost seven," he said proudly, flashing a toothless grin. "Hey! There's one." He reached into a large shrub and came away holding his finger out with a tiny red bug walking across his knuckle. "Wanna hold it?"

I gave him a big smile and nodded, too excited to talk.

"Okay, hold out your hand flat, and we'll let him walk from my hand to yours."

I followed his instructions, and he pressed his hand firmly against mine on the side where the ladybug was headed. My hand was frigid compared to his, but it didn't faze me. I was too excited to care about the cold or the rock that was digging into my knee. The moment the microscopic legs touch my skin, I gasped with a giggle. "It tickles."

"Have you held one before?"

"Yeah, but it still makes me laugh. I wish I got to hold them more. We don't have a big yard, so I don't see them very often. My favorite are the yellow ones, but they're super hard to find. I've only ever found one of those before. I like them because yellow is my favorite color. You have a favorite color?" I asked as I watched the bug make its way around to the underside of my hand.

"Probably green. That's the color of the New York Jets, my dad's favorite team."

"You know if you mix yellow and blue, it makes green? I love painting, so I know how to make all the colors," I explained confidently. "Yellow and red together make orange."

The boy cocked his head to the side and looked at me curiously. "You think if the red ladybugs and yellow ladybugs have babies together, they'd have orange ladybugs?"

I burst out laughing, making the bug on my hand fly off toward more stable ground. "You're funny. What's your name?"

"I'm Nico. What's yours?"

I didn't have to answer. My dad's booming voice called my name from the side of the house. "Gotta go! I'll see ya around."

"Bye, ladybug girl." The words followed me as I ran toward my daddy, but I hardly heard them in my excitement to get back to the car.

Daddy drove us to the movie theater to see the spy movie. I sat between him and Marco so I could sit next to both of them, which meant I got to hold the popcorn. I only had to go to the potty one time during the movie and didn't get scared at all.

By the time the movie was over, it was dark outside and *way* past my bedtime. I could hardly keep my eyes open from the excitement of the day, and the car's gentle motion on the drive home quickly lulled me to sleep. I didn't wake when the doors to the car opened and closed. It was the stillness and the silence that stirred me from sleep. Blinking my groggy eyes, I quickly realized I was alone in the car. From where I sat in my booster seat, I could see Daddy and Marco outside, walking over to two men dressed in black vests. They didn't look like any men I'd seen before with their long, scraggly beards and black tattoos on their necks and faces. But my daddy wasn't scared of them, so I wasn't. My daddy had all kinds of friends.

The men shook hands under a streetlight, my brother pretending to be one of the adults. Just before my eyelids could drift shut again, the scene suddenly fell into chaos, stirring me wide-awake. Frozen in my seat, I watched my worst nightmare play out before me like a movie with no pause or rewind buttons.

One of the men in vests began to yell. I could hear his angry voice penetrate inside the car. His face contorted, and he grabbed Marco by the hair, pressing a gun to my brother's head. The man snarled at my daddy like the neighbor's dog did when we walked by the fence. My daddy stood motionless, hands raised in surrender.

Why wasn't Daddy helping Marco? Why was the man so angry?

I wasn't sure what was happening, but I could tell it was bad. My stomach clenched viciously as fear immobilized my body.

The next moment played out in slow motion, like the cartoons where the tomcat accidentally runs into a wall when he chases the little mouse. A loud bang rang out in the night, echoing off the tall buildings and making me clasp my hands over my ears. My eyes jerked shut, but only for a second. They opened in plenty of time to see Marco's head jerk to the side and a dark liquid spray out around him.

I couldn't stop what I was seeing.

As if someone was forcing my eyelids open, I watched in horrified silence as my brother's limp body collapsed to the ground, a dark puddle quickly seeping out from beneath him.

I couldn't breathe.

All the air in the car had been sucked out, making my head spin and my vision blur.

Everything stilled.

The men seemed just as shocked as me, eyes all locked on my brother.

Without warning, Daddy launched himself at the men, stealing the man's gun and hitting them both with it over and over. He attacked them like a wild animal. I could almost have convinced myself the whole thing was a scene from the movie we'd just watched. How else could my daddy be fighting like one of the spies on the big screen?

The bad men tried to hurt him, and I wanted desperately to scream for them to stop, but I couldn't make a sound. It wouldn't have mattered. Daddy was quicker than either of them, punching and kicking, pounding on the men until both were on the ground unmoving, and still he kept at them.

Eventually, he slowed, his chest heaving up and down as he glared at the men, then lowered himself to look at one of their hands. When he stood back up, he spat on each of them and turned to Marco. Daddy walked slowly to my brother's side and dropped to his knees, placing his hands gently on Marco's chest and bowing his head, but Marco never moved.

Why isn't he moving? Why isn't Daddy taking Marco to the doctor? Why is Daddy crying? Questions and panic raced through my mind, but even at five years old, I knew the answers.

I knew that my big brother was dead.

I simply couldn't face it.

My entire world had shattered, but I was in shock.

Daddy stood and pulled out his phone, making a call before returning to the car. He thought I was asleep. I wasn't supposed to have seen what happened. I knew that like I knew my own name. What I'd seen had been very, very bad. Without a second thought, I slammed my eyes closed. I didn't want him to know that I'd been awake and wanted to hide from everything that had happened. If I closed my eyes, maybe when I opened them, I would discover it had all been a mistake.

I could feel his gaze on me as I sat there motionless, head

resting against the seat. I pretended to sleep, desperately hoping it was all a bad dream.

But it wasn't a dream or even a nightmare.

We sat silent in the car for a short while until another car arrived. In the heavy darkness, Daddy never saw the streaks of tears soaking my face. He rolled down the window, whispering softly to the men from the other car. Then we drove away, leaving Marco on the cold city sidewalk.

I never saw my big brother again.

9 781733 072137